Crazy Over You

Carol Thomas

Crazy Over You

Love can drive you crazy... in more ways than one!

To Betty
Happy reading!
Best wishes
Carol Thomas
X

Matador
9 Priory Business Park,
Wistow Road, Kibworth Beauchamp,
Leicestershire. LE8 0RX
Tel: 0116 279 2299
Email: books@troubador.co.uk
Web: www.troubador.co.uk/matador
Twitter: @matadorbooks

ISBN 978 1784624 330

British Library Cataloguing in Publication Data.
A catalogue record for this book is available from the British Library.

Printed and bound in the UK by TJ International, Padstow, Cornwall
Typeset in 12pt Bembo by Troubador Publishing Ltd, Leicester, UK

Matador is an imprint of Troubador Publishing Ltd

For Mason, Kirsti, Amelia, Madison and Edward
with lots of love xx

Benson and Milo

Chapter 1

Having finally got her girls to bed, Abby slouched on the sofa with her laptop. The computer had become a distraction, perhaps even an obsession. In her spare moments at work and in the evenings when the children slept, when she should have been doing so many other things, Abby was on the Internet.

She knew the routine off by heart – typing in their names singularly, their names together, *her* name with variations on the spelling, *her* name and *Washington* (the place '*it*' happened), their joint names and *Washington*. *Simon Turner* and *Helen Herne* were now so familiar to Abby's search terms that her computer was automatically putting them in for her after she typed the first letters. She wasn't quite sure what she hoped to find. She didn't know and didn't stop to think it through. She was fired by an obsession to find anything that would help her understand, to see who it was who had changed her life forever.

Googling, scrolling through countless pages of images and searching... Facebook, Twitter, LinkedIn, YouTube, even MySpace. Abby lurked on them all. And the irony was, she didn't actually know what the woman looked like so she was never really going to find *her*. Abby knew, in the sea of Helen Hernes she had stalked via the Internet, she could have been staring right at *her* face but she wouldn't have known it. The searches were utterly, irrefutably, mind-blowingly pointless. She knew it but she couldn't stop!

Aware she was driving herself steadily crazy with the futility of it all, Abby threw her head back and growled. Staring back at the screen, she had an idea. A different search. Same theme.

New approach. Sitting up, she typed *adultery help forums* into Google and swallowed hard as she watched the search results appear on the screen. *Wow!* There were so many of them. Intrigued, she clicked on the first site. A long list of topics appeared with titles highlighting the types of discussion threads they would reveal: *Just found out, separation, divorce, the other woman, the other man, investigative tips, reoffenders, revenge is sweet…* Abby let out a breath she hadn't realised she was holding. There was such a lot to take in.

Clicking on *Just found out,* she began to scroll through, skim-reading as she went. There seemed to be endless amounts of scorned women sharing their joint angst. And they certainly didn't hold back when it came to giving *all* the details. Abby read scenario after scenario, found opinion after opinion. It was all so compulsive and yet horribly overwhelming to read; a melting pot of confusion, sympathy, anger and conflicting advice.

Abby shivered. Noticing the you've-stayed-up-too-late-again chill in the room, she threw a cushion down to cover her cold feet and slipped Jessica's school cardigan over her shoulders. Stretching the crick forming in her neck, she realised she must have spent several hours scrolling through it all; even the dog had given up on her and gone to bed. *Thanks for the company Bramble!* Abby knew she should follow, but the thought of going up to her empty bed and trying to sleep seemed even less appealing than continuing on through her list of search results.

On opening the next site yet another pop-up window appeared, trying to encourage her to sign up or log in. Abby crossed it off, just as she had all the others. She didn't actually want to join in. She didn't want to be part of their sect. Perhaps it was denial but joining in, becoming part of the 'victims of adultery' gang, would make it all too real. She didn't want to be a fully-fledged member.

2

The sites were all very similar. She knew what she would find as she opened each new one. Despite the fact each seemed to have its own angle – *coping with infidelity for...* insert your religion, gender, sexual preference or ethnic origin here (apparently infidelity had no bias) – the topic list was largely the same. Abby was running out of steam. She knew she should stop; sleeping wasn't going to be any easier with everybody else's anger in her head as well as her own issues.

About to close her laptop, she noticed a thread titled *Tears are us!* That was a first. She opened it. The first comment simply said, *Found this and thought I'd share...* Abby read the quote that followed. Sitting back, she read it again. It was hard to focus her tired mind but the more she read it, the more she liked it. It seemed to speak directly to her. She wanted to remember it. She read it again before leaping from her seat, fuelled by an idea.

Rummaging in her bag, she found her notebook. When she'd taken it from the stationary cupboard at work, more than a week ago, it had seemed so full of promise. She remembered the brief feeling of determination she'd had as she'd sat in her empty classroom and written her first words in it. Opening it now, she read: *I'm writing this because I hope it will show my journey back to me – to being positive, happy and not confused. I hope I will find a day where my head is not scrambled, full of a name I hate, a name I don't want to hear and horrible imagined images I don't want to see!*

Since then, Abby hadn't known what to put next or where that journey might begin. But now it was clear. With no words of her own to write, she should copy the quote instead. It wasn't quite what she was supposed to be using her notebook for, but putting something had to be better than nothing. She couldn't bear staring at all those empty pages any longer.

Notebook in hand, she rooted round for a pen. Cursing the fact that the contents of her pen pot amounted to a few old fuzzy-ended felt-tips, three chubby crayons and several blunt pencils, she went to her school bag. At least the girls knew they weren't allowed to raid that. *Ah ha!* Armed with her green Bic Cristal, Abby returned to her discarded laptop and kicked the abandoned cushion and cardigan to one side.

Pleased to finally have something to write after her bold opening statement, she copied the quote from the forum into her notebook and read over it again.

"There is a sacredness in tears. They are not the mark of weakness, but of power. They speak more eloquently than ten thousand tongues. They are the messengers of overwhelming grief, of deep contrition, and of unspeakable love."

OK, so the language was ridiculously flowery, but she really liked its poignancy. Abby thought of all the time she had spent crying or holding back tears at inappropriate moments – like waiting at the traffic lights, walking the dog, in the middle of lessons or staff meetings, standing in the queue at Tesco... the list was endless! And yet the quote seemed to say it was OK to feel so sad, that all those tears were justified. It was a weird relief to read it. She felt pathetic and hated herself each time she descended into tears. It was so bloody unproductive. But maybe she should forgive herself for some of it... maybe it wasn't as pathetic as she thought.

Abby wanted to put the reference. She knew it was a bit anal and she didn't actually need to add it; the notebook was just for her after all. But then again she knew not writing it would just annoy her. If she didn't do it now she'd only do it at some other point. It was an ingrained habit from college; even with her mind in shreds she couldn't let the detail go.

The forum post didn't cite the reference, so she Googled the quote. Staring at the name as it appeared on the screen, Abby shrunk back from the computer, stunned by the irony.

"Washington Irving, Washington bloody Irving!" She said it aloud. It wasn't like Washington was a common name, and yet there it definitely was. What a git irony could be; it might as well have slapped her in the face. The first positive thing she'd put since starting her notebook and the man saying it shared a name with the very place her husband chose to have an affair. Abby actually couldn't believe it! Without pausing for thought she scribbled *Arghhhhhh!* in big black letters where the reference should have been.

Less than twelve hours later and too many hours spent Googling were taking their toll. Abby sat watching her class swim, thirty-two heads bobbing around in yellow swimming caps, while tears rolled down her face. She was tired from her lack of sleep the night before; it never helped her control her mind, inhibiting the energy and inclination she needed to hold back tears and remain focused.

Being the last swim before half-term, the session had been designated a play swim. Abby was only needed to supervise general behaviour and children in need of the toilet. The young lifeguards, all keen sporty types, probably awaiting college or university places, were watching the children splashing around on the inflatables, ensuring their safety in the water. Abby felt redundant and it left her mind too idle, too free, too able to think.

Sitting and watching was so very hot; the atmosphere was sauna-like. Outside the sun was shining brightly and inside the heat pricked at her nerves. It was noisy too. The children's excited voices echoed loudly as they bounced off the high, beamed ceiling. Abby loved to see them happy, and to hear them having so much fun would ordinarily lift her spirits but this time it was not enough to remove the ache from her chest, or prevent the incessant tears that stung her sleep-deprived eyes.

Thoughts kept slipping into her mind as scenes of her husband and *her* played out in her imagination. She didn't actually know the details. These images were based on things she'd seen in films and on television. She knew it was nonsense but she couldn't stop it. They were coming from that dark part of her mind she couldn't always control. She looked at the hard tiled floor at her feet and, in an Ally McBeal moment, imagined smashing her head against it. *Would that help?* She knew she wouldn't actually do it. She was too sensible; too mindful of her responsibilities and too conscious of her girls who needed her, no matter how tempting it might seem.

Shuddering at how broken she had become, Abby cringed as her dad's words echoed through her mind, as they had many times over the past weeks. *'Empowering yourself with the new possibilities created by any given situation is the only way forward.'* She had heard it all so many times and knew it all off by heart (the Scott girls were their father's daughters after all). But no matter how many times she tried to remind herself that 'problems are there to be assessed and overcome', or that 'dwelling gets in the way of fixing what needs to be fixed', the words all felt empty. The mantras of a man whose life had been spent as an engineer were no match for her current situation, no help to her thoroughly muddled mind. *Sorry Dad!*

Wringing her hands in her lap, Abby shifted in her seat.

"Look Miss. Look what I can do!"

Wiping the sweat that beaded on her skin, Abby attempted to focus on the young, smiley face beaming at her from the water. April was a happy girl who loved life and always exuded energy. Pleased to have her teacher's seemingly full attention April spun into a roly-poly in the water, followed by a flamboyant handstand with her wrinkled toes waving in the air. She was a confident girl. The type of bold, bright and spirited child Abby had never been. Her beaming face bobbed back up to its rightful place above the water as she looked over for recognition of her efforts. Rewarded by Abby's big smile and thumbs-up April splashed off happily to find her friends.

Abby knew teaching was part acting. It was a part she usually played with devoted conviction from 8:45am until the bell rang to mark the end of the day. Then she got to exhale, enter the staffroom to get a well deserved hot drink, and discuss the lighter moments of the day – like Jack in year five asking the overweight deputy when her baby was due or Mercedes in year four secretly bringing in her mum's pink furry handcuffs for show and tell. It was a job she generally loved. But lately she was struggling. Sitting by the poolside, 3:15pm seemed too far away. She scolded herself for the tears that threatened to let her façade down. The children didn't deserve to see her like that. To them she was their teacher, a person who only existed in their presence. They didn't want or need her to have a life beyond the classroom. Seeing her in the supermarket was enough to send them silly.

As the whistle blew, Abby was pleased she wouldn't be able to sit and think any longer. Ensuring seventeen girls all got changed into their own clothes, had their knickers on and didn't leave their sodden swimsuits behind was a welcome distraction. They dressed speedily as Abby encouraged them on.

Once the children were all counted onto the coach and settled ready to head back for lunch, Abby took her seat. Patty, the year six teaching assistant, who had met with groans from the boys as she led them onto the coach in a rare second place to the girls, sat next to her.

"You going to sign up then?"

"Sign up?" Abby had no idea what she was talking about. Patty was one of those people who always started sentences as if you had been present in their head for the preliminary thoughts that led to the final utterance. Abby wasn't sure she had the patience for guessing games and hoped she'd soon get to the point.

"Year six. The trip. Isle of Wight residential. The thing Brad is organising… the list is up. It's open to all teachers. You not seen it?"

"Oh!" *Why didn't she just say so?!* "No. No, I don't normally go. Jessica and Grace are still a bit little for me to go away."

"I think you should, it'd do you good to get away. Have a bit of fun."

Abby cringed at the word; her mum and sister had been telling her she needed to 'have a bit of fun' – when really it was the last thing she felt like doing.

"Your Simon could cope couldn't he?"

Abby sat for a moment, pondering this question and the wry look on Patty's face that suggested she was fishing for gossip. Rumours in school tended to spread at a speed the year six athletics team could only dream of achieving. She didn't answer.

"How old are the girls now? They'd be OK wouldn't they?"

Abby took a moment to consider the idea of going away for a weekend. She wasn't sure she'd like to be away from the girls, and she really wasn't sure she was up for any 'fun', but then again getting away from the house and all that had happened might be good. It wouldn't be like going away alone. She wouldn't have too much time to think; she'd be busy. So busy in fact it might actually be like… *escaping!*

"Maybe…" She bit her lip. *Would it work, could I?* Absolutely sure that the thought of having the girls to himself for three whole days would hit Simon like a left hook, she felt a sense of satisfied determination spread through her. She should go. She should bloody do it. Make a stand. "You're right. I should go." Her voice was full of conviction. "Simon could cope I'm sure. The girls are six and two now. They'd be OK."

"Oh… yes, yes you should."

Abby sat back in her seat folding her arms determinedly. "Thanks Patty, I'll sign up when I get back."

Having clearly not gained the nugget of gossip she had sought Patty harrumphed back against her seat.

8

As doubt began to seep in almost as soon as the coach pulled off Abby reminded herself that this could be good for all of them. It certainly wasn't that she would use the girls in a battle between herself and Simon. In fact she had been careful not to say anything to them about all that had occurred. Keeping things as normal as possible for them was another façade she was upholding. But in truth they had barely noticed he had moved out; too many hours spent working, too many hours away, always something more important to do – such was Simon's input in their lives since his business had almost gone bust around the time of Grace's birth. Clearly the girls, Grace especially, needed to get to know him better and Simon needed to know them. Abby wanted him to know all that he had discarded. What little treasures he had neglected to notice; she wasn't the only one he had let down. Jessica and Grace hadn't featured in his egocentric worldview either. And she couldn't deny the thought of him coping alone with them for a whole weekend did vaguely amuse her and spur her determination.

Chapter 2

"I never knew the snapshots of my life that made me smile would one day make me cry!" Abby read the quote she had written in her notebook and wondered if she would ever be able to reflect on her life with Simon and think about their happier times again without feeling like it had all been stomped on. Frustrated at that thought and cross that she was still filling her book with random quotes from random people, she discarded her pen. The book was meant to be for her, for her thoughts and feelings – to help clear her head. But here she was yet again, at 3:30 in the afternoon in her classroom, Googling and copying yet another quote. Putting the words of some anonymous contributor to an adultery forum where her own words should have been.

Inspirational at first, it was all becoming miserably frustrating now. She wondered when she would be able to find her own voice and write what she truly wanted to. Maybe if she could clear a path in her mind, unscramble her thoughts and put them into words, she would actually start to be able to move on.

A cleaner appeared at the door, interrupting Abby's thoughts. "Is it OK?" she asked tentatively, waving her vacuum plug in the air.

"Of course, come in." Abby flustered with the computer, trying to close the forum page, log out and shut down before the woman, not the usual cleaner, saw what she was up to. As the vacuum sprung noisily into action, Abby closed her book and gathered her bits together.

Looking round the room she realised that constantly trying

to keep her mind busy meant that she actually had nothing left to do – it was a rare state for a teacher to be in. Her marking, planning and assessments were all up to date. The room was tidy and everything, including the whiteboard, was set up for the following day. Abby thought about going home, but the house would be quiet, – too quiet. Jessica was at a friend's for tea and Grace was at nursery. Bramble was at home but he was thirteen and had always been a bit of a lazy Labrador. While he would undoubtedly greet her with gusto Abby knew his enthusiasm would soon wane as he sought his next comfy spot to sleep. She didn't want to be alone in the house; she knew it would simply spur her whirring mind too much.

She tucked her notebook inside her bag and assembled all of her other belongings alongside it. As she closed the clasp she let her hand slide across the soft brown leather. She loved that bag. It had been a thoroughly excessive present from Simon when she graduated. She picked it up and hugged it close – the smell of leather exuded from it and played with her senses, compelling her to picture them both in the moment she'd opened it; happy, young, full of hope and irrefutably falling for each other. It seemed a whole lifetime ago.

Forcing herself to stop – reminiscing wasn't healthy and generally led to tears, grief, anger and remorse over being unable to get back what she once had – Abby decided she should just go to a café and have a cup of tea. Maybe away from a computer (and the temptation of more forum searches) and taking a moment for herself, she could have a go at writing down her own thoughts and feelings. Being in a public place might actually help her control her mind. With others around her she couldn't easily descend into tears. Besides, the prospect of having a cup of tea in a café, out alone in the middle of the afternoon, was actually exciting. She never got to do such things. It would be a treat!

Once in her car she wondered where to go. Pondering

which of the nearest cafés offered the optimal cake-to-cost ratio she headed out of the school gates. Driving out along the dual carriageway, with Take That blaring at a mind-numbing volume, she welcomed the respite from thinking and felt momentarily in control of her mind and her misery.

It was a funny sensation, being out and about. Having no little hands to hold, nobody to consider other than herself. She liked it. Caramel slice and pot of tea purchased, Abby sat in the corner of one of the larger local cafés, trying to convince herself that her choice of seat was valid for reasons of peace and quiet and had nothing to do with her not being brave enough to sit forthrightly in the middle. She poured her tea with purpose and looked at the calorific caramel slice. She knew she was meant to be avoiding such temptations. Trimming her waist was part of the 'get over it' plan suggested by her colleague Melissa, who was at least eight years younger than her and annoyingly full of optimism.

Abby rolled her eyes. As if losing weight, a new hairdo and a whole new wardrobe, including saucy underwear, would actually help sort out her marital mess! Even with Melissa's insistence that the plan had worked for several of her college friends, Abby's attempts remained half-hearted and her attitude sceptical. She knew if she were still in college, her relationship still in its infancy, she would be reacting differently. She was more driven and decisive then. And, of course, it's easier to walk away when your lives are less entwined. Abby and Simon's worlds were thoroughly entangled. *That's what happens after fifteen years!* Abby had naively thought they would stay that way forever. She knew the impact of how suddenly that perception had come to a halt, and not knowing how to proceed in the wake of the blow was in part what was causing her such turmoil. How could Melissa begin to understand that? She was in the throes of new, untarnished, uncomplicated love, with her biggest dilemma being whether to go with the 'Blissful Love' or 'Purple Passion' boutonnieres for her wedding in the summer. At £16 a pop Abby could have easily answered that question.

The café was full of noise; the clatter of crockery and the constant murmur of conversation created a lively but not overwhelmingly busy atmosphere. The aroma of coffee filled the air. Abby brushed her fingers through her hair. The new do had not been a great success. Her new fringe hung too heavily above her eyes and the colour, only a shade lighter than her own hair, was a bit of a pathetic attempt at different. Melissa had tried to be positive when Abby attempted the big reveal but she couldn't hide the condescension in her tone when she wished her well with the weight loss and clothes shopping. Abby was beginning to regret ever saying she could and would achieve all the goals set, by the time she attended Melissa's wedding. With each day that passed both her attendance and hitting those targets seemed to be falling into greater doubt. Going to such a big event, *a posh hotel in Oxfordshire no less*, without Simon, despite the fact that half the school staff seemed to be going, would be odd and it was a wedding at that. She wasn't sure she would make a terribly good wedding guest in her present state of mind.

Sipping her tea and fiddling with the items on her tray Abby looked around the room. There was a good mix of people; elderly couples drawn in by the temptation of tea and cake after visiting the garden centre next door, mums gathering to chat while their children happily snacked and businesspeople clearly taking advantage of the free Wi-Fi and strong coffee. Watching them all simply going on with their lives, oblivious to her, made Abby feel very alone.

She wished she had bought something to read; at least that way she could have looked occupied. Sitting with a notepad and pen and no clear thoughts to write in it was exasperating. She felt foolish. Abby remembered how she always used to carry a book with her, how much she enjoyed reading and the escapism a good story could offer. But now, after all the recent events, she found she couldn't read and concentrate. Whenever she tried she found the dark voice in her head would interject (*What really happened in Washington? How did it all play out?*) reminding her of her own miserable reality and all the uncertainty in her life.

Searching for something to focus on, to gain control of her mind before it descended into panic, Abby scanned the room. Her attention was drawn to a man sitting just a few tables away. She didn't know him. She had never seen him before and it was likely she would never see him again. At that point a clear and simple thought entered her head. *How do chance meetings turn into something more? How does that happen?* She was aware that these questions were simply her mind playing a new game, contorting her thoughts back to Simon and what had happened in Washington, but she was suddenly intrigued. She didn't want to fight these thoughts. She wanted to know. *Simon had known what to do. Helen Herne had known what to do. So why don't I?* Reflecting back on her past it occurred to Abby she had never even had a one-night stand, in fact everybody she had ever dated in college, before Simon, had started out as a friend. Meeting a random stranger, getting her kit off and having impromptu sex had never really occurred to her.

She wanted all the pain and angst gone from inside her. *Would meeting someone do that?* Her mind continued with its new line of enquiry. *Could it all be as simple as getting it fucked right out of me?* She blushed, shocked at her own thoughts, but still she didn't stop… she began to wonder just how she would go about achieving that. She was one person in a world of people, drifting, needing, wanting. Who would notice her? Nobody had in the last fifteen years. Nobody unless you counted a young, rather too-hippy-to-be-a-teacher student she once worked with. He had been enough to make Simon jealous, but as flattered as Abby was she knew he was more interested in her meticulous lesson plans than her body!

What would somebody new be like in bed? It had been so long since she had been naked with anybody other than Simon. *Would it be exciting or just plain weird to touch and be touched by somebody else?* Abby looked at the man again. He seemed of similar age but taller than Simon and had lighter features, not her usual type at all. He wore a charcoal suit with a crisp white shirt open at the neck, and was clearly engrossed in his laptop. His thick, butterscotch blonde hair was slightly ruffled where he had pushed his fingers through it as he worked. Abby wondered what it would be like to push her fingers through that hair and blushed a little at the ease with which she succumbed to libidinous thoughts. She noted that he looked broad across the shoulders in a thoroughly muscular sense; there was not much flab about him. He was clearly a man who looked after himself. As he rose to get a spoon Abby attempted to look away, but she couldn't help but notice his firm thighs flexing against the tailored cloth of his trousers. Simon worked out – Abby knew about firm thighs! Ruffled by her own thoughts she forced herself to look away.

Despite the fact that it was slightly cold and had patches of dark brown teapot scum floating on the top Abby sipped her tea and glanced at her caramel slice. She knew she could be a messy eater. Sitting alone, she imagined biting into it and the whole room turning to stare as the thick caramel oozed out the sides and crumbs dropped down her top. She would have to tackle it another way. But as she passed the man's table en route to get a knife and several napkins Abby noticed the unusual way he held his coffee cup and again her attention was drawn to him. It was a firm and commanding grip, with his hand placed across the top of the broad rim. Returning to her seat she couldn't help but watch as he took it slowly to his wide, soft lips. It was then that she noticed his arctic blue eyes for the first time. Mesmerised and enjoying the moment, she realised too late that the reason she could see them so clearly was that she had been caught, practically on the verge of drooling, starring straight at him. Her cheeks blazed a deep shade of crimson and she almost choked on her tea.

Abby sat for the next five minutes in total horror, trying to look anywhere but back at him. Consumed by her own embarrassment she wondered if she should simply confess to being on day release from the attic. However it was that people took things further, she was pretty sure staring like a crazed stalker wasn't it. In her mortified state Abby suddenly felt thoroughly ashamed of sitting there with a caramel slice, all too aware that her own thighs were larger than they ought to have been. She wished she had listened to Melissa and started a diet. She had become chubby as she'd become complacent in her life, allowing the pounds to slip on after Grace's birth. She was now a size 16. The slim size 12 she had once been was a very distant memory. Abby knew she needed to take a hold of her life and herself. She needed to change her future. She had let the past happen, especially over recent years, becoming a passive player in the action of her own life. Deciding to take the caramel slice home for the girls she discreetly wrapped it in a napkin and left the café.

Grace's nursery closed at six. Abby collected her at 5:30, a little later than she usually aimed to be. Of course Grace barely noticed; she loved her nursery and always went in a bundle of giggly energy and came out smiling with chubby arms full of paintings, drawings, gluing and half the garden smeared round her rosy cheeks. Abby swooped her up in her arms and gladly received the huge snuggly cuddle she got as her little girl clung around her neck.

Settling into the car, ready to head home, Abby's phone buzzed. Without stopping to think she picked it up and went straight to her messages. It was her sister Kennedy, asking her round to try her latest culinary creation. Abby wasn't sure she could face crunchy pork chops with garlicky spinach and tomato salad, or the side order of happy families that was sure to be served up with it. Just lately, spending time at her sister's house, watching Kennedy with her devoted husband and three practically perfect sons, tended to make Abby feel like an unexploded bomb on Walton's Mountain; it was a situation best avoided. She decided to answer the text later, once she had thought of a good enough excuse to get her out of it. Noticing an earlier message from Simon, her breath caught. As she read it she could feel the familiar rush of panic as her pulse began to race: *I'd like to see the girls. Is tonight OK? I miss them. I miss you all.*

Chapter 3

Driving home, Abby's breathing felt too shallow against the tightness in her chest. She couldn't face him. She didn't want to speak to Simon. It was all too confusing. Clearly never seeing him again would be a far easier option, if only that wasn't so totally and utterly impossible. They were not only bound by their marriage, or at least they were supposed to be, there were also the material things: The house, cars, bank accounts – so many things to be undone.

And then there were their beautiful girls. Their dear sweet, innocent, unknowing girls, little bundles of love and joy whose world was changing and they didn't even know it yet. Abby knew because of their children she and Simon would always be bound together; their own genes merged in their little girls' very beings. Living and breathing, undeniable evidence of the love they had shared and the life they had together. If only she could still feel certain about that life; if only it hadn't all gone so horribly wrong.

Abby peeked at Grace in her rear view mirror. She was giggling as the breeze from the open windows buffeted her wayward blonde curls. Watching her Abby felt consumed with guilt as she remembered how in the dark depths of the night before, when her mind was left unguarded, she had thought how much easier it would have been if she and Simon had never had children. As if not having the girls would have ameliorated the whole situation, allowing her to simply walk away – start over in a new Simon-less life with only herself to think about. She hated the horrible depths to which her mind would plummet, especially when she was tired and less able to control it. Now, in greater, if not complete control of her faculties, Abby knew the girls weren't the reason she couldn't just walk away – in fact they increasingly felt like her only anchor to sanity. She knew being strong for them was sometimes all that kept her going.

Simon would have to see Jessica and Grace. She would have to face him. Abby knew she couldn't keep putting it off. But she wasn't ready. She wasn't sure how she would cope. She actually hadn't seen or spoken to him properly since that night. The night everything changed. Sitting in her driveway, she sent a text back: *Of course you can see the girls, but not tonight. We'll sort a time soon. Sorry.* She pressed send and read it back three times. *Sorry?* Why was she saying sorry? She annoyed herself with the way she always tried to placate him. It was a habit she knew she had to stop.

Throwing her phone into her bag she scooped Grace out of her car seat and took her inside. It was milk, biscuit and cuddle time. There was something reassuring about adhering to her usual routines. This was her world. She knew this. Its familiarity soothed her fractious mind. There was something so utterly calming about a cuddle on the sofa before the bedtime routine kicked in. This was special time shared between her and the girls – and sometimes Bramble who, despite his size, considered himself a lapdog. As Simon's work often meant he wasn't about, this was Abby's domain.

Grace sat snuggled into her mummy's lap, avidly listening to her favourite story. She loved to hear it over and over again, and to join in with all her favourite parts. As the doorbell rang Bramble barked and Grace leapt excitedly to her feet shouting, "Tiger! Tiger!" hoping desperately, as she always did, that this was the day the tiger had come to her house for tea.

"Not today sweetie," Abby responded automatically, her heart pounding rapidly at the thought that Simon might not have got her message. Face flushed, she tentatively opened the door and breathed a sigh of relief when she saw it wasn't him. Without stopping to say hello Jessica beamed up at her mum and instantly launched into a full and excitable account of her time at Lara's house. Abby shouted "Thank you!" and waved at Lara's mum as she drove off – her charge safely delivered.

Bath time and bedtime were a special part of the day. Abby watched as her girls played happily together, half-submerged in a mountain of white frothy bubbles, giggling at the funny beards they had made. Joining in, Abby picked up a clump of froth and blew it into the air. Jessica and Grace squealed with excitement as 'snow' splodged down onto their heads and all over their bath toys. Repeating it over and over again, Abby soaked up the normality of it all.

After the bath it was time to calm down as quiet time ensued and they all relaxed together. With brushed teeth and pyjamas on, the girls took it in turns to cuddle into Abby's lap as she brushed their hair; both so similar, beautiful blonde wavy hair which they got from neither her nor Simon.

After stories it was lights out and time to sleep. Finding it increasingly hard to walk away, Abby sat at the top of the stairs and waited until she heard Jessica and Grace's voices subside into gentle hushed breathing before going downstairs to carry out the parts of her evening routine she enjoyed less. Vacuuming (*who knew one dog could lose so much hair?*), tidying, emptying lunch boxes, making lunches for the next day, sorting the washing... All monotonous tasks made tiresome by having nobody to share the load with, nobody to talk to.

Eventually slumping onto the sofa Abby checked her phone. There was a voicemail from Kerry, Simon's sister. Abby knew Simon had been staying with her since they split up. Curiously she pressed play.

"Hey it's me, how ya doing? Look, it's none of my business but Si is pretty cut up. This has hit him hard. He wanted to come see you tonight but said you said no. Will you please just talk to him? I'm worried about him."

Staring at the phone with a mixture of disbelief and anger, expletives tumbled freely from Abby's mouth. Why the hell should she waste what little energy she had making Simon feel better? It was beyond her comprehension. There were days when she felt she could barely function. Days when going into the supermarket was too hard. Days when all she wanted was to be swallowed into a deep dark hole. Who was there to help her when she sat stranded on the roadside, unable to drive because all she could do was sob herself senseless? Did Simon's family care that she was tumbling over a precipice from which she didn't know if she would ever return? Honestly, what did Kerry expect her to do? Placating Simon was clearly not just habitual for Abby; it was quite literally a role she was expected to fulfil no matter what the circumstances. She wasn't going to do it, she couldn't! And what was the point anyway? Surely Simon's actions had made his feelings clear.

Abby decided to text back. She couldn't speak. She didn't know what she might say. Incensed, she typed, *You're right, it is none of your business, but since you feel the need to interfere I suggest you speak to your brother. Maybe he can give you the number of the woman he slept with and you can ask her to make him feel better!*

She pressed send, then instantly started another message: *And since you asked, I am bloody well not alright!*

As she pressed send for the second time she fought the urge to re-read and analyse the messages, and threw her phone onto the sofa where it would be less tempting. She had been having a good evening, she had felt calmer than on previous days but now all this had agitated her. It had thrown a bone to the dark side of her mind, which was leaping and bounding with excitement, eager to be let loose.

Abby felt restless, uneasy in her own skin. Unable to keep still, she strode into the kitchen. Gripping the edge of the sink with white fingertips, she stared out of the window into the darkness, her own reflection gazing back. Bramble stood by her side, ears pricked, sensing her tension. Anger and frustration grew inside her, possessing her. Unable to contain it any longer, she flew into what could only be described as a tantrum. A full-blown tempest of a temper tantrum! She pulled at her hair, hit her head repeatedly, kicked at the kitchen cupboards, stamped her feet and flailed her arms, all the time letting out a noise which sounded purely primal; a noise akin to that she had only ever heard herself make in childbirth. Bramble shrank back to a safe distance and watched, thoroughly perplexed. Abby felt utterly crazy, but at the same time she was enjoying it, relishing her great big self-pitying, self-satisfying temper tantrum. It felt so good to let it all free. To own her anger and let what she felt must be the crazy person inside her vent the way she really wanted to.

When she could sustain it no longer, when the noises turned to sobs and the hair-pulling, head-hitting and flailing turned to hugging herself, she sunk onto the hardwood floor in the corner of the kitchen. Bramble gingerly moved closer and lay down, resting his head on her feet with a whimper. Big brown eyes stared up at her, attempting to take away her pain. She sobbed big, long, loud sobs, arms cradled around herself, her head throbbing. Her mind didn't focus on any one thing; she just felt engulfed by it all – stranded in a loss too vast to contemplate and completely alone. The sound of her own sadness rang out into the stillness of the house as she continued to give in to her basic and desperate urge to simply be downright and abjectly miserable.

As time passed, and Bramble nodded off at her feet, Abby's focus began to settle on the noise, her own noise. She became increasingly aware that nothing was actually going to happen to make her stop. There was nobody to come and scoop her into their arms, nobody to tell her to pull herself together.

She realised, as she pondered this, that she was observing the sound as if somebody else was making it. No longer the outlet for her frustrations, it was just a noise, a silly, rhythmic noise. She decided to stop, just like that, and as abruptly as it had all started the tantrum and the tears were over. She wiped her hands across her sodden face and dried her palms on her jeans. As she went to stand her whole body felt stiff; she was exhausted from the physical exertion. Her head pounded as if suffering the aftermath of a great trauma, but she felt strangely better for it.

Composing herself, Abby poured a glass of water and greedily drunk in the cold, soothing liquid that eased her burning throat. Feeling steadier on her feet she turned and added the words *martini* and *lemonade* to the shopping list on her fridge. She needed that. It was her drink of choice whenever comfort was sought, having acquired a taste for it while sipping from her mum's glass in her early teens. She liked the deep, dark colour and the warm, sweet taste as it slipped down her throat, warming her from the inside, numbing her senses. Oh, how she needed that!

Settling with her feet tucked under her amongst a pile of cushions on the sofa Abby shakily took out her notebook and pen and wrote, not somebody else's words but her own: *I am going to stop wasting my life. I have cried too many tears and I have cried myself beyond senseless! Also, I am going to stop needlessly searching the Internet. It just adds to my bloody frustration – the loss of time is ridiculous and I am not going to let them keep imposing on MY LIFE!*

She read it back and with a nod of her head assertively placed the lid on her pen. About to close the book she hesitated, looked around the room, removed the lid and added, *And I may be going a little bit crazy; I think I might need help!*

Not stopping to read that part back, she closed the book and tucked it away.

Chapter 4

Hot chocolate in hand, Abby started to download her emails. Having mostly stuck to her promise of not wasting time with needless Internet searches she hadn't turned her laptop on, in the evening, for several days. And she wouldn't have succumbed now if Melissa hadn't insisted on emailing her the following week's Literacy plans, to check over the weekend. Once she had printed them off, Abby scrolled down the remaining twenty-three items in her inbox. They were mostly advertising, discounts and special offers – *the usuals*, Abby thought as she looked at the list (Amazon, Tesco, Mothercare, eBay…). She deleted all those that didn't interest her as she worked her way through, stopping suddenly when she spotted a message from Simon. It was sent the day after her tantrum. The day after she had been so abrupt to Kerry. Abby stared at Simon's name and the subject line, that gave nothing away, for too long before she felt brave enough to open it. Putting down her drink and folding her arms, she leaned towards the screen and read:

From: Simon Turner
Time: 06:37
To: Abby Turner
Subject: Please don't delete this

Abby,
  Please, please don't delete this. I need you to hear what I have to say and since you can't or won't speak to me I thought I'd email you. Please read to the end and then read

it again, if not now then later. Please Abby, you need to hear this.

Kerry showed me your messages. I didn't ask her to contact you. I hope you know that. What she said to you, it wasn't fair. I am so sorry you are not alright. I am so sorry for the hurt I've caused you. I've been unbelievably stupid. Stupid in so many ways I can't fathom it.

I was stupid in the way I ignored you and the girls. (Oh God, our beautiful baby girls!!!) When it looked like the business was going under I panicked; I know I should've spoken to you more, but we'd just had our little Grace and I thought if I threw myself into it I could make it right without giving you more to worry about. You had already been through so much with the loss of your dad. I wanted to keep you and the girls safe, to make sure you had everything you needed. I'm sorry but you know part of me can't help the way I feel about that.

And I know that makes what I did in Washington seem even more stupid. I wish I understood it but honestly Abby, I don't. I know you deserve more of an explanation but when I think about it I don't even recognise the person I was in that moment. I am so sorry for how that has hurt you – hurt us. I wish more than anything it hadn't happened. I've tried to stay away and give you time, but Abby it's been almost two months now.

What you saw on my phone, those were her feelings, not mine. I never said I loved her. I told her to stop contacting me. And I shouldn't have run away that night, when you found out, but the things we were saying... Anyway, I should have stayed and told you then how much I love you. I shouldn't have left before you knew that. You've no idea how I wish I could take it all back.

Abby, it's always been you. I have never stopped loving you and I know that sounds ridiculous under the circumstances but it is true! You mean everything to me. Please Abby, without you I have nothing. Please forgive me. Let's just talk, no pressure, I promise. And please, I need to see the girls. It's been too long. I miss them — I miss you all.

All my love, now and always,
   Simon xxx

Simon Turner
Company Director, Turner Advertising

Abby sat back trying to take in what she had read. In some ways it was exactly what she'd wanted to hear and in others it simply confused everything. She had spent the last seven weeks trying to comprehend the finality of it all; to adjust to the fact that her life with Simon was irrevocably over. And now Simon's words were churning up the small path she had begun to make through the mess of it all. It was true that she had only seen messages sent by *her* to Simon but nevertheless, she had seen enough to know it couldn't all just be taken back so easily.

Sitting alone in her living room, Simon's words glaring at her from her laptop, Abby looked at the photographs around the walls. Each one seemed like a snapshot of a different life, a different existence, a time when she felt whole, a time when she and Simon had been totally together. Abby felt saddened that she was no longer the same person as the one staring back at her. With the breakdown of her relationship something inside her had broken too. She had lost her strength, her sparkle, her sense of self and she didn't know how to get that back. Looking at the pictures she also knew that the person she was then was completely unaware how precious the life she had was. How special it had been.

Of course Abby knew Simon's upbringing meant he would

always want to keep them 'safe', and she knew she should have pushed more to get him to speak to her when the business was in trouble, but none of that excused what followed. At least before Washington any problems they'd faced were only about them, their relationship, their issues and the two of them facing them, or not facing them, together.

In truth Abby knew she had loved and trusted Simon totally. And she had liked how important she had been to him, how he had made her feel so special. She never thought anybody could break that, undo the special bond they shared. But now it was all so different. Simon had let another person into their lives; in fact he had not only let her in, he had willingly invited her and let her trample over the things Abby held dear.

Spotting their wedding picture on top of the bookshelf Abby began to wonder what that day had meant. *Why stand in front of family and friends and make promises you can't keep? Why make public declarations only to undo them with public humiliation?* She looked more closely at her own bright, self-assured, beaming face – then suddenly unable to bear the sight of herself on that day, in that dress, with that happy, unknowing face, Abby put the laptop to one side. Holding the picture in her hand she momentarily considered smashing it, before putting it away in a drawer. No matter what the future held she was sure her wedding day would never mean the same again. Everything that had happened, everything she had read and all they had said on that night, the night she found out, could never be undone. In that moment her life had changed, she had lost something she hadn't really appreciated she had and even if she wanted it to, she wasn't sure it would ever come back.

It was all so horribly confusing. Attempting to understand why and how it had happened had become an obsession, and now throwing in the possibility of whether they could survive as a couple was beyond overwhelming. Abby had no idea what to do with this information. With her mind frequently in turmoil she felt unable to trust her own thoughts with any certainty; the voices in her head persistently fought a battle she didn't have the energy to overthrow. Increasingly she simply chose to give in, let the voices rage on and attempt to go numb to it – feel nothing, trust nothing. It was a strategy she found helped her cope, but it also meant that she actually had no idea how she truly felt about Simon beyond numbing hurt and mostly, with the exception of her major temper tantrum, quashed anger. Could she still love him and allow herself to be loved by him? *How would that work?* She had no idea. Almost dizzy from the speed at which rounds of juxtaposing thoughts spun through her head, Abby grabbed her laptop and impulsively decided to reply.

From: Abby Turner
Time: 23:45
To: Simon Turner
Subject: RE: Please don't delete this

Simon,
I got your message. I didn't delete it. I read it. I am just so confused right now. I have no idea how I feel about you, about what happened or how to begin to deal with any of it.
You need to be patient. In truth my heart feels numb, like it has no feelings...

Abby stopped. Realising she was actually going to start paraphrasing Gary Barlow and the chorus to *Patience* if she wasn't careful, she stamped her feet in frustration. *Oh God! Why can't I just say what I mean in my own bloody words?* She deleted the last line and continued.

I need to know what I want. You will have to give me time to work this out. My head is a mess.
But of course you can see the girls. It has been too long.

Come over tomorrow after lunch if you're not too busy. I can go out and give you time with them.

Abby

About to press send, Abby hesitated, unable to resist adding a final sentence. It was a small point but one that always annoyed her.

(And please turn off your company signature when you email me!)

Abby pressed send and cursed herself for not re-reading the whole message. Panic rising in her chest, she stared in dismay as a reply sprung into her inbox, her hand trembling she clicked to open it.

From: Simon Turner
Time: 23:48
To: Abby Turner
Subject: Tomorrow

Of course I am not too busy. I'll never be too busy for any of you again. I'll see you at one. Thank you xxx

(Sorry!)

What was I thinking? Abby instantly started to question her hasty response. It was as if answering by email had given her false confidence. Now she was actually going to have to face him. Attempting to rein in her racing mind and gain control of her quickening pulse she reminded herself that she could use the opportunity to ask him to have Jessica and Grace while she went on the year six residential. It was drawing ever closer and yet she hadn't mentioned it. Sticking to that when he was actually there would give her focus. And he couldn't possibly expect her to have any answers regarding his declarations in his email; it was simply too soon.

Though as Abby re-read his original message, she knew that Simon's promise of no pressure was about as likely as her remaining in control of her faculties when tomorrow came.

Chapter 5

Sixteen years ago, when Simon first came into her life, Abby was in the final year of her degree and wading her way through essays on modern women poets. She had heard a great deal about her roommate's 'best friend' and if she was honest she was a bit unnerved about Simon's impending visit. As their parents were close friends, he and Rachel had grown up together. Subsequently Abby had heard a wealth of stories ranging from them sharing potties as giggly toddlers to them comparing notes on first kisses as spotty teenagers. Rachel and Simon's was the kind of friendship Abby had always envied. It wasn't that she didn't have friends; it was just that she had never really found a forever friend. The type you shared everything with and could always rely on. Abby's school friends had all been mates who were important in the moment. None of them were ever destined to be chief bridesmaid at her wedding or godmother to her children.

Tapping her foot on the floor, Abby glanced at Rachel. "What time is he coming?"

"He said eight, he'll be on time," she confirmed excitedly.

Abby swallowed hard. Meeting Simon was beginning to feel akin to meeting future in-laws. Because of that, and the fact she had read an article in *Cosmo* which said it takes longer to order a burger than it does to make a first impression, Abby was feeling the pressure! She knew it was silly but she couldn't help it. She just didn't want anything to spoil her newfound friendship with Rachel. She valued the time they shared talking into the early hours, going out, listening to music, cramming for exams and drinking cans of caffeine-fuelled

Coke to survive lectures. For that reason she over-thought the possible consequences of Simon's visit to the extent that she felt both the need to impress him – in case his approval was important to Rachel – and threatened! Part of her really wanted to simply stamp her feet and shout, "Go away, she's my friend now," like a tormented five-year-old.

Looking at herself in the full-length mirror Abby took the towel off her head, brushed the knots out of her wet hair and slathered it with a mound of mousse. For first impressions' sake she had gone for a black skater dress with a petite floral print, believing this, paired with her black lace-up combat boots, gave just the right balance of femininity and self-assured style. (Feigning confidence was key to her plan for surviving the evening.) Turning sideways and looking at her slim waist she was pleased to note that her student diet, consisting of copious amounts of spaghetti hoops, was clearly agreeing with her. With her head bent forward she scrunched her thick hair in her hands and started to blow-dry it.

With half seven approaching and her hair remaining damp Abby wished her hairdryer, a small pink appliance Barbie would have been proud to own, could summon even half the energy output implied by the cacophonous noise it made. When she eventually gave up, throwing the drier on the bed and her head back, she was happy to see she had at least achieved the sheen and volume promised by her shampoo. Holding her hair in place she sprayed it all over with Elnett, smuggled from her mum's dressing table on her last visit home. Finally adding black eyeliner, a touch of mascara and plenty of lip-gloss, she stepped away from the mirror content that she had achieved a look that suggested a student with confidence, style and purpose; the purpose of this evening being to show Simon that she was a permanent fixture in Rachel's life now too and there was nothing he could do (she hoped) to change that.

Just before eight a knock at the door brought a shrill from

Rachel as she ran, beaming with excitement, across the room to open it. Once the obviously-happy-to-be-reunited pair had finished their hugs, tussling and hair-ruffling they both turned arm in arm to Abby, broad smiles on their bright faces.

"Here she is, the girl who has made my survival as a student possible and who has inspired me to actually do some study and get my sorry arse through a degree. Simon – Abby, Abby – Simon."

A little taken aback by the grand introduction Abby smiled, lifted her hand, waved and said, "Hi," instantly regretting the fact that, despite all her flustering over the first impression she wanted to make, she had just greeted Simon in the style of an over-enthusiastic game-show contestant. Her cheeks reddened.

Seemingly oblivious, Simon smiled. "Hi, I've heard lots about you. Thanks for looking after my Roo." He gave a squeeze around Rachel's waist as he spoke.

"Uh-ha." Abby hesitated before offering a proper response, taking a moment to absorb the 'my' and the fact that Simon had a pet name for Rachel. Abby regretted that she'd never had that type of closeness with anyone and quashed a flashback of her dad calling her 'dumpling' as a chubby child. Clearly that was not quite the same! "Roo, eh?" Abby raised an eyebrow.

"Simple Simon here couldn't manage Rachel when he was little so Roo it was and it stuck!" Rachel giggled.

Partly ignoring the explanation Abby looked at Simon, taking him in properly for the first time. "I've heard lots about you too, it's lovely to finally meet you in the flesh." As she spoke Abby pondered how in fact it *was* good to meet Simon in the flesh; flesh that from her vantage point looked like it belonged to someone who was obviously into sport and surely must work out. Rachel hadn't mentioned he was so good-looking. The only pictures Abby had seen were the ones above Rachel's bed, obscure shots in a strip of photos taken against a half-blue, half-orange background in Woolworths. They had only offered glimpses of what he actually looked like as the giggling pair had pulled silly faces in each of the four poses. It was only now, after meeting him in person, Abby wondered if Rachel's words, "Everybody falls in love with him!" referred to more than Simon's personality.

Simon was at least a few inches taller than Abby. He had thick, dark, shoulder-length hair that contrasted perfectly with his light hazel eyes and smattering of faint freckles across his nose. He wore a pair of well-loved classic green Adidas trainers; blue, faded, slightly fraying jeans that accentuated his obviously muscular thighs and a white t-shirt that fitted perfectly over his broad shoulders. He had the tone and muscle definition of a fit adolescent who was turning into a perfectly formed man. The kind of physique a single student in full possession of her raging hormones, like Abby, couldn't help but notice.

As they walked across the rugby field on the way to the pub Abby watched Simon and Rachel chat, arm in arm. They were clearly comfortable with each other. She wondered how far things had ever gone between them. Had they really always just been friends as Rachel insisted? Despite the fact that Rachel hadn't seen Simon for a long time, she had made only a limited effort with her appearance in preparation for his arrival. A quick shower, a pair of stonewashed cropped jeans, a cut-off t-shirt, her trademark pink baseball boots, a blow-dry, a bit of backcombing and she was good to go. Abby had noted her lack of fluster; clearly she was excited but the manner in which she got ready was not at all like her protracted date preparation.

As the evening progressed Abby was surprised to find she didn't feel left out at all. The conversation flowed easily and both Rachel and Simon ensured they included her. They all drank too much cider and laughed a lot. Abby had to admit it was actually a pretty good evening. She found herself relaxing, no longer worried about what impression she might make and feeling more at ease. Simon didn't feel like a threat to her friendship with Rachel and rather than feeling like an outsider she felt drawn into their circle; they shared a warmth she enjoyed being a part of.

Simon's voice was deep and smooth and easy to listen to. His eyes sparkled with an intriguing glint that drew Abby's attention and she deemed his perfectly formed pale pink lips more kissable the longer she looked at them. Simon had an open and friendly personality. He was clearly fun and knew how to enjoy himself, but not in the laddish way of lots of their college mates; he genuinely seemed more driven, more mature. Abby liked that.

They chatted about their courses as well as their plans for the future, and Simon's immediate plans were clear. "I'm still hoping the thing in America comes off; it's all looking good. I just need to clinch this final exam and I'm there."

"You'll do it!" Rachel said sincerely. "He's on for a first you know," she added, waving her glass at Abby and nudging Simon with her foot.

"Wow! That'll be great, what's the thing?" Abby enquired.

Simon fixed his eyes on her and she shifted in her seat, feeling conscious of his full attention. "A one-year placement with an ad agency. It's a great opportunity – not just the work, you know, but the experience; getting away from… you know, here. Seeing more, doing more." He paused before adding, "I want that."

Abby could feel the intensity of his words, how much he wanted it, and she knew that he was going to get it. "Do you always get what you want?" she asked teasingly, raising an inquisitive eyebrow.

"I always set out to achieve my goals, yes! Otherwise what's the point of the journey, right? I am a believer in hard work and achieving from it." Simon paused and took a breath before continuing, "To get and truly appreciate what you want you should deserve what you get." With that he sat back and drained his glass.

Abby was trying to get her head round what he had said when Rachel burst into laughter. "Bloody hell Si, that's a bit deep after this much cider."

Abby laughed too, becoming aware, as she did, that Simon's gaze had returned to her. She felt heat rise inside her and she was pretty sure it wasn't alcohol-induced.

On the way back from the pub they all linked arms, stumbling as they went, laughter drifting into the cold night air of the rugby field. Attempting to steady herself, Abby slipped her arm inside Simon's jacket. His broad back felt warm within his t-shirt and she could feel the strength in his torso. Becoming acutely aware that only his t-shirt separated their skin she quickly changed her position and grabbed Rachel's arm. Simon was a friend, actually he was Rachel's best friend and she had been allowed to share in that intimacy, but to think further on the attraction she could feel growing inside her would be wrong. Nevertheless she knew that actually convincing herself of that would be far easier if only she were a little less intoxicated by both the cider and Simon's close proximity.

Abby woke the next morning to the smell of burnt toast.

"Morning ladies." Simon entered the room wearing just a pair of unbuttoned jeans, white boxers showing underneath, no top and bare feet. It was almost certainly the best sight Abby had ever woken up to; Simon's bare torso was every bit and more than she had imagined as she fell asleep the night before. Sitting up, Abby thought what a fright she must look in her pink pyjama crop top, makeup-free and hair all natural having showered away the hairspray and pub smoke smell before bed.

She had learnt that reeking of the night before, no matter what state you were in at bedtime, would only be regrettable and vomit-inducing in the morning. Being hung over was always easier to face when clean and at least smelling human.

It was not a sentiment Rachel shared. "Bloody hell Si, cover up, nobody should look like that at this hour," she groaned, a mass of tangled hair and her face still seemingly half-stuck to the pillow. Lifting her arm sideways, she threw a t-shirt at him.

Dodging it, he laughed. "Some of us have been up, out for a run and showered you know!" Reaching Abby's bed he held out a steaming hot mug of tea and a plate of toast – the crusts were burnt and the top had clearly been scraped by the edge of a knife. The tea was too strong for Abby's taste and she didn't really feel like eating but she accepted it all willingly with a smile. As she bit into the toast and absorbed the sight of Simon in the morning she thought how she had never before eaten a breakfast that tasted quite so good.

Chapter 6

As the girls ate their lunch Abby found she could neither eat nor drink – her nerves were taking their toll on her quivering insides. She had woken early after just three hours of sleep. Five o'clock was a ridiculous time to wake at the weekend and she found it even more annoying knowing it would simply prolong her fretful morning. She showered, blow-dried her hair in an attempt to tame her fringe and selected her clothes. Her bootcut black jeans, a recent purchase after her others developed a way-too-revealing hole, were baggy, so much so that she should probably have bought a smaller pair. Looking at herself in the mirror Abby was grateful that being abjectly miserable seemed to have a calorie-burning effect on her body. The scales confirmed she had shed just over half a stone in recent weeks and it showed.

Turning back towards her wardrobe, finding herself faced with a range of rather sorry-looking supermarket-purchased t-shirts, she sighed. *Ugh! Melissa was right; I really should have gone on a shopping spree!* In sizes from 12 now ancient, to 14 now at least three years old, to 16 and even 18 – for those days when hiding behind an oversized, baggy t-shirt was the only thing that would do – they all looked more than a little tired! Running her fingers along the hangers Abby took out a chocolate brown, scoop-necked size 16 from Tu, believing it to be moderately superior to its George and Florence & Fred closet companions. Slipping it on she was pleased with the fit: slightly loose on the hips, tight on the bust and revealing just enough cleavage to show off her assets. She didn't know how she felt about Simon or if she wanted him back but there was nothing wrong with showing him what he was missing!

When the doorbell rang Abby stopped clearing the lunch dishes and took a big breath. Letting it out slowly, she checked her appearance in the kettle. Under her eyes looked too dark but she wasn't sure she even owned enough concealer to rectify that. As she hesitated the bell rang again. *This is it!* She knew there was no escaping: she had to answer it. On her way to the door Abby considered how it felt weird not having Simon simply let himself in; it was his house too after all. Nevertheless, she was grateful that he recognised the dynamic had changed; his actions had placed him outside their world and he couldn't just take it for granted that he was welcome back in.

As Abby opened the door an uncharacteristically enthusiastic Bramble took a diving leap from the bottom of the stairs, launching himself towards Simon. Revealing an energy level he had barely mustered even as a puppy he leapt and bounded frantically around his 'Daddy's' feet. Holding aloft a large bunch of freesias and obviously grateful that Bramble's onslaught had lightened the moment Simon smiled.

"At least someone's pleased to see me!"

"Sorry, come in."

Abby realised she had been staring, motionless for too long, taking in his appearance as he stood at the doorstep. He was so familiar to her and yet somehow he looked different. Simon had lost weight; he looked darker around his hazel eyes and lacked the usual confidence he generally carried so easily in his demeanour. He actually looked older than when Abby saw him last, with possibly more grey flecks in his dark hair. He had also dressed in jeans and wore a navy blue Marmot t-shirt that hung a little looser than when Abby had last seen it. Taking in his broad shoulders, strong chest and muscular arms Abby remembered how it felt to be held close to that body, to be scooped up in those arms. She knew the weight of Simon's body pressed against hers; she knew it all so intimately – which parts caused the most pleasure when touched and kissed and teased.

As these thoughts slipped easily into her mind, so they were seized upon, blasted away by the ugliness of images of that night. The evening she found out. The darkness in her own mind forcing her to remember, to shut down – she must not forget it all, every detail. Looking at his face it was all brought back to her. That nasty, stunned, horrified face when he realised she knew. That staring, caught-out face she would never forget; it was burned too deeply into her mind. Familiarity, good looks and a bunch of freesias would not overthrow the dark side of Abby's mind. It had a point to prove, and one it was determined to stomp into her every thought.

Tentatively, passing Abby the flowers, Simon stepped inside.

"Thank you, you shouldn't have." With her head spinning, Abby was unsure how to respond. It all felt so awkward. "The girls are in the lounge."

Excitedly, Jessica and Grace greeted Simon with cheerful squeals. "Daddy! Daddy! You're back!" While they had barely asked where he was, clearly they had missed him and were delighted to see him.

Needing a moment to compose herself Abby headed to the kitchen to put the flowers in a vase. She loved freesias. She had carried a large bouquet of them at their wedding. Inhaling deeply, she took in their heady floral scent, a smell she had said many times put her in her happy place. Abby was unsure how it made her feel to have something she associated with happy times bought into their current mess, but she appreciated the sentiment and the freesias with their pretty yellow and purple hues were undoubtedly beautiful. Opening the cellophane she saw, tucked just inside amongst the delicate stems, something else. Something made and placed so precisely, waiting for her to find it. Pulling it free, she realised it was a small paper giraffe; a perfectly made, delicate origami giraffe. Around its neck was a small gift tag with the single word *SORRY!* written carefully on it. She looked at it, a tear welling in her eye and she knew… she knew exactly why the giraffe was there.

After their first meeting, after the staying in contact and late-night phone calls had turned to catching up in person and blossomed into dating Abby and Simon had spent the day at the zoo together. It was a gloriously hot day, after Abby had graduated and Simon had completed his final year with the ad agency in America. The animals had mostly been lazing in the shade but for Simon and Abby, newly together, the heat added to the intensity of the feelings building between them. They spent the day drinking in the fresh air and enjoying the sights around them, all the time inwardly focusing on the need they shared for each other. Holding hands, linking arms, hugging, kissing and teasing each other with their longing looks and tantalising embraces.

Anticipation building inside them, they pitched their slightly-too-small, holey beige tent in the nearby forest. The evening was still. As the sun set into a pink sky full of promises their own giddy heat enveloped them. Both lost to everything but their own passion, and despite their obvious yearning for each other which had built throughout the day, they made slow, sensuous love – savouring the closeness of being totally at one with each other for the first time; playing out their intense desire with every tender caress, every taste, every intensely intimate movement they shared. By the time the moon rose high into the sky Abby felt completely captivated and supremely content beyond anything she had ever felt before. Locked in Simon's embrace she knew she was hopelessly smitten, totally in love with him!

In the morning when Abby woke, next to her makeshift pillow were three small, slightly wonky-looking origami animals – a lion, an elephant and a three-legged giraffe. Making them for her was a totally silly, but quite lovely plan Simon had hatched in the gift shop, before discovering when he woke early and decided to surprise her with them that his talents at origami were somewhat limited.

"I tried!" he laughed, pointing to the pile of discarded attempts in the corner of the tent as Abby leaned over to plant a big kiss on his flushed cheek.

She still had the animals, stowed away in the attic. Holding the perfectly made giraffe from the freesias in her hand, she was pleased they were safe up there amongst the dust and cobwebs, along with their other forgotten possessions, otherwise she might have shredded them in her recent erratic state of mind.

"I made it for you."

Abby jumped, and dropped the giraffe, as Simon stood in the doorway watching her. "Yes… thanks – you've got better." She began separating the freesias and trimming their stems, trying not to show that her hands were shaking. She attempted to fill the awkward silence, "The origami I mean; it's not wonky and it's got four legs and everything." Annoyed that she had revealed that she made the connection to their past, she forced herself to stop rambling.

Simon walked across the room and stood beside her, close enough that Abby could feel the heat of his skin and smell his familiar and quite lovely aftershave.

"I mean it you know, I am sorry. Abby, I want you back." He attempted to hold her gaze, but she looked away.

"Simon, this isn't fair, not now, please."

He let out a deep sigh and put his hand gently on her arm. Part of her wanted to melt into his warmth, just give in and let all the angst slip away, but she knew she shouldn't.

Forcing herself to gain control, she stepped away. It wasn't right. Abby needed to know and feel that she still loved him;

that she could still be with him without being tortured by her unforgiving mind. Being in need of a hug and longing for the physical connection they used to share wasn't a good enough reason to take him back. She needed to have a clear head – something she wasn't entirely sure she would ever possess again.

Changing the subject, she decided to stick to her plan of getting him to agree to have the girls while she went on the residential, and getting out of the house as soon as possible. "I have to go and collect Mum, Kennedy's expecting us." She poured water into the vase of freesias and inhaled their scent before placing them on the side and turning back to face Simon. "But I need to know first if you'll have the girls while I go on a school thing… a weekend residential. You know, as I haven't been for years, the head expects it," she lied. "Will you do that? I'll email you the details."

Slightly taken aback, the conversation clearly having taken a turn he was not expecting, Simon responded hesitantly. "I'll need to know what to do – you know, what they eat, when they eat, stuff like that."

"Simon, they're not babies, they eat at meal times and they eat food – just like you."

"Of course, yeah, sorry." Clearly torn between agreeing to please Abby and placing himself in a position way beyond his comfort zone, Simon pushed his hand through his hair.

Sighing, Abby added, "Don't worry, I'll put it all in the email. You'll be fine!" Having affirmed his decision for him before he was able to back out, Abby calmly kissed and hugged the girls. "I'll be back to put you to bed, be good for Daddy." Then she said goodbye and left the house.

Once she reached her car she let out a big breath and gave in to the trembling that had been building inside her. Placing a shaky hand inside her pocket she took out the giraffe she had

43

been unable to leave discarded on the kitchen side. She looked again at the word written on the tag: *SORRY!* She shook her head and sighed. *Bloody hell, I'm going to have to keep my wits about me!*

Abby felt ill-equipped to pitch her frazzled mind against Simon on a quest. She knew he could be a formidable force when he wanted something and that he knew how to persuade people to comply with what he wanted. It came naturally to him. It was part of what made him so bloody charming and so very good at his job. And of course, he knew too much about her; he was extremely well-versed in the likes and dislikes of his target audience for this campaign. Summoning every ounce of determination she could muster from her confused mind, Abby tucked the giraffe away inside her bag. One thing was clear: she needed to know her own thoughts. She needed to understand her own mind and she needed to do that soon.

Chapter 7

Abby wondered why she had agreed to spend an afternoon in the company of her mum and sister, helping at her nephew's cycling club, when she knew her mind would be in a state. Drinking coffee, a beverage she usually avoided knowing Simon didn't like the smell, she was buzzing and trying extremely hard to remain calm. Kennedy on the other hand was in her element. She was busily arranging sticky squares of lemon drizzle cake, moist carrot cake, chunks of rich fruit cake and a variety of elaborately topped cupcakes – all baked at home in preparation for the event – on floral-printed cardboard cake stands. Abby watched, bemused, unaware until this point that such items even existed in disposable form.

As Kennedy placed her carefully written price lists alongside her offerings Abby couldn't help but tease her. "Oh no, they might get greasy; I could have laminated those for you, you know!"

Kennedy's sincere panic made her feel just a little bit guilty as she grinned.

Her mum had been put on tea-and-coffee duty and was eagerly preparing polystyrene cups and two huge brown teapots that wouldn't have looked out of place at a post-war street party. Abby liked to see her engaged so keenly; it kept her busy and stopped her from quizzing her about how she was – and from telling her to write to Denise Robertson for advice (as if sharing her problems with the viewers of *This Morning* was something Abby would find helpful).

Abby wished she could share her mum's enthusiasm for the job she'd been given, but quite frankly the monotonous task of putting safety pins on numbers and then putting them in piles of ten ready for the riders to collect before the race simply didn't occupy her mind enough. She found it frustrating and pricked her finger too many times. All the while the positive and negative voices in her head battled, creating a din akin to white noise as a background to any other thought she tried to sustain.

For Kennedy this weekly routine, along with washing Morgan's cycling top until it was window-test-white, featured highly on her Mum-of-the-Year-ometer. Five years her senior, Abby's sister was in every way her opposite. Her long, wavy blonde hair framed her peaches and cream complexion and contrasted with her bright blue eyes. Dressed in a wispy, floral Cath Kidston tea dress that showed off the slim physique she retained from her years of training as a dancer, and with her hair pulled into a casual topknot, Kennedy looked every part the domestic goddess. She clearly dominated the race headquarters' kitchen. The other mums were obviously more than a little intimidated by her and seemed to steer clear of the area until everything was set up and they could no longer resist the call of the homemade cakes. Only then did they approach and make idle chat about the pending race and their boys' previous performances.

Abby watched as the club leader, a man who possessed a leathery tan she feared belied a white torso and thighs beneath his shorts and t-shirt, fiddled with his laptop. Clearly he was going to be in charge of recording and posting results. Abby remembered watching her dad race when she was a little girl. In those days she and Kennedy would wait eagerly for the results to be scribed onto a blackboard, but today they were going to be instantly displayed on an interactive whiteboard, similar to the one Abby used in the classroom – *how times have changed*. Morgan's interest in cycling had filled Abby's dad with pride. Abby knew she would always be grateful for the distraction supporting his grandson had offered him in the tough year before he died; she also knew she would always regret not making it to watch one of Morgan's races with him. All those things that had occupied her time and made her too busy to go along seemed so very insignificant now.

With the race about to start the riders all headed towards the door, walking clumsily in their cleat-soled cycling shoes. In these post-Chris Boardman days with British cyclists dominating the sport they readily emulated their heroes and looked like Lycra-clad aliens about to leave the mother ship as they approached the light of the door.

"Good luck!" Abby and her mum called in unison as Morgan turned and waved. Keen to see Morgan off, Kennedy momentarily left her post and followed the throng.

Seizing her moment, Abby darted behind the cake table but in her hurried attempt to feign purpose she knocked the entire stack of napkins across the floor, which instantly made her blood run hot in her veins and her body tense. Increasingly she found she had a much shorter fuse than usual. She didn't like it. Having the ability to remain calm had always been an asset she was proud of, but these days she felt like a grenade whose pin had just been pulled. Certain that Kennedy freaking out at her would tip her into a rage nobody in the room deserved to witness, Abby quickly bent to pick them up.

"A tea and one of your fine buns please."

Bottom stuck in the air and taken quite by surprise, Abby went to stand and hit her head on the table. "Bugger!" Rising with a red face, aware that the word had come out a little too loudly, and only just managing to steady a cake-laden stand before it toppled its contents into one sticky heap, she snapped, "What?" and looked up. As her eyes met the bemused gaze of Bradley Hunter she froze.

Unable to hide his amusement, and with a distinctly cheeky sparkle in his eye, he replied, "I was just admiring your buns, Mrs Turner!"

With cheeks still ablaze but her anger undoubtedly subsiding, Abby rubbed her sore head and smiled. "Blimey Brad, you made me jump! What are you doing here?"

"I'm in the next race. You know me, can't resist a bit of healthy competition!"

Abby smiled and was about to speak when Kennedy caught her eye, her pace clearly quickening when she noticed her once pristine but now slightly dishevelled cake stand.

"Uh-oh!" Abby rolled her eyes at Brad.

Reaching the table in what seemed like only three strides, Kennedy gave her sister a thoroughly disapproving look. "Abby! What happened? I've only been gone a couple of minutes."

"I was, umm… helping…" Abby responded weakly, feeling like a naughty child and quite sure that her cheeks must be turning purple as she spoke.

Kennedy's wide eyes flicked from Abby to the napkins spread across the floor and then to the offending cake stand, before she placed her hands on her hips and took another breath.

"It's my fault. I knocked it." Bradley leapt in before she could speak. "Sorry. Abby was just trying to put it right, weren't you?" He glanced at Abby, grinning, eyes urging her to follow his lead.

Smiling innocently, Abby added, "It's true!"

Kennedy stared at the pair of them, raising her eyebrows, looking like a teacher fully aware that her pupils were getting one over on her.

Abby decided to quickly change the subject. "Kennedy, this is Bradley Hunter, he's the PE co-ordinator at school. Brad, this is my big sister Kennedy and technically these are her buns!"

Abby motioned at the cakes and moved aside, enabling Kennedy to say a quick hello to Brad and bluster past her to rectify the damage she'd caused.

"There's a while before my race, won't you join me for a coffee?"

"Oh… ummm." Abby brushed the crumbs from her top and swept her fingers through her hair in an attempt to regain the poise she'd lost in her battle with the cake stand. She wished she didn't always feel like the frumpy, slightly dumpy younger sister in Kennedy's presence and regretted introducing her to Bradley.

"Come on, you owe me after that performance." Bradley smiled and motioned towards the chairs at the side of the hall.

But before Abby could respond her mum appeared with two steaming cups of coffee. "Here you go, you deserve a break!"

Abby looked at her mother, unsure why, when all she had done was put blessed safety pins on numbers, she suddenly deserved a break.

"I'm Eleanor Scott. Abby's mum." She smiled at Brad. "Call me Eleanor."

Abby stared, eyes wide, at her mum.

Brad grinned. "Lovely to meet you Eleanor, how much do I owe you?"

"Oh no, these are on the house!" she added determinedly before passing the cups to Abby with a smile and heading back to the kitchen.

With the polystyrene squeaking as it rubbed together Abby set the hot coffees down on a nearby table and sat down.

Bradley smiled keenly as he took the seat next to her. "So I see you are down for the year six trip this year. It's great you're joining us."

"Oh yeah, I don't know what I was thinking! I saw the activities list this week – can you imagine me climbing, abseiling…? It'll be a disaster." Abby rolled her eyes; she hadn't thought about actually having to *do* the activities when she'd signed up. The thought of attempting any of them made her shudder, but the sudden thought of attempting them in front of Bradley made her positively cringe.

"You'll be great! And if you have trouble I'll be there."

Trying to avoid revealing that this was exactly what she was afraid of, Abby laughed nervously.

"Seriously though, it will be good, you'll see!" Bradley looked directly at Abby, his fixed gaze reinforcing his words.

"I'm sure you're right," Abby added unconvincingly as her neck flushed and she looked away. An awkward silence fell between them and Abby sipped her coffee.

Bradley took a breath. "So your sister takes this whole 'twee and cake' thing a bit seriously doesn't she?" Stifling a giggle he added, "If she wasn't so blonde I would have thought she was Kirstie Allsopp's evil twin!"

With that they both laughed.

Abby hadn't genuinely laughed out loud at anything for so long, and hearing her own release, she suddenly felt very self-conscious about sharing this moment with Bradley. She had spoken to him and joked with him hundreds of times at school and yet here, out of their usual staffroom context, it felt wrong. Feeling ready to laugh again felt wrong. Abby suddenly found herself ill at ease in his presence. Picking up her coffee she motioned towards the kitchen, pretending to have seen Eleanor beckoning her.

"Oh look, my mum needs me and you better get ready. Good luck with the race."

As she began to walk away Bradley called after her, "Maybe I'll see you after, then? Remember to save me one of those buns!"

Try as Abby might to busy herself and to definitely not look in Bradley's direction as he got ready for his race, she couldn't help herself. Of course she had seen him in shorts and a t-shirt countless times before; she had even seen him in his swimming shorts at the school gala. She knew, as did everybody that laid eyes on him, that he had what could only be described as an incredibly fit body, but actually seeing him strip out of his clothes and wrap a towel around himself in preparation to remove his black Diesel hipsters was something else! Something, in fact, she decided she should not be watching. With a polite, "You OK here Mum?" she picked up her bag, slipped her hand in to feel for the giraffe tucked inside and walked through the kitchen. Once through the fire exit she welcomed the cool afternoon breeze on her hot cheeks.

Chapter 8

"Well done. You have made the first, and what will probably be the hardest, step towards resolving the issues you face. You have reached out for help and I am here for you; working together we will help you move on from your current state of disconnection and confusion towards a greater understanding of yourself and the pathway you wish to take in the future!"

Abby found the contact details for Mallory Atkins while surreptitiously peeking at a little blue book in her GP's waiting room. The unambiguously named *Directory of Qualified Counsellors in your Local Area* sat glaring at her, begging to be unearthed from its half-buried position amongst old copies of *Woman's Weekly* and *Reader's Digest* while she waited to be called for her quarterly B12 injection. The good thing about taking a 7:45am appointment was that the waiting room was empty; there was nobody to see her slowly pick up the little blue book, gingerly open the front cover and quickly take a photograph of the first page with her phone. Obtaining the information, provided you wanted a counsellor whose surname started with A, was as easy as that. Actually phoning a counsellor and admitting she needed help Abby found much harder.

"It's all so bloody American and I am purposely holding a grudge against all things American," she had protested.

But Melissa was having none of it. "You cannot possibly blame an entire country for the misdemeanours of your husband and one woman of limited morals, and being as you are clearly not taking 'get over it' plan A seriously," she paused momentarily to eye Abby up and down, "then it's time to bring plan B into action."

Abby dismissed both the need for plan B and the concept of seeing a counsellor. "The new wardrobe is coming soon; I have put sticky notes in my Next directory and everything." A fact which was true: she had tucked them inside the front cover of her Next directory before she popped it away in the cupboard. "And I don't need a counsellor, honestly Melissa… what would I say? My mind's a mess!"

"But that's the point, you're confused. A counsellor will help you with that. Now stop making excuses and give this Mallory woman a call!"

As the already-dialled phone was thrust into Abby's face she had no time to back out before she could hear the chirpy voice of Mallory Atkins in the earpiece.

Mallory seemed to Abby to be an overly optimistic, flamboyant woman, probably in her mid-forties. She was little more than five foot and had an amply rounded figure. Her cheery voice, edged with a slightly condescending tone, was largely unthreatening. In truth Abby soon found that she quite liked Mallory's habit of hyperbolising every little bit of praise she readily lavished upon her £40 an hour clients. Besides, she was the only counsellor in the A section of the directory who did home visits after the children were in bed. She was Abby's only option!

Dressed entirely in sky blue and wearing chunky gemstone jewellery Mallory carried a large carpetbag that reminded Abby somewhat of Mary Poppins. Thankfully she had no measuring tape with which to summarise Abby's state of mind – "*Abby Turner, practically crazy in every way!*" Mallory's kit bag contained the paraphernalia of counselling: a notebook and pen, a large box of man-sized tissues and a bottle of Evian. Thankfully there were no hidden crystals or incense sticks to burn – which Abby had sworn would have seen her counselling debut come to an abrupt end.

By their second meeting they were no longer discussing the particulars of Abby's situation; they were onto the nitty-gritty and it was time to discuss her feelings. This was not an easy thing for Abby to do, particularly as the confusion that frequently took over her mind and her subsequent emotional shutdown meant she didn't have a clue how she truly felt about any of it.

"Are you angry Abby? You don't seem angry. Do you feel anger? Resentment perhaps?"

"Yes, I suppose, all of those things."

"Can you show me that anger? Do you want to get cross? Show me how you feel."

"I can't."

"But why? You feel those things, don't you? Don't you want to let them out?"

Abby took a breath. Yes, at times she felt all of those things. At times she was so angry she barely knew what to do with herself. But could she summon all of that on this Tuesday evening at 8:30pm? No! What did Mallory want to see? If only she could replay her tantrum; she was sure the praise Mallory would bestow upon her would not only see her nominated for an Oscar for her performance but would also see her ascending the steps of the stage and making her heartfelt acceptance speech. But in truth, on this Tuesday evening she felt empty. Devoid. Nothing to report and she was paying for the privilege of sharing that with Mallory. Feeling somewhat that her emotions had been darted with a tranquiliser big enough to fell a bull elephant, Abby felt out of her depth and sought to distract Mallory.

"I have a book."

"A book? What sort of a book?"

"A book I am using to help unscramble my feelings. At least, I am trying to."

"That sounds wonderful, tell me more about… about your book." Mallory clasped her hands together in anticipation.

"It's silly really—"

"Uh-uh, nothing is silly," Mallory interrupted, waggling her finger, causing her gemstone bracelets to clang together. "Remember that in these sessions we can share everything in the confidence that all things are valid! Please... carry on."

"I got the idea from the Oasis at school. It's a place we send children when they can't cope – you know, with their emotions, things at home, that kind of thing. One of the ladies in there told a child in my class to keep a book. A book where he could put his feelings, you know, to help get them out of his mind. I thought it was worth a try. I thought it might help me too."

Mallory's eyes widened. "What a wonderful idea! I am so proud of you!"

Abby felt relieved that she had offered Mallory at least something to lavish praise upon; it seemed important to her and Abby didn't like to disappoint her.

"And tell me, has it helped? Have you put your feelings in it?"

Oh bugger! Abby knew Mallory's wide eyes and excited anticipation were not expecting a few quotes and one statement of intent that she had only partially kept to.

"Really, it's just notes, you know – not much of importance."

Mallory shook her head, drawing Abby's attention to the wiry grey streaks that caught the light amongst her thick black hair.

"But your feelings are important! You must understand that Abby. If you would like I could... I mean, you could show me your book, share your thoughts with me."

Abby shifted uneasily in her seat. She should never have made it sound so grand.

"Your thoughts and feelings – they matter Abby; understanding that will be the key to setting your mind free."

Unable to cope with much more counsellor speak Abby went to her bag and took out her book. Nervously, she handed it over. Mallory opened it. The giraffe Simon had made her fell out onto Mallory's lap.

"Oh, what's this?" She held it up inquisitively.

"That? Nothing," Abby insisted, "just something for the children; it must have slipped in there when I popped it in my bag at school." (*Or*, Abby thought, *my husband made it for me as a reminder of the first time we made love, when everything was new and special, and when I was sobbing over it the other night I decided to put it in my book to keep it safe and far away from the inquisitive hands of my children!*) She took the giraffe and placed it in her pocket. Some things and some feelings she simply wasn't ready to share.

Mallory turned her attention back to the book and read with interest. Raising her eyebrow, she picked up her pencil and made a note in her own notebook. *Oh Lord!* Abby wondered what on earth she had revealed about herself.

Mallory tapped her pencil against her lip. "I like this! We can use this."

Hmm. So perhaps she wasn't as disappointed as Abby feared she would be.

"How would you feel if I gave you some homework?"

Homework? Abby wasn't sure she liked the idea. "What would you like me to do?"

"I would like you to write a letter, either to your husband, or to the woman – Helen, you said, didn't you? Tell them how you feel. Tell them your thoughts and feelings."

"I couldn't, I can't; it's too… too much."

"Oh, not to send, oh dear no – in your book. Write as if it is to them. It might help you unlock some of your frustration and give us something to work from. Can you do that?"

No! Abby felt quite certain that she absolutely couldn't, and yet the words were out before she had time to stop them and she agreed despite herself. "Yes, of course!"

Mallory clapped her hands together and beamed.

Chapter 9

Dear Simon,
I am so
I feel
I just want to say – Arghhhhhh!

Stamping her feet and growling through gritted teeth Abby tore the page out of her book and screwed it up. Her homework, despite her best intentions to let her feelings out, was not going well and she was running out of time to get it done before the residential. Leaving homework until the last minute was not a concept that sat easily with her, but with a shopping trip and beauty treatments with Melissa arranged she had more pressing matters to panic about. Despite the fact that most women she knew would love the day she had planned Abby felt it was all way beyond her comfort zone. With a queasy feeling growing in the pit of her stomach she questioned exactly how she had let herself get pressured into it. She thought back over her conversation with Melissa who, with a persuasive insistence Simon would have been proud of, had convinced her the beauty treatments were essential pre-wedding research and the clothes shopping was (apparently) just essential.

Abby rolled her eyes at how easily she had given in, but also reminded herself that going out with Melissa had given her a valid excuse to decline lunch with Simon, Kerry and the girls. She wasn't ready just yet to let Kerry off the hook for her thoughtless message and she certainly wasn't ready to play happy families with Simon either. In fact she enjoyed telling him she had other plans and the questioning look on his face when she didn't reveal what they were. But more than that, she was actually in need of some grown up girly time. Admittedly she didn't find the prospect of beauty treatments and shopping as relaxing as catching up over a long, gossipy lunch with Rachel but Abby was increasingly enjoying the time she spent with Melissa. Before her troubles with Simon they had just been colleagues, but now they had become closer. Melissa had frequently been there when she needed someone – she had propped her up and helped her prepare to face the day on more than one occasion after finding her crying in the toilets at the start of school. And her advice, although it hadn't always been welcome, had at least given her something to think about, an opportunity to look forwards rather than back.

Without Melissa she would have felt Rachel's absence even more keenly. Rachel's job as a personal assistant to Rebecca Giles, the renowned author riding the wave of her hugely successful erotic novels and very much in demand across the globe for promotional events and book signings, enabled her to travel extensively and Abby hadn't seen or heard from her properly in what seemed like too long. Maybe her decision not to contact her about her problems with Simon had been a mistake but she didn't want to make her feel caught in the middle, as if she had to take sides. Instead she determined not to call and to keep her emails jolly (as much as she could muster in her state of mind) and short. The fact Rachel hadn't called her either, as she surely would have done if she'd known, made her think Simon must have decided against telling her too.

Tooting her horn outside, Melissa took off her baseball cap, lifted her thick-rimmed sunglasses and waved from her gleaming white Mini convertible.

"Bramble, it's down to you, save me!"

Raising his heavy eyelids at Abby, Bramble let out a sigh without lifting his head from his paws.

"Hopeless!" Giving him a goodbye pat on the head and accepting her fate, Abby picked up her bag and fleece and went to the door.

Melissa, who was dressed casually in skinny jeans, a tailored open-necked shirt and pumps, greeted Abby excitedly and moved her navy Radley tote bag, which Abby was pretty sure would have cost more than her own entire outfit, to the small footwell below the back seats.

"There's a cap in there if you want one." Tucking her wavy auburn hair back into her hat, Melissa motioned to the glove box.

Abby declined: she didn't want to contend with hat-hair for the rest of the day, having just spent twenty minutes blow-drying it all into place.

After just a couple of roads, with her hair thrashing around her face, Abby realised her mistake and gave up trying to keep it tame. She also realised Melissa had the strange habit of very slightly pressing the accelerator and brake in a weird scissor action while driving, giving a kind of rocking motion to the journey. Secretly enjoying the fact that Melissa, who always seemed so together and sure of herself, was in fact a terrible driver, Abby started to giggle. Her giggles turned to laughter and she soon found herself holding her stomach, practically convulsing as the peals of laughter burst from her. She didn't want to stop and quite possibly couldn't even if she tried. Tears streamed down her face. Glimpsing herself in shop windows as they drove by only made it worse. Her hair was practically standing on end; everything about her looked in chaos compared to Melissa, who wouldn't have looked out of place if they had been filming for a car commercial.

Abby had no idea if her tears were happy or sad, she simply felt out of control, verging on hysterical. At first Melissa looked bemused; she rubbed her hand on Abby's upper arm and initially went for a sympathetic "Ahhhh", but after a while Abby's infectious laughter caught hold of her too and she was joining in. By the time they were parking in town, they had both laughed so hard their chests ached and they were gasping for breath.

"Spending time with you is like playing emotional roulette. You are fabulously bonkers!" Melissa panted.

"I know… I'm sorry… I've no idea what that was about!" Abby wiped her face, trying to regain some composure.

"Who cares? It was good to see you happy!" Melissa threw the comment back as she went to get a ticket for the car.

Abby looked at herself in the mirror. The wind had fixed a grin onto her face; she had a fringe that stuck up in the air and a mass of knots where her carefully straightened hair had been. She didn't know if she felt happy, but she suddenly found herself feeling surprisingly optimistic about the day ahead and decided not to overthink it.

Melissa was full of energy and enthusiasm as she excitedly reeled off a list of shops they could explore before their two o'clock appointment at the somewhat intimidatingly named *Prrrr*imp Your Hide salon. Abby listened intently, attempting to take it all in.

"You know Melissa, what we need is a plan of action for the day. Let's stop off in Costa and get organised, that way we won't miss anything out." It was a cunning plan and Abby was quite surprised when it actually worked and she found herself sitting in Costa sipping coffee and breaking a chocolate tiffin in half (reducing the calories to just over two hundred!), only half-listening while Melissa listed the shops she wanted to cover.

"So how is the weight loss going?" Melissa asked, changing the subject and taking her half of the tiffin off the plate.

Suddenly the chunk in Abby's mouth didn't taste so good. She swallowed and took a swig of coffee to help push it down.

"Well, I have lost a stone now," she exaggerated, "and I am down a dress size."

"That's great!" enthused Melissa. "It's really starting to show. You look great... today."

Today! Abby considered mentioning the fact that Melissa was implying she generally didn't look good, and then reconsidered as flashbacks of her own bedraggled image over recent months came into her mind. Instead she chose to continue to focus on her weight loss.

"Thanks, I wish it would shift more off my hips instead of my boobs though, I don't want them getting any smaller." She laughed, pulling out the neck of the t-shirt and shaking her head at her shrinking bust.

"I know what you mean, I'm having the same problem with my pre-wedding diet. I really don't want the bust of my dress to be the only part which needs taking in at my next fitting."

"Imagine if they have to take the bust in but let the waist out!" Abby exclaimed with a big laugh – realising almost instantly that Melissa hadn't found it funny. Instead she was looking stunned and had put the remainder of her half of the chocolate tiffin back on the plate. Abby cringed from the bottom up, stopped laughing and quickly added, "But that won't happen!"

Melissa's mouth curved as she offered a smile that didn't reach her eyes and a light, fake laugh. If it was intended to make Abby feel better it didn't work.

"Oh Melissa, I'm sorry. I didn't mean it. I have a terrible sense of humour. You look stunning. You'll look great on your big day!"

It was true; Melissa was about a size 12 and always looked gorgeous. In Abby's opinion she certainly didn't need to diet. Melissa's face softened and Abby felt the tension inside herself ease. It was a reminder that her friendship with Melissa was still new – they didn't always quite get each other yet. *Note to self: weddings and weight jokes don't mix.*

The awkward moment having passed, Melissa looked at the list of shops she had added to their itinerary and appeared to spring back to her usual bubbly self. "It's OK, I'm feeling a bit sensitive this week; you know, just a lot on." She picked up her tiffin and started to nibble it before continuing. "Anyway, this is one of my fab five days. Yay, I get to eat!"

Abby gave her a quizzical look.

"You know, five and two; eat for five days, restrict yourself for two. The terrible two are a killer!"

Abby nodded and grinned, not so much because she had heard about the 'fab five, terrible two' diet but more because only a teacher would use alliteration to help her diet become more palatable.

"Ooh, you know what we need?" Melissa's face lit up, as if she had the answer to all their problems. *If only!*

"No… What?" Abby asked, fearing the answer.

"Exercise! It will keep us going. Especially you. You don't want the weight slipping back on now you are starting to be less miserable."

That statement surprised Abby. Not the exercise part – she wasn't sure why she hadn't already considered the fact that exercise would be the next torture Melissa lined up for her – but the part about being less miserable. Was she less miserable? Abby pondered it. *Maybe.* Or maybe she was just learning to accept the misery as part of her. She had stopped fighting it so much; she was more accepting of the voices in her head and her imagined images of what Simon had got up to in Washington. She hated them, but she also knew that part of her didn't want them to go. She needed to remember all that had happened.

"I am NOT joining a gym. I don't have time!" Abby imagined herself in the clothes of a 1980s Jane Fonda with the body of the dancing hippo in *Fantasia*. It was not a pretty sight!

"No, OK, but I'm sure we can think of something – leave it with me. I'll get us fit!" With that Melissa stood up decisively. "Ready to hit the shops?"

Abby sighed.

Chapter 10

Being a Saturday, the High Street was busy. It was a hot day and there was a lot of flesh on show – some of it definitely worth sharing, some of it definitely not. Abby felt comfortable in her cropped jeans, navy t-shirt and sandals. With the array of shops spread before them she looked at her favourite haunts: ELC and Mothercare (shopping always included getting something for the girls); M&S (she loved the food hall and café); Waterstones (even though at present she found she couldn't concentrate long enough to read, she was still buying books she hoped to read one day). These shops would have all been on her own itinerary, but today she had placed herself in the hands of Melissa and while she had only half-listened to her outline for the day ahead she was pretty sure such shops didn't even feature in Melissa's world.

Abby was also pretty confident that some of the more teenage-type clothes shops wouldn't feature either, and for that she was grateful. Clothes shopping in general filled Abby with dread. The thought of humiliating herself in front of a young, orange-faced, gloriously thin shop assistant, scantily clad in clothes which wouldn't look out of place on an X-Factor wannabe, fuelled her fears. While Melissa was younger than her, Abby knew she would be relatively safe in her hands; she was one of those people who went for understated elegance and chic, her look undoubtedly more Kate Middleton than Katy Perry.

"Right, what shall we attack first: the fact that summer is approaching and you have the winter wardrobe of a fifty-year-old librarian, or those bloody mandals you insist on wearing?" Melissa thrust out her hand, pointing at Abby's sandals.

Abby lifted her bag to her chest. "Miiiiiaaaaa-ow! Don't hold back on my account Melissa, say it like it is!" she laughed. Abby knew Melissa was teasing but she also knew there was an element of truth in her analysis of her clothes; there was no point in arguing. Feigning insult she continued, "Anyway, I'll have you know these are women's sandals and they're really comfy, great for walking!" Abby waggled her foot in Melissa's direction, showing off her lightweight, chunky Velcro-strapped sandals.

"Abby. Honestly, unless I'm mistaken you are not about to go hill-walking in the Hebrides!"

They both laughed.

"OK. Let's start in Next; your order must be lost in the post!" Melissa gave Abby a wink and a knowing grin.

Abby appreciated the safe option to start. She knew Melissa was easing her in, treating her like her own little special needs clothes project and building her confidence before pushing her further. She also knew Melissa had contrived reasons for their day out, and despite her own fears about the day she was grateful for it.

As they set off in the direction of Next Abby's phone buzzed. She reached for it and discovered two messages from Simon:

Lunch would taste better if you were here. I love you Mrs Turner! x
You are all I can think about. I miss seeing you; I miss holding you close. I want you, and I want you back Abby! x

Her breath caught, heat rose in her cheeks and she hurriedly slipped her phone back in her bag as Melissa raised a quizzical eyebrow.

"It's nothing, just my Mum," Abby stated, unsure why she felt the need to lie. She missed Simon; she especially missed this side of him. When he was away working they would often send each other flirty texts. They were good at it; Abby knew just how to answer to get him wanting more. She thought of at least two different responses she could give that made her heart rate rise a little. But this was wrong! She wouldn't answer; slipping too easily into old habits wouldn't help her. She decided to ignore it. Her phone buzzed again; she bit her lip and clenched her hands at her sides, forcing herself not to automatically check the screen. But she needn't have worried: her mind soon took over and the simple thought – *did he send messages like this to her?* – swept over her warm body with the chill of a cold shower! Fuelled by frustration and anger she decided to throw herself into the whole shopping experience and determined not to look at her phone again.

Clothes shopping really wasn't as hideous as she had imagined. Once she got over the embarrassment of revealing her size and realised that Melissa had obviously missed her calling as a personal shopper she actually started to enjoy it. Melissa readily selected, evaluated and reselected outfits for her – it was all rather effortless on Abby's part. She was being pampered and weirdly, she liked it. She hadn't realised how tired she had become of being scruffy and dressing in whatever she had time to grab for herself while at the supermarket. She had forgotten how good she could look. Melissa chose clothes and colours Abby would never have chosen for herself. She liked trying on the range of styles, dresses, skirts and shirts Melissa chose and seeing herself looking so very different. As her dad would have said, she scrubbed up well! She was fascinated by how even just a change of clothes could make her feel different – more confident, more in control. It was all superficial, she knew, but even superficial confidence was better than none!

Feeling a little bolder Abby approached shoe shopping with greater enthusiasm than she otherwise might have. She looked at the range of styles on display and wondered what she should be going for. Her shoe collection consisted of a pair of well-loved trainers, a pair of black loafers for work (which

Kennedy loved to tease her about), her practical but apparently unstylish sandals and a pair of bunny slippers the girls had got her at Christmas. She had never really felt the need to purchase shoes without a purpose; on the rare occasion she went out in the evening she generally wore black trousers and polished up her loafers – Imelda Marcos she was not!

Abby wandered along the aisles of the shop, her eyes searching the laden shelves, unsure if she had ever seen so many shoes in her whole life before. Noticing a pair of red glitter courts in her size, with a slim three-inch heel, Abby grinned, slipped one on and called to Melissa.

Snapping out of the shoe-inspired trance she appeared to be in, Melissa spun around. "Wow! They're stunning, would you have much opportunity to wear them?"

Never! But as Abby looked at her foot in the little mirror on the floor she felt hypnotised by the sparkles and how positively girly she looked.

"I love the style but you need to go with something you will actually wear and can walk in," Melissa continued.

Abby smirked. Prior to her combat boot-loving student days she had in fact often worn stiletto-heeled shoes. She wore them every day to secondary school – in those days she liked to copy her older sister's style and enjoyed the fact that the grumpy old caretaker cursed whenever she wore them into the school hall.

"I might just surprise you!" Abby laughed as she slipped the shoe off and headed towards a display of more understated wedge-heeled shoes. There she found some black crossover sandals and a pair of black patent courts, with a slim ankle strap. They were classier than anything else she owned, and she liked how they felt and the increased height they gave. It was another boost to her newly found faux-confidence.

With their time at the shops almost over Abby held her shopping bags proudly, excited by their contents: her new shoes which increased her existing collection by fifty per cent; two skirts, a dress, new jeans, a tailored jacket and three tops, all sporting labels to shops she'd never even considered entering before and, depending on the cut of the shop, all in one or two sizes smaller than the too-baggy-clothes she was wearing. Proud of the achievement, she made a mental note to surprise Kennedy and give her a ring later to tell her she had actually been clothes shopping; she knew she wouldn't believe it!

"Hmm, now have we got time to fit in underwear shopping?" Melissa looked ponderously between her watch and the lingerie shop in front of them.

Abby looked at the mannequin in the window. The featureless woman was dressed in a deep purple lacy babydoll with chiffon bra and satin straps, and through the sheer material Abby could see a matching suspender belt and stockings. In that moment an image of Simon and a woman dressed like that flashed into her head; they were kissing, hands all over each other. The woman's face was shielded by her proximity to Simon and her loose wild hair. Abby choked back the urge to be sick as bile rose in her throat. She ran to the curb and held onto a nearby lamppost to steady herself. Melissa followed.

Abby caught her breath and swallowed the moisture rising in her mouth. "I can't! Not today!"

Melissa must have recognised the determination in Abby's voice, as she didn't question her. "Hey, it's OK," she said, stroking Abby's back. "How about we do lunch instead?"

Abby didn't feel hungry but welcomed the opportunity to move away from the shop and regain her senses.

As they entered the already busy restaurant Abby's phone rang. She didn't want to speak to Simon, but she also didn't want everybody staring at her as it rang on. She picked it up and decided to turn it off. As she did she noticed Bradley Hunter's name illuminated on the screen and quickly answered it.

"Hey Abby, it's Brad."

Despite the fact that he'd simply confirmed what she already knew, part of her was surprised to hear his voice. "Hi Brad, you OK?"

Melissa's eyebrows rose and she stared at Abby as the waitress led them to their table.

"I was just wondering if you needed any help with packing; you know, about what to pack... I'm pretty sure you can pack a case." He laughed. "For the weekend away – the residential I mean. I wasn't suggesting I was going to whisk you away for a... Oh God! I didn't mean that. Not that I wouldn't love to but um... hey, don't laugh at me! I'm trying to be nice but it's all gone a bit wrong. Anyway, let me know if you need any help with packing or anything. You seemed nervous about it and I'm trying to help."

Abby fought back a chuckle, having never heard Brad in such a muddle.

"Thanks Brad, that's good of you but I have the kit list you gave out. I'll be all set, don't worry."

The phone went momentarily silent before he replied, "Sure... OK. Well, you know where I am then."

"Sure, thanks. Bye." Abby ended the call and turned her phone off.

Having heard the entire conversation, Melissa inhaled and blew her breath out slowly, a teasing glint in her eye. "Well, what have you done to be offered personal help from our PE co-ordinator? I am going on the residential too and yet all I got was a piece of paper with what to bring!"

Abby flustered around, tucking her phone back into her bag. "Oh, he's just being friendly. I told him I was nervous about the activities. He's frightened I am going to bail and he'll be searching for another member of staff at short notice, that's all!" she explained, accepting it as an entirely plausible reason for the call in her own head.

"Uh-ha!" Melissa paused, but as Abby didn't fill the silence she grabbed the menu and continued. "Ooh look at the time, we better just get something light; maybe a starter, we don't have time for a proper lunch before the salon."

Abby groaned at the thought of skipping lunch, her appetite having surprisingly returned.

Chapter 11

The *Prrrr*imp Your Hide Salon was not at all the type of place Abby expected Melissa to seek beauty treatments. It was extremely pink and had a pink-bowed fluffy white kitten (Abby was convinced was Marie from *The Aristocats*) as its logo. If she didn't know better Abby would have thought it was a pet-pampering parlour. Nerves getting the better of her, she blurted, "Wow! I bet they can do all sorts with your pussy!" Cringing and not quite believing that had just come out her mouth, she grinned widely at Melissa, who also seemed to be attempting to take in the very pink sight.

Guiltily, she looked at Abby. "OK, so I should've confessed that this is my cousin's salon. It's a new venture and I said I would pop along sometime." Lowering her voice, she added, "It's not really my first choice."

Abby stifled a giggle at Melissa's obvious embarrassment. She knew families could be extremely diverse and thought it was sweet that Melissa was willing to let her beauty salon benchmark drop to support her cousin.

As they walked in a woman with almost luminous blonde hair greeted them. Her broad, glowing smile made Abby wonder if she had used the same bleach on both her hair and teeth. She had long legs, a perfect figure and large breasts that, under the circumstances, Abby was surprised actually looked real. She wore a black mini skirt highlighting her long, toned legs and a pink salon jacket with *Prrrr* flamboyantly embroidered across the pocket. Her pink lipstick matched her jacket and contrasted with her copper-tanned skin. Stretching out a hand she welcomed them, introducing herself as Mindy.

Melissa stepped forward, shook Mindy's smooth hand and stated that she was Lucy's cousin. Excited by this revelation, Mindy bounced off to get her boss.

People actually do this for pleasure all the time – so it can't be that bad! Abby reminded herself repeatedly. As she looked at the three doors leading off the reception her mind began to wander and she lost the rhythm of her mantra. *Hmmm, so what tortures lie behind there? What if it's a cloning room? Melissa and I are not going to leave here until we look like Barbie and whatshername. What was that other doll's name?* The first of the doors opening drew Abby's mind back to reality and she shouted out the name "Sindy" before she could stop herself. Melissa jumped and turned to look at her, perplexed. Abby bit her lip to hold back the rambling explanation she wanted to give, as from behind a slightly puzzled-looking Mindy, her much shorter and more rounded boss stepped forward.

"So you have met M I N D Y!" she stressed, nodding at Abby, clearly believing her name blurting was in reference to her assistant. "I'm Lucy." She grinned, greeting Abby and embracing Melissa.

Abby rolled her eyes, aware that yet again she had made a great first impression.

While Mindy returned to her desk, the two relatives chatted. Dressed entirely in black with pink accessories and a pink trim to her salon coat, Lucy seemed to grow in stature as she presented her mini-empire to Melissa and proffered the list of treatments available to them. Seeing Abby's unsure expression Melissa stepped in and selected a manicure and pedicure as safe options for them. It wasn't that Abby never took care of herself, it was just that she had never felt the need to let anybody else loose on her when it came to personal grooming; she was quite happy with her own simple routines and had no idea where to start when it came to salon treatments.

Abby looked at the picture of fish nibbling at somebody's

feet displayed on the wall. "When you say pedicure, you don't actually mean…?" Her words trailed off as she looked wide-eyed at Melissa, nodding her head towards the poster.

Melissa glanced up and giggled. "Don't worry, no fish involved. I promise."

"Phew!"

"Oh, but are you sure you don't want your legs waxed?" Melissa teased. "You never know who might be looking at you in your shorts, you know… when you're climbing, abseiling…"

Holding her expression, Abby didn't take the bait and simply stated, "A manicure and pedicure will be fine, thank you," words she had never imagined coming out of her own mouth!

"Fab, that's decided then," Lucy interjected, "and how about we throw in an eyebrow wax – on the house? We've a girl in on training this week. She's lacking volunteers," she added, pleased with her own generosity.

"Well, we'll see how time goes," Melissa stated, attempting to sound supportive but really not wanting to let a student loose on her pre-wedding eyebrows. Abby decided that she most certainly did not have time for that, no matter how long the other treatments took.

With the arrangements made and a promise to look in on them shortly, Lucy took their shopping bags to stow away in her office and left them in 'Mindy's capable hands'. Abby felt a little reluctant leaving her newly acquired stash of clothes but followed obediently as Mindy led them through the second of the doors leading off the reception. Entering a small but flamboyantly decorated room Abby wiped her hands on her jeans and wished they felt less clammy; going for a manicure with sweaty hands felt a bit like going to the dentist after a candyfloss – it was just wrong!

As they walked in Abby had expected to smell nail varnish and chemicals, but instead she was hit with the distinct smell of Parma Violets, a smell she hadn't experienced for years. She'd never really liked the sweets but her mouth watered; she welcomed the sensation across her dry tongue and wet her lips. *Ah, still a chubby child at heart*, she thought, allowing the smell of sweets to ease her nerves.

Taking in the room, Abby's attention was drawn to two white, swooping desks, each with a pink towel draped over them. *Hiding whatever tortures lie beneath*, she thought. In front of the desks were two chairs that wouldn't have looked out of place on a 1980s Athena poster. They were white and actually shaped like hands; the palms forming the seat and the fingers – complete with painted pink nails – stretching up to form the back. They dominated the room. The facing wall was bright pink and contrasted with the white tiled floor. Behind where they stood was a wall entirely covered in a collage of black-and-white shots of manicured hands, perfectly pedicured feet and other equally *prrrrimped* and elegantly presented body parts. It was dramatic and a bit daring in places, much more grown-up than the pussycat exterior of the salon. Abby liked it; it felt almost voyeuristic to look at it. She forced out the thought – *I wonder if she…* – before it took root.

Once Melissa had been made comfortable Mindy guided Abby to the second of the large chairs. The seat felt almost flexible, moulding round her as she sat; it offered a perfectly comfortable upright position.

"I'll be working with Melissa and you'll have Tanya," Mindy explained.

As if on cue the door behind them opened and a young girl walked in, wearing the same *Prrrr*imp Your Hide uniform as Mindy but looking somewhat less polished. *Hmmm, so this could be the student.* Tanya gave a warm smile and took her place opposite Abby.

About to proceed, Tanya spun from her stall and headed

for the stereo. "Hold on! Let's pop on something classical, it'll help you ladies relax," she exclaimed.

As the music drifted into the room Abby observed that Tanya's take on classical music actually meant classic movie themes; with the theme to *Harry Potter* dancing around them Tanya returned to her seat and positioned an anglepoise lamp above Abby's hand with a flourish. Then in the style of a trained double act, both she and Mindy lifted the pink towels from their desks, revealing a buffet of beauty products. For somebody who didn't even own a nail file, it was all rather fantastical. Abby's eyes goggled.

"Right then, let's get started." Tanya took hold of Abby's hand. When the first hit of the cleansing alcohol spray landed she had to stifle a nervous giggle. Just as she relaxed and decided it was actually quite a refreshing sensation, it began to seep in. At that point Abby wished she had listened to Kennedy and used a hand cream day and night as her big sister, who always knew best, advised.

Setting about Abby's nails with a file, Tanya paused and tutted. "You know, your nails…" she hesitated as if pondering the delivery of a momentous verdict before continuing, "are not in great condition!" She tutted again, this time adding a sombre shake of the head. "It's important to eat a good diet you know. Have your five a day!" she stressed.

Feeling thoroughly reprimanded and somewhat embarrassed, Abby felt the need to justify her neglected nails. "I am now. Honestly. I had a spell of not taking care of myself, of not caring enough, but that's changing. Honestly. Fruit and veg and multivitamins are top of my shopping list," she overstated, ignoring a vision of chocolate digestives being the number one item on her shopping list at home.

Despite Tanya's insistence on asking Abby where she was going on holiday, if she had plans for the weekend and other such trivial questions which made Abby want to drop the 'my husband's had an affair so my life's a freakin' mess at the moment' bomb, the rest of the manicure slipped by with her actually enjoying the experience. From the array of nail varnish on offer Abby chose a soft, luxurious taupe. It was pretty and practical; not only would it go with most of her clothes, it would also suit most occasions, teaching and abseiling included! She hadn't worn nail varnish since she was a child and moved her hand as if feeling the weight of it on her fingers as they dried. Melissa had gone for a deep lavender hue, which Mindy described as 'thoroughly on trend' and 'the perfect colour to show off her engagement ring'. Abby couldn't deny it suited her long, slim fingers.

With a slight adjustment in positioning, the pedicure was next. Having ignored and managed to mute the sarcastic voice in her head as she listened to the themes to *The Way We Were* and *The Bodyguard*, the theme to *Romeo and Juliet* felt a step too far. Luckily, just as Abby began to compose a letter for *Our Tune* in her head, Tanya took that moment to remove her from the foot spa and began to massage her feet with cooling peppermint cream. The sensation made her desperately want to return to the giggly state she'd been in earlier in the day, and it took every effort she could muster to stay focused and remain looking sane. Moisturiser and the same sumptuous taupe nail varnish were applied, and Abby's feet were looking and feeling like they belonged to somebody else.

"How's it going in here?" Lucy asked, poking her head round the corner as Abby admired her own matching fingers and toes.

"Lovely, thank you," Melissa enthused.

"It's actually been great," Abby added, sounding a little too surprised.

"I'm so pleased! Come find me when you're done." Lucy grinned. With a spring in her step, she closed the door.

Watching her, Abby couldn't help but feel a pang of jealousy.

Lucy must have only been in her early twenties and yet here she was with her own business. Clearly she had set goals and achieved them. Being nearer forty than thirty, and her recent change in circumstances, had made Abby begin to question her own achievements in life. As awful as she found her current situation she hoped that in the future she might find the strength to use the catalyst to alter her life for the better. Maybe change her work-life balance, see more, do more, dare to have some fun (like everbody kept telling her to). She just had to figure out where the strength might be hiding to actually achieve that. *Hmm!*

Feeling more than a bit bolstered by her new immaculate fingernails and elegantly pedicured feet Abby shocked herself by not wanting the experience, the very experience she had dreaded so much, to end. She was enjoying being somebody else, somebody not like herself at all. It was all new to her and far removed from her usual realm of experience, one small step for most women but a giant leap for Abigail Turner. The day had been a revelation and going home meant facing Simon and reality.

"Is it still possible to have that eyebrow wax?" she asked, the words slipping from her lips before she had quite thought through their consequences.

Excited to be getting her hands on Abby's virgin eyebrows, Tanya flew into action while Melissa scrambled for excuses to avoid having hers touched and asked Abby several times if she was quite sure about having it done.

Fuelled with determination and deciding resolutely not to let the theme to *Edward Scissorhands* inflame her nerves Abby assumed a reclined position and awaited Tanya's full attention. Attention which, prior to feeling Tanya's warm breath on her cheek, Abby hadn't realised would be quite so in her face; the moment made more awkward by the fact that Tanya stuck her tongue out as she concentrated on carefully smearing on the warm wax.

"Be careful! You don't want it in the hair you want to keep," Mindy interrupted.

An unwelcome quiver of nerves rippled through Tanya's hand before she sucked in a breath and assured, "Don't worry, I know what shape I'm going for."

Once the wax had been applied, Tanya smoothed a little strip into place and waited for it to cool off. Tension building, she eventually took hold of one of the unattached corners and Abby braced herself.

"Don't pull up. Remember, pull along," Mindy advised, now also leaning over Abby and taking on the role of tutor.

The interruption caused Abby to breathe, lose focus and release the tension from her body just as Tanya held her skin taut and pulled.

Abby screamed, "Holly fuck!" Eyebrow burning and eyes streaming, she stared at the now three stunned faces looking down on her – even Melissa hadn't quite expected that!

"What?" Abby demanded. "What is it?"

Momentarily they gazed at her, stunned, before Melissa replied, "You swore!"

Relief flooded through Abby as she spoke.

Chapter 12

Abby felt a sensation she hadn't felt in too long: beneath the layers of confusion still present in her mind, she sensed a touch of pride. She felt a bit silly about it. As if the word and the funny feeling she had inside outweighed her achievements, but nonetheless it was there – like the first tiny flicker of light before a match blooms into flame, it was there. She was well aware that all she had actually done was have a manicure, pedicure and an eyebrow wax but in doing that she had forced herself beyond her usual realm of experience, beyond where she felt comfortable, and enjoyed it. Baby steps, Mallory had advised, and baby steps she had taken. She also felt proud that thoughts of Simon hadn't dominated her day; yes, there had been flashes of insecurity, wobbles, even moments of feeling utterly overwhelmed (almost throwing up outside the lingerie shop was a low point, she had to admit), but on the whole she had made the day her own.

As Melissa pulled away, Abby stared at Simon's car in the driveway. Having left her phone off until the journey home Abby had missed his text saying that the girls were getting bored, and his subsequent offer to take them home and do their tea. She hadn't answered but presumably he had taken her lack of response as acquiescence because now he was there. Despite the thump back down to reality of knowing she was going straight in to face him Abby took a breath, glanced at her array of shopping bags clasped in her neatly manicured hands and determined that nothing was going to let her little glimmer of light get snuffed into darkness.

Entering the house undetected, Abby quietly popped her

shopping bags into the cupboard under the stairs. She didn't need to hide them from Simon, he wouldn't have minded the money being spent; in fact he always tried to encourage her to treat herself, insisting that despite the huge disparity in their salaries the money was equally theirs to spend. Even in their current circumstances he hadn't questioned any of their finances and had promised that no matter what, Abby and the girls would never want for money. She believed him too. Simon had watched his mum lose everything when she and his dad divorced and he never wanted his family to experience the same; they would never have to live as he had as a child. No, it really wasn't about the money. Abby stowed the bags away because she just wanted to keep them hers; her day and her new things bought for her to enjoy.

Still undetected, Bramble being under the table awaiting any chance crumbs, Abby stood in the kitchen doorway watching them – her family all where they should be, together in their house. She stared, more than a bit amazed that Simon had cooked spaghetti bolognaise. He was being the perfect daddy, all smiles and time to share. The girls were lapping up both the attention and the dinner without complaint – even though Abby could see he'd forgotten the cheese they always insisted she sprinkle on top.

"Mummy!" Grace's eyes sparkled as she spotted her mummy and bellowed the word.

"Hey gorgeous girlies, have you been good?" Abby greeted each of the girls with a kiss on the head.

"Of course!" Jessica responded cheekily.

Simon looked surprised and was momentarily thrown by Abby's appearance. "Wow! You look… great; so… so relaxed."

Abby smiled. "Thank you, it was a good day."

Simon waited for more but Abby wasn't forthcoming with a further explanation. Filling the silence, he sprung from his seat. "Would you like a tea? Have you eaten? Kerry sent it round; I've heated enough for you too."

That explains the sudden culinary skills. Abby declined the offer of food despite being hungry. "I'm good thanks, don't worry though, it'll freeze. The girls seem to love it." Guilt spread through her as she saw the wounded look on Simon's face. She busied herself with the mail to help fight the urge to retract her response.

Agreeing to let Simon stay and help put the girls to bed made sense on one level – Simon seeing their routine in action saved Abby explaining it all in an email for when she went away – but on another level she found it exacerbated her frustrations. Watching Simon behave like the loving, sweet daddy he had been when Jessica was little, the daddy Abby knew he really was, and having him there with her was exactly what she had wanted for so long, but under the circumstances she knew it wasn't real. If her heart wasn't already in pieces it would have shattered.

Abby wasn't sure why she asked Simon to stay and have a drink with her after the girls were settled. Maybe it was to say thank you for taking them for the day, maybe it was because she was enjoying the happy-family mirage and didn't want it to end, or maybe it was simply that she hated the thought of watching him leave again; at the time she didn't question it. But as they sat on the sofa, Bramble nuzzled between them, relishing their attention, she began to think she had made a mistake. There was an awkward silence in the room as the weight of things unsaid lay too heavily in the atmosphere. Previously, she had always felt so at ease in his presence – comfortable to simply be with him – but now the silence compounded how strained things felt between them.

Abby sipped her martini and searched the room for a distraction. As she looked at the bookcase she wondered if Simon would notice that their wedding picture was missing. Before he could follow her eyes she looked away and noticed that the answerphone was flashing. *Good, something to break the silence.* Leaning across, she pressed play. There was a message from her mum asking if she would see her before she went away, and one from Kennedy:

"Hey, what have you been up to? Sounds exciting. I need details!"

It was a response to a text Abby sent on the way home, hinting at her day. Simon raised an eyebrow and Abby smiled. But as the third message began to play, her smile faded and she froze.

"Hey, it's me, just wanted you to know I meant what I said earlier, and I'm happy to oblige any time." Bradley's voice, too teasing, too jolly, too friendly, spilt into the already laden atmosphere of the room.

Simon sat completely still, staring at Abby. She didn't look at him but she was well aware he was looking straight at her. A hot flush blazed across her neck and cheeks. Wanting to be free from his gaze she went to stand, but Bramble tumbled to the floor and stretched at her feet, preventing her escape.

"Abby, wait! Who was that? What… What is it? What did you do?" Simon scrambled for words, trying to fathom the messages and Abby's response.

Abby couldn't believe the implied accusation. Instantly cross that she was suddenly erroneously feeling like the one with a guilty secret to hide, she turned. Anger burning in her eyes, she seethed, "Really Simon? Really? You want to question me? Question my behaviour? Because let me tell you, I am not the one in the wrong here. I have so many questions firing round my head all the bloody time I can barely think straight. My mind is a mess, most of the time I think I am going crazy, and where are my answers? Where the hell is the explanation you owe me?" Aware that she was hitting him repeatedly with a cushion as she spoke, Abby forced herself to stop. She sat, fighting back angry tears and staring wildly at him.

Simon looked on, stunned, taking in Abby's anger – the hurt branded in her eyes, the fury on her face and the ferocity with which she spat every word.

"Abby, I'm sorry! I am so, so sorry." Tears welled in his eyes. "If I could take it all back I would. I hate what I did. I hate myself, but most of all I hate how much I've hurt you. I know it's all just words…"

Like wedding vows, she seethed inwardly.

"But I mean it, please Abby, I love you. Let me prove to you that you can trust me. I know I don't deserve it but please… Abby, give me – give *us* – a chance." He spoke each word fired with determination to make her listen; she had to know how much he regretted what happened.

Abby didn't respond. She couldn't trust herself; who knew what would come out of her mouth if she spoke – something fuelled by anger, words she couldn't take back, or worse, she might say something to make him feel better and she had sworn to herself she wouldn't do that. He didn't deserve it. He should feel bad, he should be sorry. Only the sound of her breathing was audible in the room as what felt like several minutes passed before Simon spoke again, quieter this time, less desperate.

"What do you want to know? Abby… You could ask me. I'll answer what I can."

"Don't be stupid. The things in my head… I need too many details… it'd be too weird. You wouldn't answer."

"Abby, I want us to get over this. I want you to love me again. If it will help I will answer what I can."

For the first time in weeks Abby's mind went completely blank. She tried desperately to think of all the things she wanted to know as nothing instantly sprung to mind; instead the saying *be careful what you wish for*, one of Eleanor's favourites, spun over and over in her head. Abby sat, momentarily unsure that she actually wanted to know anything. Then it struck

her: her mind was crippled with not knowing the details –
would knowing really make it worse? Perhaps it would make it
better? She stopped holding back. She took a deep breath and
before she could think on it any more she released the spectre
of morbid curiosity that had yearned for this moment.

Chapter 13

Dear Helen – younger, thinner (who knew my husband would be such a midlife crisis cliché?) Helen,

Earlier this year you slept with my husband. After your chats in the bar you knew I existed and that we had children but you didn't care!

Until that moment Simon had only ever slept with me and our wedding vows were unbroken. Does that mean anything to you? Because it did to me! I had loved him since I was twenty-one and he was so very important to me. Not always a great husband, not always a great daddy, not always perfect but MINE! My best friend, my husband, my forever. For almost half our lives we had been together; it had always been just the two of us – our dreams, our family and our future.

I hope sleeping with him was worth it because in that moment, in that drunken, selfish moment, the first time you did it, you knew about me and yet you didn't care. How nasty do you have to be? How narcissistic to think only of your gratification? To sleep with someone – not yours – and not care about my life, my family, my beautiful girls! Almost half our lives spent together, fifteen years, all gone just to have sex, all thrown away so easily. All meaning nothing for the pleasure of cumming!

And after that first night the two of you concocted your lies together, extending his trip to Washington – how clever you must have felt! How easy for you both it all was – just lie to me, I'm worthless, who cares about me? I am so stupid, so trusting, so unsuspecting. Who cares if I am left home, alone, to do EVERYTHING?!!!!! I'll cope, I'll get on – it's what I do!

Did you enjoy your week with my husband? Sleeping with him again and again, holding him, kissing him, touching him, waking up with him? I hope it was truly worth it! And how truly nasty do you have to be to keep speaking to him, to text him, to call him after – once he was home – all the time knowing I was here and we had a life together?

I didn't know it then of course but the countdown was on. It took me – stupid, loving, trusting me – a few weeks to realise, to put it all together, before I managed to actually catch him in our bed reading your text! To see it all so plainly, spelt out for me in your horrible I-love-and-miss-you-babe casual, uncaring, unthinking, selfish, stomach-churning text!

Nothing will ever be the same again. You broke my heart and destroyed my love and trust. You shattered our lives together. I hope it was worth it because now, months on, I still don't know how to live with it. I think about it every hour of every day! Did you feel special? Did you feel like you were important having him lie, lie, lie, LIE for you? Changing his plans, missing work to spend time with you – just to fuck you?

What a horrible, nasty person you must be! You ripped our world apart. I hate you so much. I hate what you did. I hate the nasty lies. I hate you being in my life, the things you have done to me and the fact that the horrible, disgusting, selfish things you did are in MY FUCKING HEAD!!!!

Abby stopped. She put the lid on her pen. She didn't read back over what she had put, but she looked across the page, enjoying the sight of her own words, her feelings, in her book. She hadn't expected to get her homework done before the residential but her talk with Simon had inspired her; her head had been left reeling and she had to let it all out, let the rancour in her mind spill word by word onto the page. What Mallory would make of it Abby didn't know but writing it had at least been a huge release!

Before going to bed Abby knew there was one more thing she must do. Opening her diary she sighed, removed the lid of her pen and made a note: *Visit the clap clinic!*

Eurgh! Simon had said they had been safe but hearing the sordid details made it all so horribly, disgustingly real. Abby had slept with Simon after his trip to Washington, before she knew, and she wanted to be sure she hadn't caught anything. She looked at the words in her diary and wished she knew the proper name; she was sure 'clap clinic' wasn't right. She would have to check the *Embarrassing Bodies* website to see if that enlightened her. It was all so horrible, another experience beyond her comfort zone that she had never expected to face – only this one she was pretty sure wouldn't turn out to be enjoyable.

Chapter 14

The forty-minute ferry ride to the Isle of Wight was choppy to say the least. Ninety children bustled around the café as they were allowed to leave the coach, stretch their legs and visit the toilet. The teachers seized the moment for a hit of caffeine and kept watch for children going green as the boat rolled from side to side. Abby already missed Jessica and Grace but as she watched Portsmouth disappear from view she was pleased to be heading off on an adventure – a fabulous distraction from everything at home. Encouraged by the bubbling children she felt an air of anticipation growing inside her, maybe even a touch of excitement! As the dramatic Jurassic coastline grew in the Solent-splashed window they returned to their coaches and waited expectantly for the final part of the journey to begin.

Twenty minutes on and they were winding their way along a sparse country road, enthusiasm waning as the coach swayed from side to side; even the cheekiest children in the back seat had given up pulling faces at the teachers in the coach behind. "Are we nearly there yet?" droned with increasing frequency from the travel-weary children. Abby watched carefully, wondering which of her three known motion sickness sufferers might erupt first. Ironically, as she attempted to calculate how many hours it had been since their foreboding parents had dosed them up and waved goodbye she couldn't help but notice Jake Price, a child not on her ones-to-watch list, turn a pasty shade of grey. Realising this was not a good sign she flew from her seat, sick bucket in hand, and reached him just as the entire contents of his stomach left his mouth in one huge heave.

Relieved to find most of it had landed in the bottom of the bucket, Abby fought back the impulse to retch building in her throat and attempted to ignore the warm, moist seepage she could feel across the top of her trainers. Recognising the imminent danger of others following suit – Abby included – Patty flew like a woman on a mission into salvage operation mode. The ever-prepared teaching assistant instantly set to with paper towels and disinfectant before passing out her entire – and as Abby couldn't help but notice, somewhat considerable – supply of chewy mints in an attempt to appease everybody's senses. If she weren't still holding the sick bucket Abby would almost certainly have given her a hug!

When they finally arrived at the activity centre and left the coach everybody breathed a refreshing sigh of relief before being pounced on by an extremely enthusiastic instructor who magnanimously ignored the stench they were omitting and keenly introduced himself as Justin – their leader and number one port of call for the duration of their stay. The children were instantly in awe of him and hung on his every word as he rallied them into cheers for each of the activities on their itinerary. A list of events that made Abby fear that her perfectly manicured nails were doomed and instilled her with more than a touch of trepidation, despite her best intentions to retain a spirit of adventure. Following Justin's lead they all collected their luggage and walked towards a large, slightly shabby-looking building.

"Not the usual one then," Patty lisped, holding a chewy mint to the side of her mouth and strutting up next to Abby.

"Sorry?"

"This building – we're normally on the other side, the newer bit," Patty added, gesturing towards the opposite direction to where they were walking.

Typical! Abby sighed as they entered the maroon double doors leading to the place they would call home for the next three days.

The room Abby was designated was down a long corridor, apart from the other teachers but opposite a room of giggly year six girls. It was small and a bit scruffy. Abby sat on the slightly damp, too-soft bed and looked around. It wasn't great but it was a bit of space she could briefly call her own. A few months back she would have hated the thought of the solitude but now she was learning to control the equilibrium of her mind more, albeit with varying degrees of success, and felt she could cope.

As Abby considered unpacking her bag and the likelihood of spiders crawling amongst her things if she did, there was a knock at her door. She opened it to be met by Bradley.

"Hi, I've been sent this way as male lookout to protect you ladies. I am stationed to the right of the stairs should you need me." He gestured through the double doors to the stairwell and the boys' corridor beyond as he spoke.

"Thanks Brad," Abby smiled, "but I think us ladies," she motioned down the girls' corridor, "will be just fine."

"Well, I'm just saying, because you never know..." he mused, reaching up to the corners of the doorframe. The shift in stance accentuated his strong physique and his t-shirt lifted just enough as he stretched to reveal a hint of his firm stomach.

Abby blushed as she realised she was overly staring at the fine hairline of his happy trail. *Oh lord!* She felt a strange tingle as she blinked, attempting to shake off the image. Gathering her senses, she put her hands on her hips. "Now I am sure you have unpacking, or organising or something to do," she stated in her best I-am-not-fazed-by-you voice.

Bradley grinned an infectious, cheeky grin and lowered his voice. "You know, if you keep refusing my offers, Mrs Turner, I'm going to start taking offence!" he teased.

"Oh, is that so?" Abby giggled.

Bradley Hunter was one of those people who commanded attention through their cheeky front and charm, and generally got it. He had the male primary school teacher X factor. He was the one who had the children right where he wanted them, behaving, ready to listen and eager to please. In fact most of the staff, the Head included, responded to him similarly. He did a good job, he was clearly passionate and a good teacher. Abby had always slightly envied his energy and enthusiasm.

Over Brad's shoulder Abby could see mayhem erupting in the room opposite as eight year six girls attempted to choose beds, unpack and put duvet covers on quilts, a task many of them had never done before. They had been placed together because they were friends but the way things were going Abby knew that wasn't going to be the case for long. She pointed over Bradley's shoulder. "I best sort them."

"Ouch! Good luck with that!" He laughed and went to walk away. "Just kidding," he added, stepping back into view. "I'll help." Dropping his bag outside Abby's door he joined her as she ventured into the pandemonium of the girls' room.

Several demonstrations, one child stranded in a duvet cover, a disaster averted when a lost teddy was found and the job was eventually done. With fifteen minutes left until their team briefing and activities started, Bradley returned to rally the boys and they all set about putting on trainers and grabbing waterproofs ready to take on the great outdoors. Before leaving her room, wishing she looked more Lara Croft than Ray Mears in her shorts, Abby checked her phone; there was a voicemail from Simon. Worried that something might be wrong, she pressed play. When she heard Jessica's chirpy voice she stopped panicking and grinned.

"Hi Mummy, I miss you but Daddy is being funny. He is taking us to the park later and doing pizza for tea. I love you.

Hope they are being good for you! Bye. Oh, and Grace says hello." At which point Grace could be heard chipping in with, "Hello Mummy!" in the background. Smiling at her phone, Abby also noticed a text from Simon:

Hey wife, I bet you look great in khaki, feel free to send a pic – I always knew you had a thing for the crocodile hunter! Be careful and have fun! xx

Considering the nature of their last proper conversation the playful tone of the message took Abby by surprise; at first she was unsure about it, feeling that she should be cross when really she just felt amused. It was refreshing. She was tired of so much tension between them. As horrible as her talk with Simon had been, knowing more of the details somehow made her feel more able to deal with it (perhaps her Scott traits weren't going to let her down after all... empower yourself with the facts, assess and overcome!) and she didn't want to be bogged down with the complications of their relationship while she was away. That was what she was escaping, after all. She answered Jessica and Grace with a text – she didn't want to speak to Simon if she called – and then pondered answering Simon's message. Biting her lip, unsure whether she should actually acknowledge it at all, she typed a quick response and pressed send before she could change her mind.

Crikey!!! You should be so lucky; all evidence of me in khaki is staying in the IOW! And don't worry, I will look out for danger, danger, danger!

Rather pleased with her homage to the late Steve Irwin, she left the room.

The team briefing turned out to be more chanting with Justin and being introduced to six equally keen instructors in their late teens to early twenties – a kind of crossbreed between sporty and hippy types – who stood on a wall and called out the names of their activities. The children, already in groups chaperoned by teachers and teaching assistants, fell into line depending on their activity timetable. Up first for Abby and her group was the zip wire, an activity she felt confident she could do with all the enthusiasm of Julie Walters in *Educating Rita* – minus the pink pyjamas. After that it was the welcome campfire, hot chocolate and toasting marshmallows. That she knew she could do!

Chapter 15

With the first activities complete at the end of what had been a long day, the children finally settled down around ten o'clock.

"You'd think they'd be tired after all that." Melissa sighed as she launched herself into an armchair in the makeshift staffroom.

"The first night is always the worst," Bradley added. "By tomorrow they'll be knackered."

Abby felt strangely exhilarated. The fresh air had been refreshing and the campfire had reminded her of happy days in the girl guides with Kennedy. She would have loved to have joined in more with all the singing but her voice was still hoarse from screaming her way across the zip wire, much to the amusement of the year six children who had managed the task with a lot more decorum than their flailing, screaming teacher.

"In the absence of anything stronger, anyone for more hot chocolate?" Abby asked.

They all decided to indulge; Melissa offered to help but Bradley stood, offering to go, before she left her chair. As they bustled around the kitchen rinsing cups and sorting various requests for a little chocolate, a large spoon of chocolate, extra milk, sugar and so forth Abby became very aware of being alone with Brad. The realisation made her feel suddenly hot and more than a bit flustered; feeling all fingers and thumbs she had to force herself to concentrate. She couldn't believe that simply being in such close proximity to him was making her feel so hot and clumsy. Inwardly she reprimanded herself; she had worked with this man for a few years and he hadn't affected her this way before, so why was he making her feel like a fumbling teenager now? Thoughts of brushing up against him, in the style of the movies, naughtily slipped into her mind. *Oh lord, Abigail Turner, you ARE going crazy! Your imagination is running riot due to the fact it has been… ummm, too long!* Heat rose in her cheeks.

Eager that Brad didn't see her crimson blush she asked him to fetch the milk – ensuring he had to move away from her to go to the fridge. *That's better,* she thought, until she turned and caught a glimpse of the smooth base of his back and the dimples that sat just above the line of his shorts as he bent forward. Abby dropped the mug she was holding and chocolate powder puffed up into the air and snowed back down onto the side and floor. Clearing that up at least made her refocus on the task, albeit that despite her protestations Brad insisted on helping and their hands touched a little too often, sending tingles through her body as she felt his skin on hers.

As the head teacher returned from corridor patrol they all drank their hot chocolate and at Patty's suggestion experimented with melting Quality Street into it while sharing their funniest stories of the day. Abby's sick disaster and screaming like a banshee on the zip wire featured alongside Justin being run over by Jake Price in his go-kart and Melissa accidentally setting fire to her marshmallow – something she wouldn't be living down in a hurry. With breakfast scheduled for eight am, but no guarantee that the children wouldn't be up hours before that, one by one they headed off to bed. Only Patty, Abby and Bradley remained.

Abby drank the last of her hot chocolate and caught Brad's eyes smiling at her from above his mug as he sipped the last of his. Abby held his gaze for a moment, feeling what she felt must be the heat from her hot chocolate spreading within her. Sitting between them, Patty glanced from one to the other.

"Doing it then?" she asked excitedly.

Abby looked aghast, while poor Brad positively choked on the drink he had barely swallowed.

"What?" they both asked, cheeks ablaze.

"Abseiling, tomorrow? It's a challenge but I love it!" She grinned.

"Oh, that!" they chorused, both stifling embarrassed giggles as they noticed she was holding the next day's itinerary.

"Oh, yes, of course," Abby said, catching up with the gist of Patty's conversation.

"Oh, for sure," Brad stated.

"I knew you would." Patty slapped Bradley's thigh as she laughed, allowing her hand to linger a little too long, Abby thought. "It's Abby I wasn't sure about. You know she's been all nerves since she saw the activity list," she added, a bit too gleefully.

Feeling more than a little affronted and not wanting Brad to know quite how nervous she had been about the whole trip, Abby leapt to her own defence. "I am definitely up for it!" she affirmed, adding more conviction to her tone than she actually felt.

"That's great Abby," Brad offered sincerely, before turning to Patty. Seeing the slightly smug smile that lingered on her face he added, "You shouldn't underestimate Abby, Patty... I think she can be pretty amazing when she puts her mind to something!" A warm grin spread across his face, reaching his eyes, causing them to sparkle.

Abby looked at Patty, who appeared positively put in her place and for once speechless. A little taken aback and fighting the little lump which swelled in her throat at the sweet compliment Abby stood and grinned at Patty – *ha, who feels affronted now?* – and announced she was off to bed.

Still feeling buoyed by Bradley's words, Abby got to her room and enjoyed a steamy shower before slipping into her panda print short pyjama set and a pair of fluffy slipper socks, both bought a little too hurriedly from the supermarket in preparation for the trip. Feeling thoroughly refreshed but wishing she had considered her pyjama choice a little more fully, she checked her phone. There was a message from Simon:

Hope you've had a good day. Jessica and Grace have been great. They are a credit to you – so bright and funny. I can't believe I haven't done this before; you know, with the two of them. Sorry. And sorry is not really enough. I've missed out on so much. And I miss you. I love you. I hope I get to prove how much I love all my girls!

Abby stared at his words, feeling thoroughly discombobulated. She missed her girls – her 'best things', she liked to call them – and in all honesty she missed her husband. The thing was, she wasn't sure that the husband she missed was the one she still had. She scrolled through the pictures on her phone; pictures of Jessica and Grace, some of Simon on his many trips – Mexico, Las Vegas, California, all places she would have liked to visit too, if only she'd been invited – and one of them all together taken last Christmas. *Yes, they are bright and funny*, she thought; *they are special and lovely and you didn't notice until now! And now… now you want us, I'm not sure I can do it – just accept what you've done and move on. What if I can't do that?* After a few moments of staring at her phone, frustration building inside her, she growled into the empty room.

Almost instantly there was a knock at the door. Embarrassed that perhaps one of the children had heard her, she opened it slowly.

"Are you OK? I was just passing and thought I heard you say something." It was Bradley, his voice a husky whisper.

Abby quickly became acutely aware that she was standing there in what now felt like her way-too-short panda print pyjama set and little else, and attempted to hide herself behind the door as she spoke. "I'm fine, honestly. Just venting. Sorry. I didn't mean to disturb you. Hey, thanks for earlier, you didn't have to—"

Bradley took a step closer, causing Abby to lose track of what she was about to say.

"Abby," he breathed, brushing her arm with his fingers, causing her skin to tingle, "I know I'm full of it, always joking, always making people laugh. But I know you have been through a lot lately. If you need anyone, I'm here. Honestly. Just say."

His face was just inches from hers as he whispered. She could smell hot chocolate and a hint of his lingering aftershave mixed with the fresh-air scent of their afternoon spent outdoors. Abby imagined how easy it would be to kiss him, his lips already so close to hers. She didn't offer an answer; she didn't know what to say. She froze. Bradley held her gaze with his deep brown eyes and let out a sigh that brushed across her cheek.

"You are an amazing person Abby Turner, don't forget that." With that he turned and walked away.

Abby let out a breath. *Bloody hell!* Using all her strength not to call him back, she stood staring after him. She had expected teasing and joking but sincere, sexy-as-hell Bradley was something quite new. Feeling too warm even in her distinct lack of clothing she slumped, perplexed, on her bed, unsure what she had ever done to give Bradley Hunter the impression she was an amazing person. Of course, she told herself over and over, he'd got it wrong; he just felt sorry for her and was being kind; she definitely didn't feel amazing, she hadn't handled things amazingly and she knew she looked far from amazing. People like Kennedy and Melissa they were amazing – she was just ordinary, often out of her depth and generally not even in control of her own mind. Amazing, she determined, she was not!

But as she sat there, alone in her room, she couldn't help but feel a little touched that he had said it. Bradley Hunter

– lovely, funny, cheeky Brad with the thoroughly fit body – had said she was amazing. In fact he had said it twice in one evening! As silly as she knew it was, she giggled to herself as she let that thought linger.

Chapter 16

The words *I am definitely up for it* played mockingly on repeat in her mind as Abby stared up at the huge tree which she was pretty sure put Jack's beanstalk to shame. She knew she had to do it – backing out wasn't an option. Not in front of the year sixes cheering her on, not with the memory of Patty's smug grin still in her mind and certainly not after Brad had called her an amazing person. No, she was a woman with something to prove: to them, yes, but also to herself. She wanted to climb that tree and abseil down it; she needed to do it and she damn well would do it even if it bloody killed her. *And it just might!* Her mind interjected evilly.

With the year sixes spurring her on Abby stood, harnessed and hard-hatted, ready to go. She felt slightly ridiculous in the gear and was grateful at least that only the children and instructors were there to witness her looking like a ready-to-roast turkey. Taking a deep breath she approached the rope ladder flanking the trunk and took hold of it in her shaking hands. As she put her foot on the first rung her legs felt heavy and uncooperative, almost as if she was trying to move them while numb. The rope ladder wiggled as she clung to it; it was fastened in places but still felt too precarious for Abby's liking. *Come on, one step at a time,* she told herself as she took a big breath, urging her legs to move.

The higher she got the more she could feel the breeze around her. The children whooped and cheered from below, but Abby zoned out of the noise, hearing only her own heavy breathing and the murmur of voices in her head. She had to focus on the task in hand and controlling her mind. That and climbing the ladder was making her feel exhausted. Her legs trembled. Again Melissa was right, she really was in need of some kind of exercise routine. At the halfway point she faltered; the ground was already too far away and seemed to spin as she glanced down. Her hands were feeling cold with nerves and her head slightly swimmy. Glancing at the children looking smaller on the ground she growled in frustration. In her mind she envisaged Simon's face and felt the frustration at what he had done, how much it still hurt her and how irrevocable it all was. Anger building inside her, she forced herself onwards and upwards. The platform that had looked tiny from the ground grew tantalisingly closer with every step.

Eventually she reached the top rung and the children roared with excitement. Abby scrambled onto the platform as the awaiting instructor, Libby, heaved at her arm. Thankful to be off the rope ladder and having something firm to sit on Abby became aware that her whole body was convulsing. Nerves and exertion taking their toll, she attempted at least to steady her wild breathing. Libby, a girl in her early twenties, perfect figure, blonde plaits and seemingly completely unfazed by being on a small platform tens of feet off the ground, greeted Abby.

"Awesome, you made it!" Her overly jolly American nasal twang stung at Abby's ears as she stared, dumbfounded. Not quite believing her luck, Abby suddenly felt that leaping off of the platform was going to be easier than she had initially imagined.

Trying hard to forgive Libby for being American, Abby slowly stood to full height, adding five feet, six and a half inches to what already felt like the thirty-five to forty feet she was off the ground. Abby held her breath and looked out across the view. Fearing her courage would fail her she determined not to look straight down. She was aware she was sweating but felt decidedly cold at the same time. The breeze, which remained thankfully calm, met her face as she took in the rolling green view and the sparkling blue sea beyond. It was beautiful. In contrast to her still-quivering body her mind felt oddly tranquil. Not a voice, not a murmur interrupted her moment; she soaked it up. A small smile crept across her face as she looked out, barely noticing Libby as she went about adjusting her harness and ropes ready for the descent. Feeling momentarily revitalised Abby waved at the children, regrettably looking down and flipping her bacon and egg breakfast into a spin as she did.

"Ready then? You just need to lean out and let the harness hold you." Libby grinned.

Caught off guard, her breakfast rising in her throat, Abby felt a hint of panic building inside. She could feel herself, despite all her earlier determination, losing the battle to remain focused and in control. Her fear showed in her white face and panic-stricken eyes. Libby steadied her.

"You can do this! Look how far you've come," she said, not knowing how deeply her words penetrated Abby's mind.

She was right of course. Abby had come too far just to give up now, and besides, what was the alternative? A wobbly, shamed descent of the rope ladder, or worse, staying with Libby and listening to more of her overly jolly American accent. Steeling herself, Abby took a long, deep breath and decided to go for it.

Guided by Libby, Abby stepped to the edge and leaned back. It was a weird sensation of air and empty space below her but she felt her harness and the rope take the strain and felt reassured. Slowly, taking baby steps, she edged gradually down the tree, staring at the deep ridges in the bark – the life of the tree and all it had experienced etched into its being. *Like my new wrinkles round my eyes from not enough sleep and too many tears*, Abby mused. Inch by slow, steady inch she gradually moved herself closer to the ground. *You are bloody doing it*, she chanted reassuringly over and over in her mind, until she finally felt her foot hit the floor.

The children cheered wildly. Abby felt elated. Grinning, she bent over to take deep breaths, not realising she had hardly dared breathe for the entirety of her descent. She started to laugh and then tears sprung to her eyes. The children, still congratulating her, looked on, at first bemused but then gradually falling silent as Abby, seemingly losing all self-control, laughed and sobbed in hysterical breaths. The on-the-ground instructor, barely out of his teens, was unsure what to do and attempted to move the children away, but they wouldn't budge.

Eventually, Chloe, one of the more confident year six girls, stepped forward and put her arm round Abby. "Miss, you... you OK Miss?"

Abby felt Chloe's arm across her back and all the children's eyes staring at her. She looked up, taking a shuddery breath, like a toddler after a tantrum, and seized control of herself. "Not entirely," she gasped, "but I am going to be!" she said, smiling.

The children cheered and laughed, not really knowing what their teacher meant but glad that she at least seemed to be verging on normal again.

Grinning from the exhilaration of completing the abseil (and managing to control her inner demons along the way) Abby thanked the instructor, gathered her senses and her group and headed for the refectory. The children were all very sweet to her. Lavishing them with chocolate and biscuits Abby told them how proud she was of them, and herself for controlling her mind and concurring the abseil – letting them assume her tears had purely been the result of her overcoming a fear of heights. *Damage limitation done!*

The staffroom that evening was more sombre than on the previous day; it seemed it wasn't only the children who were feeling tired as the residential progressed. Having decided a morale boost was in order the head teacher had gone to the gate to collect a Chinese he had ordered in from the nearest town. While everybody got ready to eat, and Melissa went to fetch her mini-manicure kit to salvage what she could of her damaged nails, Abby found herself alone with Jo Simms, a teacher who had only joined the school in the previous term. Jo seemed to leap towards Abby and held onto her arm, clearly having something she wanted to say.

"Are you OK?" she asked, searching Abby's face.

"Yes, all good thanks." Abby didn't know Jo well, having only ever previously shared chitchat with her while on playground duty, and wasn't quite sure what she was referring to.

"It's just, you know, I heard about your husband... and the children today, well they mentioned you cried and—"

Abby's throat tightened; she really didn't want to drag everything up and attempted to cut Jo short. "Thanks Jo, but really, everything's fine. It's been tough recently but today... today I was just scared of heights and—"

"My husband had an affair, the bastard!" Jo interjected.

Abby was a little stunned by Jo's outburst and didn't like the turn in conversation. "Sorry to hear that," she replied, feeling increasingly out of her depth. She felt ill-equipped to deal with her own problems, let alone somebody else's.

"Five years it had gone on for, five years, when I had waited for children and he said we'd be ready soon. What a nasty bastard." Jo was clearly on a charge and not going to give up the conversation easily.

"Oh... When? I mean... how did you find out?" Abby asked shakily.

"Three years and two months ago. I caught him in my bloody bed with her, the bitch whore from hell." Jo's words were venomous and yet she spoke them with a slow, cold resignation, as if she were delivering the facts to a jury.

Abby looked at the door, desperately hoping that somebody would come in and rescue her from this conversation. She reached out and touched Jo's hand – it felt cold. Abby really didn't want to enter a deep and meaningful conversation, and especially not on this subject. Apart from anything she was tired and always found it hard to control her mind when she was tired, but curiosity got the better of her. How people coped and moved on after affairs interested her. She had read on one of her adultery forum skulking sessions that it takes at least two years to get over your partner cheating on you; one to relive the anniversaries of when it all happened and another to start to make new ones. Clearly Jo was beyond this and still more than a little possessed by the trauma she had faced.

"I'm so sorry, I know how hard it is. Are you with him now?" Abby couldn't help but ask.

"No, I pretty much swore off men from that day, they're not worth the effort," Jo said firmly. "The good thing about not having children, though, is I never have to see him again. At least the bastard did me that favour."

Abby looked at Jo's angry face. She could feel the tension in her words. Was she going to be like that? Would she always allow Simon's actions to haunt her, possess her? She hoped not. She didn't want to be that person. What he had done had affected her life, yes; she knew she was a different person now, she knew that her mind could plummet to new depths now and maybe she would never be able to stop that, but watching Jo she also knew she couldn't let his actions define her life. She was worth more than that; she deserved more than that. She had to move forward, no matter how hard that might be.

"Hungry anyone?" Brad came through the door with a huge grin on his face, followed by Melissa, and the head teacher carrying a large box of Chinese takeaway. The smell of food wafted into the room and Abby felt relieved to be joined by the others. On the pretext of an after-dinner manicure (as if that was something she did all the time!) Abby excused herself from Jo and went to sit with Melissa. Brad joined them with copious amounts of food at the table and the evening took a decided turn for the better.

Chapter 17

Feeling in great need of a shower after the journey back to school Abby heaved her rucksack, now full of washing, onto her back and followed Melissa to the car. She couldn't wait to see her girls and catch up on some much-needed cuddle time. But as she neared her car Melissa dropped her bag on the floor and stared in disbelief.

"Oh no, it's flat!" she exclaimed, taking in the sight of the deflated tyre on the driver's side of the car. "I pumped it up hoping it would last until I sort a new one. Adam told me I should just let him change it but I didn't dare tell him the spare was flat too. I can't call him!" Imagining the knowing look her fiancé would give her, she swore under her breath. Car maintenance wasn't really her thing but neither was giving in and letting a man sort it for her!

Abby felt deflated too: while she had really enjoyed her time away she now very much wanted to be home, but not wanting to make Melissa feel bad, she smiled. "Come on, we'll find a lift and sort it tomorrow. It'll be fine here for one more night." She spoke cheerily, attempting to sound positive. With being home feeling tantalisingly close she really hoped Melissa would agree.

Scanning the car park it quickly became apparent that most people had made a hasty retreat as the last of the children had been collected. Being due back in school in the morning meant everybody was feeling in much need of recharging their depleted energy supplies before the onslaught began again. Abby spotted Jo but looked around, hoping to find somebody else to ask for a lift. She was quite simply too tired to handle her intensity. It seemed there was nobody, until the last of the coaches drove away revealing Brad's car behind it. Realising he must have popped into school to return sick buckets and medical forms, Abby decided he was their best option for a quick ride home. She pulled at Melissa's arm.

"Look, Brad's still here; he'll probably give us a lift home."

With that Melissa returned from her dumbfounded state and laughed. "Oh, I'm sure he's up for rescuing a damsel in distress," she teased.

The lift all sorted and directions given, Melissa insisted on climbing into the back seat; her house was closest and she would be dropped off first. Abby sat in the front of the car and looked around. It was a very masculine domain, black leather, matt brushed metallic inlays, sporty and yet spacious; no children's car seats, no baby wipes, no sweet wrappers or used tissues in the door pockets, and Radio 1 not a Roald Dahl story CD playing on the stereo. The car still smelt new. Despite feeling fatigued they all chatted easily just as they had the night before. In what seemed like no time they were pulling up outside Melissa's. She got out of the car, thanking Brad for the lift and unnecessarily apologising again to Abby about the flat tyre.

Despite the continued murmur of the radio, as Melissa shut the door the car suddenly felt too quiet. Abby smiled at Brad and looked out of the window, watching Melissa's house slip away into the distance. The easy conversation had stopped, the shift in dynamic of three becoming two became increasingly obvious as they drove and Abby felt very aware of being in a relatively confined space completely alone with Bradley. She shifted in her seat and fiddled with her seatbelt as she tried to think of something to say. Glancing at Brad, she noticed the stubble etched across his chin from the weekend and pushed away the thought of it rubbing against her if they kissed.

"I hope you had a good time," Bradley said, breaking her wayward thoughts.

"Yes, it's been good thank you; quite cathartic," Abby responded, instantly wishing she had said something less pompously cryptic. Trying to think of something sensible to add, she glanced down and glimpsed his smooth, strong hand clutching the gear stick and the muscles that flexed in his thigh as he changed gear. As blood rushed and tingled at the surface of her skin she added, "But I can't wait to get home now."

"Sure, I bet your girls will've missed you," he responded easily.

"Yes, and Simon," Abby cringed, wondering why she had felt the need to say that.

Bradley barely grunted in response and Abby tried to think of things to say to make her comment sound less pointed. "You know he's had the girls all weekend and the dog, the house and work…" About to add, "he'll be relieved to see me," she stopped as Bradley interrupted her.

"Like you do every weekend you mean?"

Abby looked at him, surprised by his tone. "Yes, but I'm used to it. Simon's not. He's really trying. They've all had a great weekend and the girls have loved having him all to themselves." She knew she sounded too abrupt but she couldn't help herself. She also knew she was jumping in to defend Simon as usual, despite promising herself she wouldn't, but she couldn't help it; it was simply one of those I-can-complain-about-my-family-but-you-can't responses. She felt strangely on edge; the atmosphere in the car had changed and she didn't like the fact that she suddenly felt on the verge of an argument about her personal life when really it was none of Bradley Hunter's business. She folded her arms and wished she had taken a ride with Jo.

As they drove into Abby's road Brad pulled the car over, switched the engine off and turned the radio down, before shifting in his seat to look directly at her.

"Thanks for the lift, I'm fine from here." Abby didn't want

to talk any more; she wanted to get inside and see her girls, and went to undo her seatbelt. Brad caught her hand in his and she looked up in an attempt to give him a frosty glare; a look that she was aware would have been more effective if it wasn't melting so easily at the sight of him.

"Sorry!" he began.

Abby inwardly sighed – she had heard too much of 'sorry' lately.

"It's none of my business I know, but you've looked so sad lately, I just think you deserve some fun."

Fun, it actually sounded tempting.

"It's been great to see you smile this weekend. And well… I mean… would you like to come out with me sometime? We could just have a drink or something, away from school. Just us."

Abby felt on the spot. Was it wrong that a part of her wanted to say yes? What would Simon think if she did? He was still her husband after all and she was still his wife.

"Look Brad, I'm hugely flattered. But really, it's just not a great time for me at the moment," she started.

Brad smiled and squeezed her hand. "Not a great time to go for a drink?" he teased, unleashing a thoroughly cheeky grin.

Abby considered her response and noticed his thumb was stroking across the back of her hand. "Just a drink? Nothing more. Just friends," she affirmed, aware that removing her hand would have perhaps reinforced her point more.

"Strictly friends." Bradley grinned and glanced past Abby through the passenger side window. Abby followed his eyes and saw Simon and the girls on the front porch putting up a homemade banner, and Bramble busily sniffing round the garden. The sight of her family tugged at her heart and made her grin.

"I better go," Abby said, pulling her hand free and very much wanting to be swooping her girls up into a cuddle.

As she opened the car door Bramble turned and spotted her. Not being one to break into an excited run he stood on the grass barking in her direction. Jessica and Grace looked over, saw their mummy, and sped towards her. Realising all the commotion was because Abby was home, Simon pushed the last of the pins into the *Welcome home Mummy* banner and followed them, stopping abruptly when he saw Bradley, now out of the car, holding Abby's bag and saying hello to the girls. Unaware that his friendliness towards them was simply based on them meeting at the school fete where they had greatly enjoyed throwing wet sponges in his face, Simon felt instantly jealous at the whole scene. He wasn't about to let anyone else carry Abby's bag and he wasn't going to let anyone else appropriate his girls. Marching purposefully towards them, he looked directly at Bradley.

"I can take that!" he snapped, taking Abby's bag. He didn't want to make a scene in the street but he wanted to be sure Bradley felt unwelcome. Positioning himself between Brad and Abby and surprising her with a kiss on her cheek he added, "We've got a surprise for Mummy inside, haven't we girls?"

As he'd hoped Jessica and Grace instantly lost interest in Bradley and started excitedly pulling Abby towards the house.

"Thanks for the lift Brad," Abby shouted over her shoulder.

"No worries!" he responded a little flatly.

"Yeah, thanks," Simon added with a dismissive tone, pleased with how easily Abby had been led away from him.

Now it was Bradley who felt jealous. He knew he had no claims over Abby but he also knew that he would like to, if only she would let him. He didn't like the look on Simon's face and he didn't like what he had heard about the way Simon had treated Abby. About to get in his car, he stopped. Unable to help himself he called after Abby, "By the way, I forgot to say – panda print really suits you!"

With that, he smiled at Simon, got in the car and drove away.

Chapter 18

Abby barely recognised the house as she walked in. It was immaculately clean and smelled gorgeous; she always kept a tidy house, but this was quite simply beyond tidy. As the girls hurried her into the lounge, the sight of freesias on almost every surface overcame her. Their scent filled the air.

"Simon, they're beautiful!" she exclaimed, taking it all in and trying not to think how much they must have cost. The room was a rainbow of bright colours and beauty. She had never seen so many freesias in one place before. On the walls hung more *Welcome home* banners made by the girls and a poster adorned with Bramble's paw prints.

"That was my idea Mummy!" Jessica announced proudly.

"Hmm, and it seemed a good idea right up until he spotted a cat and jumped up at the window." Simon laughed, grimacing – cats were about the only thing Bramble deemed worthy of a burst of energy, especially the sight of one sitting smugly on his garden wall. Abby's mind scrambled, it was all so unexpected. Simon had always been dismissive of going anywhere near the children's art cupboard. And now he had let them loose with it and even attempted something as bizarre as paw printing with the dog, something even Abby would have found a step too far.

"Sit down, there's more Mummy," Jessica said excitedly.

"Aun—" Grace attempted to speak, but Jessica quickly put her hand over her mouth to prevent her spoiling the surprise.

"Oh Grace, why don't you come and sit with me, ready for my surprise?"

As Abby pulled her close Grace poked her tongue out at Jessica.

"Look who's here," Simon announced, pointing at the lounge door.

Abby looked over, taking a moment to register the sight of her friend. "Rachel!" she eventually exclaimed, leaping to her feet and hugging her tightly while Jessica and Grace danced around them.

Holding on to Rachel a little more tightly than she meant to, Abby realised how very much she had missed her friend. Tears welled in her eyes and she couldn't help but let out a sob of happiness as she took in the sight of Rachel actually there in her living room. "I didn't know you were coming. It's been so long. Too long!" Abby beamed. "How have you been? What have you been up to?"

Rachel laughed. "It's so good to see you. Sorry it's been a while but I'm here now." She gave Abby a reassuring squeeze as she spoke.

Simon looked at them both. His two best friends in the world together again, chatting away like old times, and knew he would be briefly redundant as they caught up. He took Abby's bag and decided to make himself useful – it was a new concept to him to apply himself domestically but he was actually enjoying it. He had even learnt to use the washing machine, and if he was honest these odd jobs around the house occupied his mind and allowed him to imagine them all being together again.

Tipping out Abby's washing he stared dumbfounded as her panda print pyjamas fell onto the top of the pile. Bradley's words stung him as the meaning of what he had said hit home.

Abby walked into the room, needing a glass of water after all the excitement, took in the scene and saw the hurt on Simon's face. He was of course jumping to the wrong conclusions again but at that point she didn't care and she really didn't want to upset him. Instead she walked over to him. "We all patrolled the corridors and went to children when we were needed, even if that was in our pyjamas!" It wasn't quite the truth but it easily explained Brad's knowledge of her sleepwear.

As Simon remained still she put her arm around his back and turned him towards her. Without speaking his body responded to hers and they embraced in a long hug. Abby pushed any thoughts from her mind other than how happy she was in that moment: she was back home, Rachel was there and her husband was in her arms. It felt so good to be holding him close, feeling his familiarity, the way they fitted in each other's arms. The scent of his aftershave, the one she had bought him, lingered on his smooth, warm skin. Knowing it was momentary, that her mind wouldn't allow her to enjoy it for long, she just wanted to soak it all up. "Thank you. I couldn't have hoped for a nicer welcome home!" she whispered sincerely.

"Bloody hell! It's good to see some things never change!" Rachel blurted from the doorway as Abby and Simon reluctantly broke from their embrace.

Putting on a smile, Abby couldn't help but consider how very much things had changed, and regretted that she hadn't been honest with Rachel before now.

Once the girls were in bed and Simon, aware that it was inappropriate for him to stay now Abby was back, had excused himself with a false errand to Kerry's, Abby decided it was time to tell Rachel the truth. She poured herself a large glass of martini and opened Rachel's wine. It was a warm evening. With the windows open the scent of the freesias drifted round the room. They chatted. Abby, aware that Rachel still didn't know what had happened, only half-listened as Rachel told her about her latest trip to the States and how being PA to Rebecca Giles and travelling from place to place for weeks on end was not nearly as glamorous as it sounded. She had heard it all before. Abby knew that as much as Rachel might say she wished they could swap lives she would soon tire of staying in one place; living a life of domesticity would never be her forte. With the night drawing in Abby decided she needed to just get on with it and say what she wanted to say.

"Rachel, Si and I…"

Rachel looked at Abby, a knowing sorrow etched in her expression.

"We, well he…" Abby continued. She told her everything about what had happened and how she found out.

Rachel listened to her intently. Abby was grateful that she never once attempted to question her or stand up for Simon. In that moment she was being Abby's friend, and she didn't need her to play counsellor or devil's advocate; simply listening was enough. As Abby spoke she was aware how guilty Rachel looked. Sorrow pulled at her expression more than she had anticipated and she realised Rachel must have been feeling awful for not being there for her throughout this difficult time. But that didn't matter, she was there now.

Chapter 19

Watching Mallory read her book, Abby felt incredibly nervous. She meant every word she had written in her letter to Helen but now she was sharing it with Mallory she felt too exposed, as if she might have said or revealed too much with what she had written. She wrung her hands in her lap and searched repeatedly for a distraction. She looked at the many vases of sumptuously scented freesias that still blossomed in the room but even they couldn't prevent her focus from returning to Mallory. Several minutes passed and still her eyes didn't falter from the page. Abby could feel tension building inside herself and began to imagine grabbing Mallory by the scruff of her sky-blue mohair jumper and shaking her for a response. Finally, she could take it no more.

"Is everything OK? I'm sorry about the language, I should have rewritten it."

"Abby, I ..." Mallory began, peering above the rim of her chunky glasses.

Oh God, what? 'I feel it unnecessary for you to swear in your homework?' 'I am disappointed?' 'I am going to have you certified?'

"I'm so pleased you did it. You wrote down your feelings; you let your mind speak." Mallory's face lit up; she genuinely looked pleased.

Abby's eyes widened. She was taken aback. With the residential to focus on and then Rachel's arrival she hadn't really thought about her achievement. Yes, she'd been pleased to see a page of her own words, but she hadn't actually considered what she had written. Her words, her own thoughts and feelings – they were there on the page. Tears welled in her eyes. Yes, she had let her anger vent and not just in frustrated grunts, tantrums and growls; she had actually managed it in words. Her words, all her own words!

"Except, I have to wonder…" Mallory broke into her thoughts. "Why Helen?"

I hate her; she slept with my husband – who else would I vent at? Abby didn't respond.

Mallory raised her eyebrows and lifted the book to emphasise her words. "Why write to Helen? Did she betray you?"

Abby felt agitated, the feelings of pride at having written her thoughts quickly disappearing as she felt as if she was about to be told off. "You said write to Simon or Helen." The words came out more defensively than she intended.

"Yes. Yes, I did. But most of what you say here, your anger about the lies, the cheating, the betrayal, how hurt you are… couldn't most of that also be directed at Simon?" Mallory suggested, her voice too calm and light for the depth of her question.

Abby wasn't prepared for this. She had done what Mallory asked and she didn't want to probe further into what she had put; simply writing it had felt like a release.

"Abby? Does it bother you that I say that?"

"… A bit."

"Why, Abby? Why does it bother you?"

Abby took a long drink of her Evian and wished it were something stronger. She waited, hoping Mallory would fill the silence but she didn't.

" Because… because…"

"Yes?… Go on."

Abby paused, trying to hold back, trying not to give way to the anger building inside her. She couldn't just succumb to it; she feared unleashing it. Now she was learning to control her mind the thought of unshackling the demons within made her anxious. Abby attempted to steady her rapid breathing.

117

Mallory's penetrating gaze remained fixed, urging her to speak. "Why does it bother you?" she repeated coaxingly, willing her to respond.

Abby shifted uneasily, desperate to speak and yet frightened to hear her own words.

"Why Abby?"

"Because I know that!" she eventually stated. "I know it!"

"You know it?" Mallory leapt on the response.

Yes, that's what I said. "Yes, I know it was Simon, of course I know it was him…" Abby spat the words; unwelcome tears pricking at her eyes, her voice too shrill, her whole body convulsing. "I know he betrayed me! I know he did it and I hate that he did that to me!" She bit her bottom lip to stop herself but it was too late; with the words out, she sobbed helplessly, unable to stop the tears.

"It's OK," Mallory reassured her, reaching across with a tissue. "It's OK." She waited for Abby's breathing to slow and her tears to ebb before speaking again. "Abby, you can voice how you feel."

"But I can't," Abby replied, her voice barely above a whisper.

"Why? Why do you feel that way? You can own your feelings Abby. You can say how you feel."

"I can't."

"But to me, Abby – as a start, you can share your feelings with me."

Abby shakily drank the rest of her Evian and waited a long moment. She felt calmer but washed out. Part of her wanted to speak, to just let the angst go. Holding on was making her weary and she didn't have the energy to keep fighting.

"But if I do… If I say how I feel… how I truly feel, if I speak the hurt I really feel, then what does that mean? If I voice those words, the words I put to Helen in my letter, to you, to myself, or to Simon, how will I ever take them back? How will that hate and that anger ever be forgotten? My words would always be there. Non-retractable. Out there." Abby gestured into the room, catching her breath and steadying the trembling she could feel building again inside. "What if that hate consumes me… or us – Simon and I? What if it consumes us?" A tear rolled down her face as the finality implied in what she was saying hit.

Mallory looked at her, not speaking, not wanting to interrupt her and allowing Abby to take the time she needed before continuing.

"And I don't know if what I'm feeling is real. I can't trust my own mind." *There, I said it; now you'll know I'm crazy!* "One day I hate him, hate what he did and know I deserve so much more and then on another I love and miss him. And what if I'm wrong, what if I say all those things but I trusted the wrong part of my mind? It'll be me who has split my family up then, it will be me who made my little girls lose the opportunity to grow up with their mummy and daddy together. He wants me back; he wants us all back together. Only I'm preventing that now."

Mallory decided to interject. Abby was clearly struggling with her thoughts and had raised a lot of important issues. Mallory wanted to explore them further before moving on. She shifted in her seat, ready to speak.

"Firstly, you can't put all that upon yourself. Your actions or reactions now are a response to what has happened; it's not fair to treat your decisions about how to proceed as if the past does not exist."

Abby went to disagree, but Mallory raised her eyebrows and continued, "Secondly, not knowing your mind is entirely understandable; you have every right to feel confused and to allow yourself time and space to find your way forward. You deserve that."

Abby listened, not entirely convinced.

"Don't you think that's understandable under the circumstances Abby?"

"Is it? I don't know. I know other people whose partners have had affairs and they've moved on, or at least they've known what they wanted," she corrected thinking of Jo Simms. "So why don't I? It's all so confusing."

Mallory removed her glasses and sat back, allowing Abby to continue.

"You see in theory, I always knew – at least I thought I knew – how I would deal with this; in my mind it was so straightforward. Books and films informed my opinions and I suppose I felt safe – Simon and I had been together forever; I never really imagined this would be my reality. It's easy to form opinions when you are judging others."

"And what is it you thought you would do? What advice would you have given to others?"

"Walk away. Don't look back. You deserve more. It was all so straightforward in my mind. But really, honestly, this is anything but. I'm completely out of my depth here." Abby lowered her voice. "To be honest I'm struggling with my own inability to cope. And of course I know this is not the worst thing in the world, so I'm scared that something might happen to put this in perspective. Not coping, it's… it's not like me."

Mallory placed her glasses back on and slid them decisively up her nose. She felt proud that Abby had opened up, and knew that on some level she was starting to reach her.

"Abby, it is OK to feel the way you do. Everybody has a trigger – something that is beyond their usual realm of expectation or experience, something that is beyond their ability to cope in their usual way. While for some it could be the loss of a loved one, a pet or even a job, for others it can be the breakdown of a relationship, or elements within that relationship. You don't have to conform in how you deal with it because there simply is no right or wrong way."

"But sometimes I feel that I am barely dealing with it at all."

Mallory tilted her head to one side and took a breath. "Be

aware, Abby, that what you are experiencing is grief. You are mourning the loss of your former relationship, a relationship which spanned almost half your life, and you have every right to do that; it was something you treasured – even if you weren't always aware of it at the time."

Abby considered Mallory's words but couldn't help but wonder why this was her trigger. She had lost her dad after all and while that was devastating it had never made her feel like she was going crazy. If it was grief she was feeling now why did this feel in some ways harder than that?

"Am I a bad person because this is my trigger and not, say, the death of my dad who had cancer?" Abby felt guilty at the thought.

Mallory leaned back and took a breath, untwisting her topaz earring from her hair before speaking. "No, not at all. You said yourself you had considered your reaction to this and yet you feel unable to take the course of action you had always predicted you would. With your father you were probably more aware of the coming loss and more accepting of your grief. It's not that you necessarily found it easier to deal with, it's that your path to doing so, for whatever reason, was clearer."

Abby sat back to take it all in. That actually seemed to make sense. Moments passed. Mallory's shoulders relaxed, and a slight grin tugged at her lips. These small breakthroughs always made her job feel worthwhile.

Having reached a moment of realisation with Abby, Mallory decided to attempt a step forward. "You say Simon wants you back. How does it make you feel to consider the possibility of you all living together again in the future?"

Abby paused, pondering the question, remembering the sight of Simon and the children at the table and in front of the house when she had returned at the weekend. "I don't know. I guess… hopeful, perhaps." She hesitated. "I mean, this has all affected him too. What if everything I had ever wanted is within my grasp now? He's changed; I mean, he says he has. It seems like he has. If I say yes, I might get the husband I loved back – the one who was mine before his company almost went broke, the one who didn't throw everything into his work, who didn't ignore us, who made me feel like the centre of his world."

"And do you think that's possible?"

Abby considered for a moment. "Maybe. I don't know. But here's the thing… to get that I have to accept our life on these new terms. He cheated on me. I know that. Simon betrayed me." The words came out more easily this time. "I trusted him implicitly, but I guess he wasn't who I thought he was. What if I can't just accept that? God knows I am having trouble coping with it."

Mallory flicked through Abby's book. "I couldn't help but notice…" She paused, opening the book to the page of Abby's letter. "You tore pages out; did you restart this many times?"

"A few, yes."

"Why not leave your first attempts in there? Why take them out?"

"It was messy. I wanted it all down in one," Abby answered, wondering why the conversation was heading off on a new tangent.

"And would you say you often do that? Start over rather than continue with a mistake?"

"I like things to be right. I find it hard to live with mess and mistakes." Abby laughed but stopped when she realised perhaps what it was Mallory was getting at.

"Moving on, starting over, would that feel more like a new beginning for you? Starting afresh?"

"Yes, I suppose so."

"But you don't yet feel able to do that because… because you are unsure of your feelings for Simon," Mallory pondered for a moment before continuing, "and to move forward with Simon, you have to—"

"Accept the mess, live with it all." Abby finished the sentence before Mallory did. Mallory smiled before continuing.

"Well, I might not have put it quite like that."

"But it's true," Abby affirmed, beginning to understand her personality in this new light. "I can't just walk away because I don't know if that's what I want and I am scared to stay with Simon in case I can't accept what has happened – to live with the mess." This made sense to Abby; this was the crux of what was causing the turmoil in her mind. Yes, she was hurt but being confused and scared of the future was what was preventing her from moving forward.

"Perhaps knowing your mind more fully will only come through understanding your mind more fully."

Abby looked at Mallory. Clearly she was turning her counsellor-speak-ometer up but what she was saying was actually making sense. Abby felt relieved; she had gained a small insight into her own mind, it made her dare to hope that she wasn't going crazy, and that she just might find a way forward.

"Only you can decide what is right for you Abby, but be aware, sometimes we have to actively *find* the answers we are seeking. Holding back, never making mistakes is safe, it's neater and causes less mess along the way, but it can also be boring and stagnating. Taking chances, making mistakes and learning from them, seeking and finding the key to your happiness – now that's empowering!" Mallory sat back, allowing Abby to absorb her words.

Chapter 20

Abby was starting a new phase in her book. She was inspired by Mallory and wanted to record her words of encouragement. Unfortunately every time she went to note them down Eleanor's old favourite *you have to break a few eggs to make an omelette* kept popping into her head. Abby would have liked something a bit more fitting to herald the change but decided the wisdom of Eleanor Scott would have to do, at least until Mallory's words came back to her.

As she looked at the new page she had turned, and her not-quite-fitting-to-the-occasion quote, she really hoped this was it: the first step in the new phase of her life. She was going to strive to stay positive, to push herself to make decisions, and to do that she knew she had to start trying things out – testing the waters of her new life to see what she wanted, what made her happy and what she could live with. To mark the change she set about making arrangements for three things she felt would be steps in the right direction. Firstly she looked up her local sexual health clinic, inwardly thanking her Internet research for providing the correct name. Finding they had a drop-in clinic that very morning led to two further phone calls: one to school saying she would be taking her Planning, Preparation and Assessment time at home (it was planning, preparation and assessment she intended doing, just not quite of the nature they assumed) and another to Simon to suggest he went with her.

It was only after the call that she considered her motives for doing that. She really didn't want to give him the wrong idea – she wasn't checking that they both had a clean bill of health because she was ready to leap back into a sexual relationship with him, but equally if that arose in the future she really didn't want to be worrying about STIs – an acronym she also had her research to thank for. She also wanted him to share in what she felt was the ugliness of it all, the grimmer side of having an affair. The reality of it was that he had put them both at risk. He had participated in what she could only presume to be the seduction, the euphoria and the illicit excitement of it all – now he could join her in facing the decidedly less attractive consequences.

Of course he agreed to go. He wanted to be moving on and despite feeling abjectly horrible about putting them in that situation, guilt had flooded through him as Abby had stated it all in such a very matter-of-fact manner on the phone, it seemed a step forward. Part of him was relieved to see Abby behaving more like her old self; more like the Abby he knew – the one who coped, who got on, who moved forward. It made him hope that his actions hadn't entirely broken her to the point where that side of her was lost.

The second positive thing Abby did was to ask Rachel to meet them for lunch at her favourite Italian restaurant in the centre of town. Having that to look forward to would help her through the clinic. And if she was honest, Abby knew Rachel's presence would make it hard for her and Simon to dwell on the tests, the reason behind their clinic visit, or their results. As close as they all were it wasn't really the kind of thing the three of them would discuss over lunch. Besides, Abby found having Rachel around was making her feel generally more positive – seeing her on Sunday evening and talking to her had undoubtedly put her in a happier place.

The third positive thing was sending a text to Melissa reminding her that she was going to find them some form of exercise to do, and suggesting that despite her initial protestations, maybe they could even check out the gym.

Aware that was all quite enough for now, Abby stepped away from her phone and focused on getting the girls to school and nursery. She knew that once that was done she had approximately twenty minutes to get home, have a shower and get ready for Simon to collect her. She wondered what she should wear – having smears and babies had taught her that skirts led to less overall nakedness when it came to revealing the lower half of your body but she also wasn't entirely sure the testing would be that explicit. Most of what she had read suggested urine samples and blood tests would pretty much be it, although she had stopped Googling when she started to imagine having every symptom she came across.

Simon pulled up on time, just as Abby knew he would. As she left the house he got out of the car and opened her door. Abby wondered if her jeans were the right choice as Simon looked smart in tailored trousers and a white cotton shirt, open at the neck with the sleeves rolled up. Neither of them knew quite how to greet each other; the result being that Simon placed a rather awkward kiss on Abby's cheek as she moved past. Abby slid onto the leather seat, noticing instantly that Simon had cooled it ready for her. It was refreshing; although it was barely 9:30 in the morning the heat of the day to come was already building. Abby looked round the car; Simon's car, like Brad's, was a very masculine domain – black interior, chrome finish and leather sports seats. The difference was that in the back there were two booster seats and the side pockets were stuffed with remnants of the girls' weekend with their daddy – Jessica's book, one of Grace's teddies, drawings and tissues. It was so cute it made Abby smile.

"Could you pass my sunglasses out, please?" Simon pointed at the glove box.

Abby automatically opened it. Inside there was a small,

perfectly made origami elephant. She faltered as she reached in to get it.

"He goes with your giraffe." Simon smiled, nervously.

"I know." Her voice came out more croakily than she intended. "Thank you." She looked at the elephant, the second in the set of animals she knew Simon was replicating for her. The elephant, though, had a little black velvet pouch wrapped delicately around its neck. Abby looked at it.

"You can open it, it's for you."

Abby carefully removed it and slowly slipped the top open. Inside was a beautiful cyan-coloured gemstone; it was highly polished and felt smooth and cool in her hand. She looked at Simon.

"It's chrysocolla. It's supposed to encourage letting go – the release of emotional sadness, and support the coming of joy, happiness and peace…" He hesitated, unsure what her response would be. "I know it's probably silly but I wanted to get it for you."

Abby clutched it in her hand. She wasn't entirely convinced about the powers of gemstones; if Mallory had given it to her she probably would have scoffed at it, but it was beautiful, thoughtful and completely apt for the new phase she hoped to be starting. "But the elephant? Aren't elephants supposed to never forget?" Drawing on humour instead of emotion she meant it to tease him, but the wounded look on his face made her wish she could take it back. She wasn't trying to hurt him. The gift really was a lovely gesture; she just didn't want to reveal how touched she was by it.

Aware the comment was more than deserved, Simon shifted in his seat and swallowed. "Well yes, happiness, longevity and patience too; but never forgetting, well that'll be for me. Honestly Abby, I'll never forget how much I've hurt you. I hope to get the rest of my life – our lives together – to prove to you that I'll never hurt you like that again."

Abby's chest ached a little; she wasn't trying to get him to apologise again. It wasn't why she had said it. But she should have known he would have thought the symbolism through. Simon had spent over half his life in advertising and he was always pointing out the hidden meaning in things. Unsure what to say, she looked at the elephant. "Thank you" was all she could manage.

Simon turned to start the engine.

"The giraffe?" She couldn't help it; she knew he had given it to her with a purpose but she suddenly wondered if that purpose had been more than she first thought.

Without hesitating, he replied, "Sticking your neck out, patience and sturdy footing in life's rocky terrain." He smiled.

Abby looked at him. His eyes looked green in the light, and had a little extra sparkle from his response. She had always liked how his mind worked – perfectly apt, of course. Trying to hide her smile she turned to put her seatbelt on.

Simon started to drive, scrolling through and selecting music as he went. As Take That began to play, Abby laughed.

"And I suppose this just happened to be on your iPod?"

"Well…" Simon shrugged his shoulders as a slight blush crept over his cheeks.

Abby momentarily forgot where they were going. Simon was being so sweet it was almost like they were on a date. As the second song started and Abby recognised the beginning of *Patience*, she leaned forward and skipped to the next track. Reality would hit home soon enough once they got to the clinic, and she didn't need anything to give her mind an excuse to get out of control.

Sitting outside the hospital felt weird. The last time they had done that together Abby had been in labour. She remembered it so clearly, all the hope and promise in that moment, knowing that when they came out their family of three would be four, and how much she had awaited Grace's arrival and the completion of the family she had always wanted. It was just over two years ago and yet it had all gone so horribly wrong in that short period of time. She thought about all that had occurred, all that had led them to this situation, sitting outside the hospital again under very different circumstances.

"Ready then?" Simon asked decisively.

They both very much wanted this to be over.

"Let's do this thing," Abby replied, clutching her gemstone and quashing the fear building inside her.

They followed the signs towards the clinic. Of course it wasn't actually called the sexual health clinic; Abby had learnt from the hospital website that she was looking for the Wilson Unit. *Obviously a better name to ask for should you get lost en route*, she'd mused. When they finally found it Abby took a deep breath. About to enter the door, she felt a tug on her arm and swung her head round.

"Hello, it's you isn't it? Mrs Turner from up the school. You taught my Shelley – ooh, must be six years ago now! She'll be chuffed I've seen you. Still teaching then?"

Abby stared at the small, overly excited woman gawking happily at her. She couldn't believe her misfortune: caught by a parent, with her hand on the door handle of the Wilson Unit. There was no way she could pretend she wasn't about to go in.

Let the ground swallow me now! Please... she inwardly implored. "Oh yes, Shelley Peters, a lovely girl. Please tell her I said hello." Abby faltered, her cheeks aflame as she attempted to reassure herself that a) Mrs Peters might not know the nature of the clinic she was heading into and b) she might by some miracle be less of a gossip than she had known her to be six years ago.

Seeing Abby's mortified face Simon stepped in, cleared his throat and spoke with a distinctly masculine air of authority.

"Mrs Turner, the leaflets you need for your class are this way. We must get them now as I'm due in surgery in ten minutes." With that he opened the door and motioned for Abby to go in, turned to Mrs Peters, shook her hand and told her how lovely it was to meet her.

Abby seized her opportunity to escape and practically ran inside, closely followed by Simon, leaving Mrs Peters calling her farewells and slightly swooning in the corridor.

Abby couldn't help laughing. "My class? Simon, the eldest children in the school are only eleven!"

"It worked though, didn't it!" He laughed.

Turning to face the receptionist, their smiles soon faded. They had forms to fill in with their details, and the visit began in earnest. Abby had to remain calm and concentrate. She and Simon, the only person she had slept with for fifteen years, her husband of ten years, were actually in a sexual health clinic to be checked for sexually transmitted infections. The idea that either of them could have contracted something was a reality she didn't want to consider, but nevertheless she knew that finding out for sure was part of moving forward. She didn't want to live with the shadow of not knowing.

"If it helps, she told me she had been checked, that she didn't have anything," Simon whispered.

Why the hell would that help? You having never spoken to her would have helped. Not having to be here would have helped… In fact you saying that actually makes me think you weren't safe – otherwise why have the bloody conversation?

"No, not really!" Abby stated honestly.

Abby realised her mind was in danger of spiralling, and took a breath and a slow look around the room. *What a strange mix of people*, she thought. She looked at the teenage boy opposite who seemed to be there with his grandparents, and the two young girls, who looked too innocent to be at a sexual health clinic, busily texting to her right. These were all just ordinary people. Just like her. What had she expected, scantily clad women and men in raincoats? She chuckled at her own absurdity. The waiting area was just like any other waiting area in the hospital – newly painted but showing the strains of an NHS budget. She didn't want to be there but she was grateful at least that it didn't feel like she was being looked down upon or judged in any way.

Simon shifted in his seat; he swallowed a little too often and repeatedly pushed his fingers through his hair. In truth he had been hit for the first time by the prospect that he had put Abby at risk, and he knew no matter how safe he felt he had been, she had not known what he had done the last times they slept together. He had removed her element of choice with regards to taking risks with her own body. And for that, as well as everything else, he felt guilty.

It was clear to Abby that he felt uncomfortable; it was strange but his nervous fidgeting made her feel strangely bolder, braver even. Maybe it was occupying the upper moral ground in the situation, maybe it was simply seeing him squirm. Whatever it was she seemed to be feeding off it and was surprised by the way she managed to control her mind and stay calm.

With some tests being gender specific and because of their private nature, they were to go in separately. As Simon was called first he gave Abby's hand a squeeze before he left the waiting area. When Abby's turn came she followed the nurse into a side room, where she had to answer a few questions regarding her sexual history – one of which asked if she had participated in sexual relations with partners outside of the UK. She answered but felt cold at the realisation that Simon's answer would be different to her own. As her own sexual history shed no light as to why she felt the need to attend the clinic she then had to reveal that her husband had had an affair. It was odd how saying it to this stranger somehow made her feel like a failure, like she hadn't kept him happy – that she wasn't good enough. It was the only part of the experience she found degrading.

As the nurse went about her business she was calm and reassuring. In Abby's opinion the tests required nothing more intrusive than having a smear, though she did wish she had worn a skirt because her revelations about her husband had made her feel exposed enough before she was asked to take off her jeans. As she lay on the bed trying hard not to tense up, the nurse looked at her.

"You know, for men these tests require a urethral swab – pop some cotton buds on the bathroom side, even the memory will make his eyes water," she said with a wink, and Abby couldn't help but giggle.

At the end of it all Simon and Abby left with the knowledge that they would receive a text with their results. *A text! How very blasé is that?!*

Chapter 21

Gennaro's Italian restaurant was bustling with the lunchtime crowd. Abby felt a pang of envy as she took in the scene. She generally spent her forty-five minute lunch break in the staffroom eating a sandwich while marking or photocopying; these people were lunching in style. Rachel had found them a table near the large open-fronted windows, which meant they could benefit from the warmth of the midday sun without sitting directly in it. She looked relaxed as she put down her large glass of wine and stood to give each of them a kiss.

"So how was your probing morning?" she queried.

Both Abby and Simon groaned at the inappropriate joke and decided not to answer. Instead Simon pulled a chair out for Abby and waited for her to sit before taking a seat himself. Almost immediately a waiter joined them, deftly handing out menus while reciting an enticing list of specials. It all sounded delicious, and was made even more tempting by the deep rhythm of his rich Italian accent. They gave their drinks order – a slightly rebellious skinny latte for Abby (*Ha – look at me drinking coffee!*) and water for Simon – before pondering what to eat. Abby looked at the healthier options but eventually decided on a chicken and mushroom risotto; she had reminded Melissa about exercising and that had to count for something after all! Simon ordered the lobster and crab tortellini and Rachel, ever mindful of her figure, ordered a baked mushroom starter as her main. *Oh great!* Abby rolled her eyes.

Rachel hardly ate and seemed to thrive on work, a weakness for wine and the occasional cigarette – a habit she actually indulged in more than she liked to admit. It was a well-established routine that she insisted worked for her and nobody could deny that she generally looked great. In the years since leaving university it was as if their roles had reversed. In those days it had been Abby who seemed the most driven and took the most care over her appearance. Now it was Rachel. Over the years Rachel had perfected the distinct look of a person who woke each day with the single consideration of getting herself out of bed and dressed to impress; a fact Abby liked to joke about and compare to the mummy-on-the-run look she seemed to achieve on a daily basis. With her self-esteem already at a low ebb she wished she had dressed up a little more in preparation for lunch. She knew that she ought to actually start wearing the clothes she had bought with Melissa.

In contrast to Abby's safe option of trusty trainers, jeans and t-shirt, Rachel wore a pair of black patent Jimmy Choo pumps, fitted three-quarter length cotton trousers and a pink camisole with high neck and keyhole back. The material hugged her petite figure in all the right places and revealed a toned body with firm breasts that saluted the fact she'd never had children. Her sandy blonde hair was loose, the subtle layers making it fall around her face in a tousled, slightly sultry manner. Despite the heat she wore what Abby considered to be a lot of makeup, but her routine of exfoliating, moisturising and priming, before layering colours and contouring to achieve maximum definition, ensured a result that to those unaware of her daily routine oxymoronically looked thoroughly natural.

With the drinks delivered they began to chat about Jessica and Grace. As it had been a while since Rachel had seen her goddaughters she mentioned repeatedly how much they'd grown and how they reminded her of Simon when he was little. As the conversation turned to work and Rachel's recent travels, Abby couldn't help but notice Simon's posture stiffen in his seat. Instead of joining in he frequently looked out to the street, attempting to draw the conversation to things he'd spotted. Rachel seemed oblivious and continued with her tales of overexcited Americans accosting Rebecca Giles and getting her to sign blindfolds and to pose with them in handcuffs. Abby thought it was silly. It wasn't like she was never going to hear of anyone travelling again; even with her anti-America and all things American stance she knew she would have to learn to cope with that. Abby watched as Simon pushed his hand through his hair. Perhaps it was his over-protective streak, not wanting her to get upset, or the talk of kinky sex aids – though Abby didn't want to think why that might make him feel awkward; either way he looked uncomfortable and obviously decided he'd had enough as he excused himself to the bar, seemingly fancying something stronger than water after all.

As Rachel spoke Abby realised she should turn her phone on. She was supposed to be at home doing her PPA, so she ought to at least be available should the school need to contact her. As her phone sprung into life three texts pinged into her inbox: Eleanor checking she would be taking the girls round for tea, as she had promised, and two from Melissa:

Brad says the teachers' netball team could do with some new "talent" – ooer! I phoned the gym: induction for Wednesday at 5:30, unless you fancy pole fit; another suggestion from Brad xx

Abby stared at her phone and scrolled to the next message.

Not really but I couldn't resist that, though I do hear it's a great way to get in shape! xx ;-)

Abby laughed out loud, stopping Rachel mid-sentence and causing her to look at her in surprise.

"Something to share with the group?"

"Not really, just my friend Melissa; we're going to start the gym together."

Rachel almost choked on her wine. "You? Really?!"

Incredulous that everybody seemed to have so little faith in

135

her ability to take on a physical challenge, Abby went on the defensive. "Yes, it's to continue the good work we started while we were away – you know, the abseiling and stuff. Melissa's great like that." She knew she was being childish and really didn't need to play the 'Melissa is obviously more supportive than you' card, but she couldn't resist. She was getting fed up with some people's obviously limited expectations of her. Rachel continued to have a smirk on her face. Abby took a gulp of her latte, wishing she'd opted for a nice cup of tea, before continuing.

"We were going to do pole fit but the class is busy, so the gym it is – you know, while we wait for a space." *What are you saying? Stop now, seriously; quit while you're ahead!*

Rachel looked at Abby as if she were some new species. "Who are you and what have you done with Abigail Turner?" She laughed.

"It's the new me," Abby affirmed. "Things have changed and I need to change too." She sat back decisively, swigging down the last of her almost-cold coffee, trying desperately not to wince.

"Good for you sweetie! Personally I loved the old you but if you want to change you go for it!"

Abby felt a little guilty, and as much as she was grateful for the distraction of the food arriving she hoped desperately that as Simon returned to the table Rachel wouldn't mention pole fit; she wasn't sure she could keep up the pretence and be thoroughly convincing in front of him.

Abby's new homework from Mallory, as well as the challenge of attempting some small but positive steps, was to make a list of the ways Simon had made her happy. Much of what they had discussed so far had focused on how unhappy he had made her. This new stance was intended to help Abby focus on a more rounded picture of their relationship. As Abby tucked into her risotto, attempting to ignore Rachel picking at her mushroom, she started to wonder what she might write. Perhaps if she focused on how he used to be with Jessica when she was little and the nice things he had done recently she could write a bit. The freesias, the gemstone, the origami, it was all very thoughtful. Then again she didn't want Mallory scrutinising her every word and telling her off again; she was learning that counsellors read as much into what you don't mention as what you do! Maybe she should write more about the ways he used to make her happy, things he had done in the past, not things wrapped in apologies. Things before 'it', *slutgate*, happened. A few ideas popped into her mind but she found it hard to think about the past in a positive light when things that had happened since overshadowed it. It was frustrating.

"Anyway, it seems the world loves a bit of BDSM wrapped in a gushy love story."

Abby's mind flipped into the present as she caught up with the fact that Rachel was now referring to Rebecca Giles' continuing book tour and where she would be off to next.

"Have you read it yet Abby?"

Rachel's attempt to draw Abby into the conversation caught her off guard. She went to take a drink and ponder her answer, but remembered her cup was empty. She didn't want to seem a prude by saying she hadn't read it, but she also didn't want to reveal why she hadn't; especially when it seemed most of the female population had.

Abby decided on a noncommittal, "That would be telling." She grinned, aware that she was probably fooling nobody but pleased not to have revealed that her only attempt at actually reading the book had ended abruptly when she realised it was set in the US and the lead characters referred to each other as 'babe', reminding her all too much of the *I love and miss you, babe* text.

"Anyway, it's Europe next and there's even mention of

Australia in the spring," Rachel stated, thankfully saving Abby from further explanation.

"That's quite a tour!" Abby was pleased for Rachel. Despite all her protestations she knew she loved to travel and was lucky to have a job which allowed her to do exactly that, but she also felt a little saddened at the thought of losing her friend again so soon. She attempted a positive answer. "I always wanted to see more of Europe."

"Venice was amazing!" Simon looked surprised by his own words – he'd obviously said it on impulse and seemed unsure how Abby would react.

Abby grinned back but didn't speak; Venice had been amazing. Their trip, arranged by Simon as a birthday surprise, had resulted in one of the best holidays she'd ever had and the birth of Grace nine months later. Ironically it was the last time she could remember them sharing a really lovely time together; no outside stresses of work or children, just the two of them. Maybe she should write about that for Mallory.

Unsure that Abby wanted to relive past events Simon continued quizzing Rachel about the book tour. While they spoke, the Italian food, the music, the waiter's accent and the warm sunshine played with Abby's senses, encouraging her to slip too easily into remembering the long weekend. For a moment she longed to be back there, in Venice, just the two of them. She remembered walking hand in hand through the labyrinth of alleyways shaded by tall buildings, their voices echoing up to the colourful strings of washing stretched between open-shuttered windows, and the contrast of stepping out of the shadows into bright sunshine as they traversed the countless footbridges. She had loved soaking it all in: the sights and sounds of everyday life were totally unique in a city with no roads. Of course they had done the gondola ride and the way-too-expensive bitter hot chocolate in St Mark's Square, where Simon insisted on paying extra so the orchestra would play while they sat. But those moments alone, away from the crowds, exploring the hidden corners of the city were what she remembered most. That and the long, hot afternoons spent entwined together in cool sheets in their hotel room, the sound of the lapping canal drifting through the open window. How far away it all seemed now. Abby wondered if they would ever share a moment like that again.

"You OK?"

Simon's hand on Abby's arm made her jump. She realised tears were welling in her eyes.

"Yes, sorry; just popping to the ladies'." In a fluster she excused herself and left the table.

In the washroom Abby splashed cool water on her face. The mirrored alcove around the sinks meant her reflection stared back at her to infinity as she looked up. Her fringe had grown and sat less heavily above her eyes, but her hair needed dyeing again. She had definitely lost weight and her face looked thinner. Cheekbones were actually reappearing after being hidden for too long; she sucked in her lips and made a fish face, imagining how they might look should she lose another half a stone. She turned her head and caught sight of her bottom. The harsh lighting was not terribly flattering and the fact she was still wearing her old clothes meant she hadn't optimised on revealing her new slimmer self, she knew Gok Wan would not approve. *Hmm, so things have changed and I need to change too*, she thought.

Abby took out her brush and fluffed up her hair. She didn't own a makeup bag but she rummaged in her handbag and found some lip balm that she smeared on to give her lips a more luscious sheen. She took out her phone and text Melissa:

And there I was all excited about pole fit! ;-) All good for Wednesday. I'll meet you there; not so sure about the netball, at least the gym will be inside.

She sent it, rather pleased with herself, and wondered what on earth she would wear to the gym. She looked at her tired trainers; they certainly didn't look ready to be put through their paces. She would have to stop at the shop when she got the girls – *You must be able to buy gym gear at Tesco!*

Opening the door from the ladies' brought Abby out onto a mezzanine floor looking across the restaurant. She paused, feeling the childlike urge to wave from her new viewpoint, she attempted to catch Rachel's eye. It was then she noticed that she and Simon seemed locked in some kind of heated debate. Abby stared, trying to fathom what they could be discussing; there was no way she could hear them over the general hubbub of noise but their body language definitely suggested some kind of altercation. Simon was leaning across the table; Rachel was holding her ground, sitting upright in her seat, her body rigid. Both had flushed cheeks. Rachel seemed to motion to Abby's empty seat a few times which gave her the distinct impression they were talking about her. Simon shook his head; whatever it was Rachel was saying he was clearly disagreeing.

Abby was intrigued. She couldn't remember ever seeing them cross at each other; generally they sorted out their differences in a half-mocking, half-joking manner as if they had never moved on from being at school. But this seemed like something more. Abby cringed, hating the thought that she could be the cause of any bad feeling between them. She hoped she hadn't revealed too much to Rachel; she didn't want what was happening between her and Simon to affect their friendship. She hurried down the stairs, hoping to interject before things went too far.

Walking towards them she couldn't help but notice that her nearing presence caused them both to move back into their seats, swig at their drinks and look in opposite directions. "Everything OK?" she asked, cutting through the tension surrounding the table.

"Yeah. All good... aren't we Simon!" Rachel spoke with a tight smile.

Simon nodded.

Whatever it was that had upset them they clearly had no intention of continuing their argument in front of her.

"Good," Abby affirmed, unconvinced by their performance. "Who's for dessert?" She knew the answer was probably just her, but she hoped the distraction might help.

Chapter 22

Abby pulled her slightly-too-shiny Lycra leggings out of her bottom and yanked down her too-baggy faded black t-shirt in an attempt to hide the floral motif embellished with the words *fit as* across her hip. She didn't need her sarcastic mind interjecting with exactly what she was as fit as. She wondered whether to put her hair up but decided that keeping it down meant she could hide behind it. Her new trainers felt soft and springy. They were white and silver with pink flashes and probably more suited to a teenager than a grown woman, but she liked them. They undoubtedly looked like the keenest and most exercise-ready thing about her. Melissa in contrast looked like she had stepped off the glossy pages of a gym-wear catalogue, already the picture of fitness and hair scooped into a springy ponytail.

They walked through the corridor of the leisure centre. Abby felt nerves creeping in as she had flashbacks of her own school PE lessons. In an attempt to stay calm she quashed an image of herself as a chubby child being forced to crawl through the gap under the balancing beam while imitating a snake in what her teacher called 'musical movement'. It was a task the seven-year-old Abby had embarked upon with trepidation, bowing to the authority of her teacher but pretty sure she was never going to fit. Unfortunately, judging by the look of horror on Mrs Garner's face this realisation didn't occur to her until it was too late – right about the time Abby's bottom got stuck in fact! Much embarrassment ensued on both sides as Abby wriggled and Mrs Garner pulled in desperation to heave Abby out of the humiliating situation and herself out of having to call the fire brigade. Abby knew this was the reason why her own pupils saw her as a pushover when it came to PE; she never made them do anything they didn't want to.

Inside the gym Abby had expected dim, hopefully flattering lighting enabling her to hide and skulk in the shadows. What she discovered however was very different. The room was bright, not just ordinary sixty-watt bright but glaring, operating theatre bright. There was clearly nowhere to hide. To add to the intensity MTV blared out on four large televisions strategically placed so with the help of mirrors you could watch from any angle. Abby conceded that seeing Beyoncé Knowles shake her booty did seem to be having an inspiring effect on the sweat-ridden onlookers who pushed, pulled and pounded with an impressive verve on the range of machines sprawled before her. She swallowed hard and noticed goosebumps prickling at her skin. Rubbing at her chilly arms and about to put it down to nerves she realised she was standing under an air vent blasting cold air at her. *So much for the gym being the warm indoors option!*

Looking round she was pleased to see that she actually didn't look out of place. There was a range of people sporting an assortment of outfits from hardcore types wearing Lycra as if it were a second skin to those, like her, who had fashioned an outfit together aiming for optimum body coverage at minimum cost. She loved the fact there were middle-aged women, *Heat* magazine spread across the output display on their exercise bikes, juxtaposed with fit young people in their twenties powering through the burn. *Do people still say that?*

She was also pleased that she wasn't the biggest person in the room. She knew it was a shallow way to make herself feel better but sadly it worked as a morale boost. Besides, she blamed Kennedy for the thought. The game was her invention when they were in their teens. Basically, as you entered a room the idea was to mentally calculate where you would come if you lined everybody up from skinniest to chubbiest. For Kennedy, who was eternally skinny, it was a bit of fun. For Abby, who didn't share the same naturally skinny genes (or jeans), it generally wasn't. Lately, however, she had allowed the realisation that she was no longer pushing depressingly towards the top end of the scale in most of the rooms she entered to boost her deflated self-esteem. She knew she should know better – judging others by size alone was cruel, even if the results did inflate her ego more than it should!

"Age, weight, height and fitness goals popped on there please, ladies." George, as his nametag denoted, was dressed in the obligatory canary yellow leisure centre t-shirt and a pair of navy shorts, revealing sporty and possibly shaved legs. Abby grimaced at having to reveal her offending credentials to him. As for fitness goals, she had no idea – *survive the induction?* She peeked at Melissa's. She'd convincingly gone for *Toning, improved cardio fitness and maintaining weight loss.*

Ooh, good answer. Abby copied it, minus the maintaining part, lied slightly about her weight and passed the form back. George sorted them a key each and passed them over, along with the cheesy and well-practised line, "These, ladies, will be the key to your fitness!"

About to ask if the machines would be motorised, Abby realised it wasn't really the time for unleashing her bad sense of humour, especially as it always deteriorated further with nerves.

"Right, my colleagues'll be up shortly to get you started."
What? That wasn't it? Oh lord, here comes the exercise!

In actual fact the induction wasn't as bad as Abby feared. She felt lucky that her instructor was Ted – sweet, verging on retirement, ex-security guard Ted. He led her round the gym, introducing her to each of the machines. The cross trainer you had to step onto from the side, the wave machine you approached from the back, the rowing machine you had to sit on without letting the seat slide away from you – there was a lot to take in. Each time Ted encouraged her to play with the buttons and alter the settings as she had a go and got a feel for the exercise. Once her muscles got moving Abby warmed up nicely and appreciated why they kept the air conditioning on cold. She even considered that next time she would scoop her hair up. At the end of each trial run Ted declared that "ten minutes at low impact" was the maximum to program onto her key as a starter, and that she would "soon be achieving that and beyond!" He said it with such conviction and repeated it so many times as they went round that even Abby was starting to believe it.

Unfortunately for Melissa, she seemed to be faring slightly less well under the fierce instruction of Marcia – middle-aged, jaw of steel, muscles of a man Marcia, who was putting her through her paces and setting her times and levels for each machine that were clearly as yet beyond her limits; insisting that the body needed to be, "Challenged for change." As Abby watched, gently spinning her legs on the exercise bike and chatting to Ted about his grandchildren, she felt for Melissa, dripping in sweat and coughing in that special way you do when you don't want anybody to know your lungs are on fire and you can't actually take a proper breath. She could see her limbs, swaying back and forth on the cross-trainer, glowing bright red from across the room. Her high ponytail no longer bounced but clung limply to her sodden neck. As much as she felt for her friend, Abby had to stop herself laughing out loud when she heard Marcia announce, "There's a reason why fitness comes after exercise in the dictionary!" She was just waiting for the 'no pain, no gain' mantra to follow. *Poor Melissa! Thank God that's not me!*

Abby showered, feeling refreshed and looking forward to her next session. The gym, despite its initial operating theatre-meets-*Top of the Pops* appearance, seemed OK. She liked it. It felt self-indulgent in a good way and, she decided, if she threw herself into it enough it might just give her an opportunity to vent some of her built-up frustrations and anger. Abby was sure that with Simon having the girls occasionally and the help of her mum she could keep it up. She didn't want to be one of those people who started keenly only to give up within a few weeks, leaving their bank account to be the only thing being exercised as the monthly direct debit payments continued to roll out.

Melissa on the other hand griped about her stinging muscles, mad Marcia and her thoroughly mental mantras, and the fact that the way the water dribbled out of the shower it was sure to leave her with shampoo build-up. Abby listened to her rant while she got dressed, deciding that nodding sympathetically and remaining silent was probably best. Once finished, having maligned everything she could possibly think of about her induction to the gym, Melissa looked at Abby and grinned. "Up for it next week then?"

"What? You mean you didn't discover the reason why fitness comes after exercise in the dictionary, tonight?" she teased in response.

"Don't get me started again. I was this close," Melissa presented her thumb and forefinger, parting them so you could barely see light between them, "to telling her another F word that comes after exercise in the dictionary!"

They both laughed. By the time they left the changing room they were sniggering about the vein that bulged out of Marcia's neck every time she got excited, and the blood vessel in her eye that looked near to popping as she exuded encouragement with every ounce of her overly toned body.

"At least that's over; next time you'll get to exercise in peace at your own pace," Abby reassured, thinking that actually, chatting to Ted had made the time pass quite pleasantly.

As they walked towards the door Abby was taken aback to see Bradley Hunter standing ahead of them looking at the notice board. She turned to Melissa, sincerely hoping it wasn't a setup.

"I didn't say when we were coming," Melissa responded, reading Abby's expression.

Brad turned at their voices. The smile (*Hmm, that smile*) and look of surprise on his face confirmed he hadn't been expecting them. "Hello. You started then?" He spoke with an air of sincere excitement; ever the PE co-ordinator encouraging people to exercise.

"Well, Abby fancied pole fit but—"

Brad's eyebrows went up. Halted by the sharp dig of Abby's elbow in her ribs Melissa corrected herself.

"I mean yes, just had our inductions. You?"

"Just been for a swim, I find it relaxing. The water, me, going through my paces."

Oh! Abby felt her cheeks redden as she let her imagination get a little carried away with the thought of Brad in his swim shorts, the water, and him going through his paces. She shook her head, attempting to clear the vision, and hurriedly added, "And now I have to get back."

"Oh really—"

"I thought you said your mum had the girls covered!" Melissa exclaimed.

"We could have gone for a drink or something." Brad continued, his disappointment clear.

"Sorry, I text just now and said I'd be back," Abby lied. She actually wasn't expected back at any particular time. As she hadn't known how long the induction would take Eleanor was giving the girls tea and had even offered to put them to bed if necessary.

"Next time then." Melissa smiled at Brad and rolled her eyes at Abby.

As they headed out into the warm evening air of the car park Melissa elbowed Abby. "Back to you!" she laughed. "You know he's just offering a drink. It won't hurt to have a little fun,"

Abby knew she was right. She was supposed to be trying to move forward; having fun was meant to be a part of that. Besides, she had told Brad she would go for a drink with him – as friends. Once she got to her car she sent him a text: *How about next week for that drink?*

After pressing send she stared at the message for so long it imprinted on her eyes. *Yikes!* She was actually going to do it! As her phone buzzed a reply she almost leapt out of her seat.

Looking forward to it.

Chapter 23

Booking our trip to Venice. Making all the arrangements…

Abby tore the page out and then remembered she wasn't supposed to be doing that. She unfolded it to tuck back in her notebook but it looked messy; she would have to try ironing it. She tried to start again but it was no use – she couldn't find the right words. Every time she tried to write the nice things, the ways Simon made her happy and the things she loved about him, her mind slapped her ideas down with derogatory afterthoughts. *Booking the flights – like for Washington. Keeping it all a secret – he's good at that.* She was annoying herself.

Instead of trying to please Mallory she decided to write what she wanted to. It was her book, her place for her thoughts after all. She surprised herself by starting to write as if to Simon – a letter he would never see.

Sometimes, like in the restaurant when you mentioned Venice, I can see clearly and think happy things about our life together but other times my mind twists and contorts them, like it doesn't want me to let go of how hurt I've been. It's as if, when I try to think positively, my feelings, compelled by this sadness, want to overwhelm me. It leaves me feeling twisted and angered inside – but I don't want to feel like that. It's tiring. It wears me down.

It's weird though; it's not like it was. I don't need brain-silencing loud music any more because some days my mind has clarity and that gives me hope that the peace will return. That has to be a step in the right direction, I guess.

Even though you answered some things, I still get the questions – why? Why did you do it? We were good together, you know that; it's why you want us back together. So why did you risk it all? I really have to try not to focus on that, it's too frustrating.

I think of us making love, I can see your face looking right at me and then you smile and I think of you looking at her – doing that face to her, so close, so intimate. Why didn't you care that it wasn't me? Why didn't that matter? It makes me sad.

I think the thought of being happy, enjoying myself in the past or now, actually scares me. Committing to the thought of being happy, especially with you, makes me feel vulnerable. Like it might all be snatched away again.

Abby stopped herself; she didn't want to spiral into sadness. Instead of getting frustrated she decided to focus on a positive thing to do next. She was pleased with her progress so far – going to the sexual health clinic was good to get out of the way, her lunch with Rachel and Simon, though odd at times, had been OK and going to the gym had been fun. So what next? It was like these mini-goals gave her something to focus on, a way to look forward rather than back. There was her drink with Bradley. *Hmmm* – the thought of that made her nervous. Things were complex enough; she didn't need to add to the muddle in her mind. A drink after her next gym session seemed like the best option. If Melissa was there too it would feel more casual, like colleagues going for a drink, instead of… well, whatever just the two of them going for a drink was.

Searching for inspiration Abby noticed the bit of pink paper sticking out of her school bag; an invitation to Patty's lingerie party. It was a bad idea. Abby knew it was a bad idea! Nevertheless the memory of her epic fail at buying lingerie on her shopping trip appeared in her head like a gauntlet being thrown in her path. She wanted to act while she felt brave enough and text an RSVP but she didn't really want to go alone. It said to take a friend, *but who?* It was the kind of thing Simon's sister Kerry would have been up for. But while they were speaking again things remained a little frosty, certainly too frosty to drag her along to a lingerie party.

She thought about Rachel. She could be a good laugh, especially with a few wines inside her, but she wasn't sure she would get on with her school colleagues and she didn't want the laugh to be on them. Besides, Abby thought, if she did descend into panic she really didn't want Rachel there to witness it. Telling her she'd had trouble coping was one thing, letting her see her lose control felt like another. It was too personal. It would reveal too much about how she had changed. She was only just accepting the frailty of her own mind – sharing the extent of how out-of-control and low she could feel felt a step too far; strangely more so with Rachel who had known her as another person than it did with Melissa, who had become her friend through and probably because of her current issues.

Melissa, of course! She wouldn't need to take anybody else if she could persuade her to go too. She couldn't imagine it was really her sort of thing and wondered if she had even bothered to pick up an invitation from the staffroom table. Abby tapped the invitation and considered just arranging another shopping trip, the goal being to actually make it inside the lingerie shop this time. But then she thought about skinny mannequins and young sales assistants and decided she couldn't face it. For some reason choosing underwear in a light-hearted atmosphere, under the influence of alcohol at Patty's, felt like the safer option. A grin crept across Abby's face as she thought of a way to ask Melissa that might just mean she'd go.

She sent a text: *Feeling up for Patty's lingerie party? I'm sure it will be pretty awful but I fancy the challenge of actually buying underwear this time (you have to challenge for change – grrrr!). xx*

She waited for a reply, and when it came it made her smile and feel genuinely grateful for Melissa's friendship. *Really? Hmmm, well when you apply the wisdom of Marcia how can I resist? Though if you are seriously making me spend an evening with Patty, lingerie and things that require batteries there will be strictly no running away Mrs Turner! Happy to help you face your demons. xx*

Melissa's second text made Abby laugh out loud and send a response she would never have imagined typing: *Sorry. I can't promise there won't be chocolate willies! xx*

The ring at the bell and Bramble's bark sent Abby into a panic as she tried to hide first her book and then all evidence of texts about chocolate willies. By the time she opened the door her cheeks were warm and she wondered if she looked as flustered as she felt. Mallory – *of course!* With her busy week Abby had forgotten that Mallory had changed her appointment. Not even trying to do her homework had jogged her memory. *Oh bugger, homework!* Abby wasn't even sure what she had written technically equated to having her homework done. Her heart rate rose a little.

Mallory, excelling herself in a turquoise jumpsuit, matching sandals and hair scooped into a low sideways ponytail, settled into the leather chair by the window. Anticipating that Abby would take her usual place on the sofa she angled herself in that direction. Abby chose not to sit straight away; instead she offered Mallory a cup of tea. It was a ploy to use up some time and give herself a moment to get her head into counselling mode.

"Shall I read what you put while you do it?" Mallory pointed at the corner of Abby's book sticking out from the side of the sofa where Abby had just shoved it.

Realising that seemed a strange place to keep it, she bluffed. "Yes, I popped it there ready for you." Aware that actually made no sense, Abby left the room. She filled the kettle more than was needed – *that should make it a bit slower to boil* – and set about slowly making the tea. She really didn't want to watch Mallory's expressions as she read, and she really wasn't looking forward to being told off about her lack of homework.

Eventually returning with two mugs of steaming tea, Abby sat on the sofa, bracing herself, staring at Mallory's feet, not wanting to meet her eyes.

"Abby, it's so honest."

Abby looked up in surprise. Mallory gave a warm smile.

"But I didn't do what you asked."

"No, not really. But you wrote what you wanted to say, and that's better. You considered your feelings, tried it my way. I can tell that from the piece you tore out… and… ironed." Mallory paused to give her a gentle chastising tut. "But when you couldn't move forward with that you found a way through. Something you *could* put. Something I am guessing felt more honest, more relevant for you right now."

Abby was confused; this really wasn't what she had been expecting, but she liked it. Mallory in praise mode was always more welcome than Mallory on a mission.

"Well, I didn't think about it too hard really, that all just kind of came out."

"But do you see? That's better, Abby. It just came out. That's you allowing your mind to speak. Owning your own feelings."

"Only to me… and now you. I haven't actually said those things to Simon." Abby felt the praise was a bit misplaced and wanted to make sure she hadn't given Mallory the wrong impression.

"But how you feel is not necessarily about telling Simon how you feel, it's about understanding more of yourself, your feelings and what you want."

"I suppose… but when you read that don't I still sound confused to you? I still feel it."

"I read that you are achieving greater clarity, I read that you are achieving greater equilibrium, I read that you are finding a way through. And yes, the thought of finding and losing happiness again is scary but Abby, for the first time you are talking about taking that chance. When we first met I don't think happiness was something you had considered regaining." Mallory was beaming now. Pride oozed from her.

Abby sat back, absorbing some of Mallory's praise and noticing a strange feeling she thought might be her self-esteem having a little stretch.

"Now tell me, how has your week been? Did you manage to try any small positive steps?"

Now Abby knew this was going to go well because she really had pushed herself to try new positive things. Deciding that Mallory perhaps didn't need to know about the sexual health clinic she focused on lunch with Simon and Rachel and her trip to the gym. It was a refreshing session, very different to last week's. Abby felt buoyed by Mallory's encouragement. Nevertheless when Mallory announced that she would be unable to offer sessions for the next two weeks due to family commitments, Abby felt a rush of nerves. Momentarily thrown adrift, she felt panic rising in her chest.

Sensing Abby's unease Mallory reassured her. "Abby, you will be fine. Use your book and keep working on those positive steps. I'm sure you will surprise yourself."

Abby remained unconvinced.

"Would you like the number of a colleague, as a safety net? In case you want to talk?"

Abby thought about having to start over with somebody new. Explaining it all again. She was comfortable with Mallory; she felt like they had moved forward. If she spoke to somebody else she would have to explain everything again. She wasn't sure she had the energy for that. And what if somebody new interpreted things differently? Mallory didn't seem to think she was crazy but somebody else might!

"No thank you," Abby responded weakly, trying to convince herself it was just another small positive step. She went to her bag, took out her cyan-coloured gemstone and squeezed it in her palm.

Chapter 24

"Well it's not a chocolate willy!"

Melissa rolled her eyes and looked at Abby with a thoroughly bemused, I-am-going-to-kill-you expression on her face.

"At least it's Cadbury's!" Abby realised her attempts to add a positive spin on this would be more convincing if she weren't wishing the ground would swallow her up.

"Ladies, when the hooter goes, start sucking!" Leah, the party rep, was clearly the most excited person in the room at the prospect of this game, and held aloft a squeezy boob-shaped ball as she started her countdown.

On the *huh-huh* of the 'hooter', Melissa, Abby and the eight other apprehensive party guests started sucking on their chocolate fingers like women possessed. As the wine already spreading warmth into their bellies, the hint of competition and the reassuring taste of chocolate set in, they went for it despite themselves. No wonder Leah had been excited – within moments of sucking on a chocolate finger they had all changed from respectable adults to giggling teenagers. Her job just got a whole lot easier.

Everybody was crowded into the lounge of Patty's two-bed semi. Abby wasn't surprised to see that Patty was the kind of woman who seemingly wallpapered for fun and liked to chintz at every available opportunity. *Who knew pelmets still existed?* While the sofa was large it clearly wasn't made to seat five grown women and Abby envied Melissa for having had the sense to perch on the arm.

"Harder, harder ladies, come on!" Leah's excitement was reaching fever pitch.

Melissa and Abby were soon giggling too much to put in any serious sucking effort; their attempts to control their grinning mouths simply making them laugh harder.

"I did it!"

Everybody cheered as a rotund relative of Patty's bounced from her seat holding her chocolate-less finger proudly aloft.

The surprise shout caused Melissa to accidentally bite the top off hers and Abby, spotting Melissa's faux pas, to spit hers across the room as she burst into a new round of giggles.

"I'll have what they're having!" Patty's aunt chortled, causing everybody to join in.

Attempting to regain a little order Leah excitedly grabbed the lucky winner. "You get a prize from my goody bag!" she announced, gleefully adding, "With or without batteries?" as if it were a completely normal question.

Without hesitation the pink-faced winner replied, "OOH, with!"

Everybody clapped and whooped as she hurriedly collected a parcel and eagerly ripped it open – her pink cheeks turning positively crimson when a shiny 'purple bullet' dropped into her lap.

Abby leaned over to Melissa and whispered a little too loudly, "A vibrator for the Borrowers!"

Leaping in before everybody could descend into hysterics once more Leah honked her boob ball for attention. "OK, one more game before we hit the rails and catalogues; try a few things out… try a few things on!"

Taking her role as hostess seriously Patty refilled everybody's glasses. As hers had barely had time to empty before being topped up since the time she'd arrived Abby had no idea how much she'd actually had to drink. But her light head was beginning to make her regret not having tea with Jessica and Grace earlier. As Simon was babysitting she had wanted to make sure everything was sorted before leaving. For some reason, in her warped mind that meant dusting and vacuuming opposed to eating.

"Now, do we want more chocolate or a bit of action?" The choice offered by Leah seemed to be between chocolate rolls or balloons.

As chocolate rolls meant getting something edible Abby joined the calls for that, then slightly regretted it when chocolate won and blindfolds, plates and whipped cream appeared as accompaniments. Leah set about assembling them, with the chocolate rolls standing on the plate in the centre of a whipped cream base.

"Now ladies, on your knees, blindfolds on, hands behind your backs. The first to have an empty plate wins!"

"What have you got us into Abigail Turner?" Melissa feigned looking sternly at Abby but was down on her knees and grabbing a black satin blindfold before she had chance to respond.

Abby grinned – she never expected Melissa to throw herself into this – and followed her onto her knees. As the other women slipped on their blindfolds they started sniggering and making lewd references to Rebecca Giles' book. Abby was pleased she hadn't brought Rachel along; they would probably have swamped her with questions about her famous kinky connection.

Abby was enjoying herself. It was so far removed from things she normally did. While of course there were plenty of references to sex, the games they were playing and the continuously flowing alcohol meant she couldn't dwell on anything. It was all just a laugh.

"Five, four, three, two, one… nosh off!"

Please tell me she didn't actually just say that!

As Leah shouted everybody's bottom went in the air, faces thrust down towards their plates and the soon-to-be-devoured contents. Abby could feel sticky cream all round her face and had to snort some out of her nose. She found her chocolate roll and manipulated it into her mouth. It was hard to chew the whole thing at once and to just swallow bits at a time without gagging, but she soon forced it down. Once it had been swallowed she messily licked up the cream – *finally, a sweet tooth and being a messy eater pays off!*

"We have a winner!" squealed a very excited Leah.

Abby suddenly became aware that it was her arm being held aloft. She pulled her blindfold off in unison with everybody else and they caught sight of one another. They looked beyond ridiculous with cream and chocolate smeared round their faces, and peals of laughter were once again filling the room. As Abby turned to Melissa, feeling way too excited about having won, she realised Melissa's face wasn't messy at all. She was holding her phone, pointing it at Abby.

"Oh no you didn't!"

"Revenge will be sweet!" Melissa laughed.

"Oh, you wouldn't... Would you?" Abby exclaimed, snatching for the phone.

Melissa put it decisively in her bag with a fake dramatic laugh and threw Abby a packet of the wipes put out for the clean-up operation. Abby was too giddy on wine, sugar and the joy of winning to take the threat of photographic – or worse, video – evidence too seriously and set to removing the cream splurged round her face.

"With or without batteries?" Leah shook the goody bag in Abby's direction.

All eyes moved to her.

Batteries! "Without batteries," she said, thinking batteries might have been more fun.

Leah passed her over a parcel. Peeking inside, she found it contained a red silk and black lace bundle. Abby decided to open it properly at home.

The games over for now, it was time to look in Leah's

'box of tricks'. Everybody leaned slightly forward as Leah's hand slipped into the large satin case. When she pulled out something resembling the clackers Abby could remember playing with as a child everybody's head seemed to move to one side before an audible 'Oh' resounded round the room as the realisation dawned. *Jiggle balls!*

"Clackers?" Patty's auntie queried.

Everybody smirked, as if they hadn't had the same thought.

Patty leaned into explain as Leah announced, "No, jiggle balls!" before adding, "These come in hot pink, smooth silver and our new icicllllle," purposely holding the final '*lllll*' for effect and presenting a pair of glass-like orbs from her bag. Abby couldn't help but think of the Glacier Mint bear and stifled a giggle and her urge to share that thought.

They each held them in turn, passing them round and feeling the jiggling, almost resonating, sensation as they clashed in their hands.

"These can be used to work your pelvic floor muscles and build subtle sexual stimulation, in anticipation…"

Abby stopped listening. She didn't want subtle sexual stimulation – she wanted her man, and all this sex talk was making her miss Simon more keenly. Or was it Simon she was thinking of? And if it was Simon, was it Simon before or could it be Simon now? *Arghhhh!*

"Right, now try this on your nose; you'll feel the sensation as you would below." Leah held a multi-function, eight-inch pink pearlised vibrator to her nose.

Oh yes, my nose has been feeling a little neglected lately! Abby rolled her eyes. Melissa looked at her as if this might just be getting a step too far, so Abby grabbed the bottle of wine from the table and topped up Melissa's glass, encouraging her to drink. It seemed it was perfect timing as Leah announced, "Now for my rabbit out of a hat trick, ladies; you'll love it!"

Looking through the catalogues would have been a strange

experience in a room full of people Abby hardly knew had they not already shed their inhibitions through lewd acts with chocolate, and nasal experimentation with sex toys. Patty had quite extreme, mostly animal print tastes she enjoyed sharing with everybody, while Abby liked some of the more demure, subtle but very sexy babydolls. Though she found she couldn't focus on any one page in the catalogue for too long, for fear of the hint of panic she felt rising in her chest increasing, she was able to flick through. Melissa, probably a little too far under the influence of alcohol, decided to get something to share with Adam on their honeymoon. It was a bold choice that Abby tried to tell her she might regret once sober but she was having none of it. Abby felt a pang of jealousy at not having anyone to share any of the fun with and decided to treat herself to some new short pyjamas, a bit less cutesy and more come-to-bed than her panda print ones.

"Underwear!" Melissa hissed over her shoulder, looking at Abby's order form. "You're here to buy underwear and it'd better be something completely over-indulgent and super sexy or I will be sharing your antics with... hmm... let me see, whose number do I have?" She paused for dramatic effect, picking up and scrolling through her phone. "Brad!" she announced, pointing to his illuminated name on her screen.

"Oh my God! You wouldn't!" Abby felt herself abruptly sobering up.

Melissa waved her finger over the send button and Abby felt her heart leap to her mouth. "STOP! I'll do it. I'll order underwear! Please just put it away," she pleaded, aware that she sounded pathetic, as if Melissa were holding a loaded gun, but in her over inebriated state Abby couldn't be sure she wouldn't actually do it. Melissa winked and popped the phone back into her bag.

Abby skulked off to look at the underwear rail under Melissa's watchful eye. Leah obviously knew her stuff and had brought a diverse range of lingerie from size 12 to 20 – quite literally something for everyone. Abby liked the pretty matching sets which combined lace and silk in an elegantly sexy way. She chose a set in deep purple and decided to try it on. Lining up outside the bathroom (the only room with a full length mirror) she felt the need to make idle chat.

"Must be the winners line," Abby grinned. The flush of crimson on the cheeks of the young woman in front of her made it quite clear she didn't want to bring attention back to her 'purple bullet' prize. "That's pretty," Abby continued, trying to change the subject and pointing at the anything but pretty outfit the young woman was holding. *And now you are drawing attention to her Madame Whiplash number!* Abby tried biting her lip to stop herself from saying more but then noticed the size 12 label. "Pahhhh!" Realising she had actually said that out loud she hurriedly attempted to hide her pointed look at the garment's label and faked a coughing fit. By the time she finished spluttering the woman was heading into the bathroom shutting and locking the door a little too enthusiastically. Abby hadn't meant to be unkind but honestly, she knew the girl had to be kidding herself. As Patty joined the back of the line with an obviously-too-small zebra print chemise set, Abby bit her lip.

By the end of the evening Abby had ordered four sets of underwear in various sexy, sultry colours, and her new pyjamas. It was a big step forward and, of course, she had her red silk and black lace prize to investigate when she got home. She was beyond happy with her achievements. Even in her drunken state Melissa told her how very proud of her she was and gave her a few too many hugs – though that, mixed with their talk of sex toys and chocolate delights, gave the taxi driver an entertaining fare on their ride home.

When Abby woke in the morning she could barely move her head off the pillow. She generally tried not to drink to excess;

she hated the hangover feeling. She also knew she had broken her own rule of not showering before bed after a night out. It usually served to make her feel at least a little more refreshed upon waking. She put her hands to her throbbing head. *The girls!* Regretting the sudden move to sitting, she let her eyes adjust. Next to the bed Simon had left toast, a now-cold cup of tea and a note:

We've popped to the park. Back for lunch. Thought you might need a little recovery time. xxx

Abby leaned back against the headboard as the sight of the toast made her tummy churn. She grabbed her stomach. *What the FUCK?* Abby's hands clutched at the silk she could feel swathed across her stomach. Her eyes bulged and her head rushed. She was wearing the red silky number! The prize! The little red camisole and black lace knickers – she actually had them on! *Holy hell, what have I done?*

Chapter 25

While her stomach still churned Abby was feeling more sober by the minute, her head surging through throbbing pain towards raging panic. Had she slept with Simon? When had she put the bloody things on? She couldn't remember at all. Did she want to sleep with Simon? She really didn't know. *Surely I would remember!* She stood in the shower for what felt like an eternity, letting the water pour over her and desperately hoping it would clear some of the fog from her mind. *What was I thinking, getting so steaming drunk?* While she liked the numbing effect of alcohol she had learnt months back that too much only served to bring her further down when the effects wore off – like she really needed any help with that. She washed her hair, enjoying the cleansing bubbles as they foamed on her scalp and slipped down her wet skin. As the water began to run cold she got out and wrapped herself in the biggest, softest towel she could find. She needed a hug, a big consoling bear hug, which the towel didn't really provide. Her phone buzzed. She winced at the noise and the thought that it might be Simon. How could she face him?

It was safe. It was Melissa. *Abigail Turner, my head is banging. Let's stick to the gym, at least that's brutal in a healthy way! Hope Simon got you in OK. I offered but he said I was in no fit state. Harsh! I think he was enjoying having you draped over him. xx*

Draped over him! Oh God! Abby slunk to her knees. It was awful – what had she done? She had a sudden flashback of holding Simon's face in her hands and the words "*...but with your wife is the only time it is right,*" came into her mind. She tried desperately to remember what happened next but she couldn't. It was exasperating. Her head went swimmy from trying to focus and she rushed back to the bathroom to be sick. As she had hardly eaten the day before she heaved molten liquid until she could heave no more and dry-retched on her own emptiness. After rinsing her foul mouth she slumped on the bed. Hoping to relieve the emptiness she picked up her toast and nibbled at it. It had been burnt and scraped, normally her favourite way to eat it, but having been left on the side it was cold, and any moisture from the butter had long since disappeared. Toast and crumbs filled her too-dry mouth and stuck to her Velcro tongue. She gave up.

An idea sprung to her mind; her eyes scanned the room and she searched for her clothes. They weren't in the bedroom. Her head throbbed as she moved. They weren't in the laundry basket. Abby peeked downstairs. It was quiet. Treading lightly, she went down. There was no sign of Bramble; they must have taken him to the park. Her eyes bulged as she reached the lounge, finding her clothes neatly piled on the leather chair. Mallory's chair. *Oh Mallory, what would you think of me now?* There was no way she had been in a fit state to fold them there. This did not look good. Hearing a noise outside she darted back towards the stairs. She wasn't ready to face Simon, and certainly not wrapped in a towel. Her brain hammered at her forehead as she took the stairs two at a time, expletives spilling from her mouth.

Abby threw her underwear on, a pair of jeans and a scoop-necked t-shirt. She looked in the mirror and swapped her t-shirt for a high-necked, long-sleeved one. Who was she kidding? She had probably already exposed more than enough to Simon last night. Of course he'd seen it all before but that felt well and truly beside the point. She rummaged in her sock drawer; needing comfort she took out a pair of fluffy slipper socks and put them on, trying desperately for a relaxed, weekend look when really she felt anything but relaxed. She could hear the girls' voices downstairs and someone coming upstairs. *Oh God!* The door opened and Bramble thudded in. His big, ever-loving brown eyes were a very welcome sight. He waddled over to her, his happy tail making his hindquarters swing with each step. Abby knelt on the floor to greet him and wrapped her arms round him. It wasn't quite a hug but it was damn well near and it was just what she needed. Giving him an extra squeeze and a big pat she eventually stood up.

"Mummy, Mummy, where are you?" Grace's voice bounced joyfully up the stairs.

"Just coming sweetie." Abby held her head. She went to the bathroom and splashed water on her face. It was no good; she couldn't hide forever. She brushed her hair and felt thankful that her fringe had grown out a bit; with the bags already there her eyes needed no extra shadow. She decided her hair would have to stay wet; there was no way she could face the noise of the drier. About to leave the room Abby looked at her discarded silk and lace prize. Picking it up, she threw it at the bin, groaned and rolled her eyes.

"Tea? Or coffee is it?" Abby wasn't sure if it was a reference to her attempt to be rebellious or her hangover, but the look on Simon's face suggested that either way it amused him. He looked too good: refreshed from the park and carrying off the relaxed weekend look way too well.

"Water thanks," Abby responded timidly. She was a bit cross with him for having seemingly made himself at home in the kitchen, but then again it was technically his home too and she could hardly complain when he had looked after the girls all morning while she was in no fit state. Sitting at the table she wondered who was going to mention the elephant in the room first. Simon placed a glass of water in front of her. Abby noticed his hand on her shoulder as he leaned across, his breath on her neck and the lovely scent of him. It sent a picture into her mind. *Oh no, no, no, no! I can't have been straddling him.* Her cheeks flushed. Surely the dark side of her mind wouldn't have let her. It would have leapt in and stopped her, either that or plain common sense should have. But then again maybe she had drunk both into a coma.

She felt angry with herself. She panicked; what if it wasn't Simon she had come across in her drunken state? Would she have popped her new underwear on for anybody? Here she was still hurting over his sexual misdemeanours and yet it seems she had leapt out of her clothes at her first drunken opportunity. She pushed it out of her mind – besides, his wasn't a drunken opportunity, it was a fully sober, consenting encounter that lasted a week. *Would a drunken encounter have been any easier to handle?* Abby checked herself for going off on a tangent. None of this was the point in hand. Last night was. She had to know what had happened.

"Si… did we… did I—"

"Mummy, Mummy, come see this!"

Abby welcomed the interruption, unsure how she was going to actually say the rest of the sentence. She stood to leave the room as Grace's little hand clung onto her. Ah, her baby, she missed her bedtime snuggle with her last night. Abby scooped her up and glanced back at Simon, who had a too cheeky, too knowing grin on his face. *Oh, this is not bloody funny!* Abby decided to ignore him and go and get her fix of the girls. Her head was still delicate but they always made her feel better.

The next hour was spent playing in a camp that had been built out of blankets the girls had found stashed behind the sofa. Abby hadn't seen them when she came down initially. They were from the airing cupboard and their presence in the living room gave her hope that maybe they implied separate sleeping arrangements. But then of course it wasn't the sleeping she was concerned about.

After a rather tense lunch Abby could barely eat, Jessica and Grace took themselves off to their bedrooms to play and Bramble wiggled out from under the table, slumping onto his bed, aware that any hope of crumbs had now passed. Abby picked up the plates, their clattering reminding her acutely that her head ached. She grimaced at the noise.

"I'll do it." Simon attempted to take the plates from her.

"No, it's fine." Abby clung on to them; she might be delicate but she wasn't useless.

"Abby, let me."

Hmm, he was being all domestic again, the new way he liked to play happy, 'normal' families. Abby conceded. She was secretly beginning to like this side of him and her headache was returning with vengeance. As she watched him move to the dishwasher she had another flashback of her hands ruffling his hair – *oh no!* She couldn't keep avoiding it. If she had slept with him she didn't want to give him the wrong impression. Things were not alright between them. She wasn't ready to just accept what had happened.

"About last night." There, she broached it.

Simon's eyebrows rose and he smirked. *Oh, that's not good!*

"Did you have fun?" he asked through his grin.

What does that mean? When exactly? Not wanting to reveal that she had no idea what she'd done last night, she countered, "Did you have fun?"

Simon pondered momentarily. "It was entertaining and informative."

Clearly he found this funny. Abby didn't, and her head hurt too much to play games. "Simon, don't be a shit, what happened?"

Simon giggled in surprise at Abby's language; he didn't often hear her swear and had certainly never known her to get so drunk that she couldn't remember things.

"I'm not sure you want to know."

"Of course I want to know. I just bloody asked didn't I?"

"Really?"

"Yes, really! Unless you want to keep more secrets." It was a low blow and she regretted it as soon as she saw the playful sparkle in his eyes fade.

"I helped you in, I got you to drink some water."

"And?" She was losing patience.

"And you were grateful?"

What the hell did that mean? "How grateful?"

Simon's lips curved a little.

"It's not bloody funny. You took advantage." Abby regretted it as soon as the outburst was out of her mouth. None of her flashbacks suggested he had. She was accusing him to escape her own mortification.

Simon was across the kitchen in front of her in a couple of strides. He looked into her eyes. Abby shrunk.

"I did not take advantage of you! Christ Abby, I wouldn't. You know that don't you?"

"Yes." Her voice was weak. She knew he wanted her back, and perhaps that would have been a way. She pushed the thought out of her mind. He looked hurt at the accusation.

"I wanted to, of course I wanted to." He rubbed his temples, his frustration still evident. "You were being funny and sexy and throwing yourself at me."

"But my clothes…?"

"When I went to get you more water you threw your clothes off, mostly round the room, and when I got back you were standing there all silk and lace, giggling, like you used to."

Abby raised her hands to her face. She was never drinking again.

"You looked amazing." The words came out in a small voice. Simon wasn't sure how welcome they'd be but he meant them.

Abby made an *eugh* noise of exasperation, still recovering

from the revelation as an image of herself in that outfit filled her mind.

"I bent to get a blanket to cover you – I'd got them out when you text to say you were drunk."

Abby looked confused.

Simon continued, "I thought I'd stay on the sofa and distract the girls in the morning, so they didn't wake you too early—"

"Wait, I sent a text?" Abby wanted the ground to swallow her up. What had she put in the text? She didn't remember typing it.

"I think it read, *Watch out, I'm drunk and coming for you!*" Simon giggled, clearly reciting it verbatim.

Abby knew her cheeks must have been turning purple. She could hear the blood rushing round her glowing ears. She didn't want to know more, but then again she still didn't actually know what *had* happened. She let Simon go on.

"When I leaned down you pushed me onto the sofa."

Oh no, here comes the straddling! Abby closed her eyes. "Did I… did I… straddle you?"

"You do remember!"

"No. No, no not really."

"You straddled me and put your hands through my hair, insisting I look at your new underwear… You said you loved me and you wanted me, that I was yours and always had been."

"What did you do?" Abby was feeling angry with herself. Her mind was in such a muddle – why had she said that? Was it really how she felt? Abby wondered if being drunk made her mind clearer or more confused. She didn't know. She knew he had denied her, she remembered sulking – "*…but with your wife is the only time it is right.*" It seemed the low blows were coming easily to her these days.

"Abby, I love you. I want you. I want you more than you know. But not like that. I want you to want me the way you used to. To love me the way you used to. I wasn't about to take you like that."

Abby opened one eye and squirmed, looking into Simon's sincere face as it turned to mischief.

"Besides, you passed out so I covered you over and took you up to bed."

Abby giggled and hit his shoulder. She couldn't help it. He was too bloody cheeky. She let her eyes meet his.

"So you covered me… and you left me in bed?" she asked, slowly raising an eyebrow.

"OK, I may have been a bit slow to cover you and I may have let you snuggle up next to me a little bit when I picked you up and you nuzzled into my neck." He grinned.

"SIMON!"

"It wasn't my fault; I didn't ask you to get half-naked and throw yourself at me."

Exasperated at herself Abby thrust her forehead at his shoulder, hiding her red face. It was a fair point.

Simon lowered his voice, speaking on a sigh. "And it felt so good to hold you close, to have you sleep in my arms the way you used to. Sorry. But I promise that's all that happened." He took her hand in his. The gesture felt warm and delicious and ultimately tender.

"Abby, I love you. I want you back, but I want all of you. I want you conscious, I want all of your mind wanting me back."

And that was just it, she wasn't sure all of her mind would ever let that happen.

Chapter 26

Abby's body felt invigorated from the gym. Her muscles tingled and her cheeks were flushed from the exertion. Ted's estimation that ten minutes on each machine would be enough to start had been right; it was a challenge. In fact she found it bloody tough at times. She had gone at it hard, pounding away unwanted images with each step on the treadmill, powering her way through muddled thoughts on the cross trainer, sliding past old regrets on the wave machine, riding into oblivion on the exercise bike and, well, basically, just trying not to throw up on the rowing machine. It had been a workout for mind, body and soul. On the two occasions she actually felt like she might pass out she took a long, slow drink and fiddled with her shoelace; accidentally forgetting to pause the machine meant those final impossible minutes had slipped by – *oops!*

As the cool water of the shower slid over her enlivened muscles, Abby realised she was actually grinning. She was proud of herself. Not least because she made it through the exercise programme, but also because she had gone and done it alone. When Melissa cancelled it would have been easy to make excuses but she hadn't. A few months ago she knew she would have, in fact a few months ago even being a member of the gym would have seemed alien to her. This was progress. Wrapping herself in a towel she decided she couldn't wait any longer; she had to send Melissa a text: *I did it! I bloody did it! Even mad Marcia would have been proud of me!*

After pressing send she realised she should have tempered her own excitement with at least a touch of concern for Melissa's predicament. *Hope the ankle feels better – I knew heels* were a hazard. I have a pair of neglected mandals if you need to borrow them while bandaged ;-)

It was only then, coming down from her exercise high, that the thought of the drinks to follow crept over her. She had been so focused on forcing herself to go to the gym alone that she forgot to cancel drinks with Bradley. Was it too late to cancel now? Maybe there was a chance Melissa would still go. Abby fired off another text:

Are you sure you don't want to come out for a drink? I'll pick you up? xx

Melissa's response buzzed back before Abby left the changing room: Well done you! Neglected mandals are the only type of mandals there should be in this world! I'm sorry; I wouldn't be good company for drinks. I just need to keep this thing up and pray for no bruising. You should still go though. xx

Abby sighed. Melissa had twisted her ankle when her heel got caught in the string of a discarded PE bag in the corridor at school. The injury really wasn't that bad but with her wedding drawing ever closer Melissa was increasingly living in a pre-wedding portal where any issue or small problem was magnified to disastrous proportions.

Staring at her phone Abby wondered if she could still cancel her drink with Bradley. Without Melissa the whole concept felt a bit awkward. She could use the excuse that her mum needed her to get back, but it simply wasn't true. Eleanor had enjoyed putting the girls to bed last week and was looking forward to doing it again. In fact she had practically pushed Abby out the door and told her not to return so early this time; Abby had a sneaking suspicion it was because Sky was showing reruns of *Bergerac*. As she knew her mum had always had a soft spot for John Nettles she felt it her daughterly duty to comply. But going out with Brad, just the two of them – it felt so strange.

Perhaps she was just making the whole thing feel like a bigger deal than it was. She'd made it clear she just wanted to be friends and he'd agreed. So why was she worried? *Damn it, it's just a drink.* Determining to go along anyway, with the intention of sticking to soft drinks after her little escapades the other evening, Abby scooped up her bag and headed for the door.

As she entered the corridor, Abby swooned a little on her black, wedged sandals. *Bloody hell.* Brad was staring at the notice board again, not a hint of the sports kit-wearing PE co-ordinator about him. He was dressed to go out and quite possibly to impress, in a cobalt Oxford short-sleeved shirt revealing his toned biceps and a pair of charcoal jeans-style chinos. Even his regular Nike trainers had been replaced with black Derby lace-ups. His hair had been styled with a little wax but retained its slightly ruffled look. *Oh God, he's made an effort!*

Abby wasn't sure whether to panic because already it seemed like more than just a drink between friends, or be cross with herself for not making more of an effort. She looked down at her jeans. At least she had paired them with one of her new tops – no oversized supermarket special tonight. Her low-cut, daisy print bubble hem blouse with her wedge-heeled sandals might just be enough to lift her outfit to 'normal person going out' proportions. Not that she really knew what that was; she hadn't been out much since having Grace. Abby swallowed, making an effort to smile casually as Bradley looked up with a distinct sparkle in his dark brown eyes.

"I thought we were meeting at the pub," she stated, aware she was being caught mid-swoon.

"I know but I was passing and saw your car; I thought I'd wait for you, see if you fancied a walk along the beach, maybe a drink in the café instead of a pub?"

Yes please! The pub wasn't really Abby's scene these days and the walk and café felt so much more casual, a much nicer way to spend a bit of grown-up time while she wasn't being Mummy or a teacher under stress. "Sounds good to me."

"Great, come on then." Brad put his hand out to Abby.

Hesitating, she left it hanging; unless you were under the age of ten holding hands seemed highly inappropriate for friends going out.

"Your bag?" Brad looked at her, puzzled.

Abby's eyes went wide. *Thank Christ I didn't grab his hand!* She cringed.

"I'll take it for you."

Attempting to regain her composure she blurted, "No, no thanks, it's fine. I won't inflict my sweaty underwear on you." *Oh God, where did that come from?* This was going oh so badly and they had barely left the leisure centre. Abby's cheeks felt no hesitation in firing up to beacon heat as she bit her lip forcing herself to shut up before she made matters worse.

Brad let out a laugh. "Well I was attempting to be a gentleman, but—"

"I'll just go pop it in my car." Abby rushed on ahead, welcoming the cool evening air on her cheeks as she marched across the car park attempting to dispel all thoughts of her self-induced humiliation.

As they crossed the road from the leisure centre, the view of the beach was breath taking. The deep saffron sun sat heavily on the horizon, its long rays illuminating the clouds and diffusing bursts of pink and purple across the darkening evening sky. The calm sea lapped lazily at the shore, mirroring the serenity of the scene above.

"Wow! It's so pretty." Abby paused for a moment, in awe. Her children's bedtime routine had practically put a curfew on evening outings for her; the only thing she regularly went outside for past 7:30 seemed to be to pick up after Bramble. It really wasn't quite the same. "It's like…" She sighed.

"Pardon?" Bradley looked at her, puzzled.

"Oh… nothing… I do love a pink sky."

Brad watched Abby, intrigued. She seemed miles away. He thought how lovely she looked glowing from exercise, her eyes captivated, enraptured by the evening sky. She looked thoroughly at peace in the moment. Suddenly aware he was overly staring, he flicked his eyes down towards the beach for a distraction.

"How are you at making ducks and drakes?"

"What?" Snapping out of her daze, Abby's mind scrambled to make sense of what he'd said. "What are you on about?" *Is it rude? It sounded rude.* She really didn't know what he was referring to.

"Ducks and drakes… you know!"

"No I don't." The words came out more sharply than she intended.

"Stone-skimming, skipping a stone across the water. Ducks and drakes… how are you at it?" Brad gestured to mimic the action, looking at her as if she must be an alien not to know what he meant.

Her shoulders relaxed as she grinned broadly. "Oh, stone-skimming! Why didn't you say so?" Abby felt hugely relieved and couldn't help but giggle. "Who calls it ducks and drakes?"

"Me, my dad, my brother, my granddad… *EVERYBODY*," he added indignantly.

Abby laughed harder.

"Well, I guess not you." Brad watched her, bemused, letting her laugh herself out before raising his eyebrows and folding his arms. "I think you are avoiding the question Miss Turner."

Miss? "What question?" she managed breathlessly.

"How are you at du… stone-skimming?"

Abby attempted to regain her self-control. She'd never really tried. She had lobbed stones into the water with Jessica and Grace to see who could make the biggest splash. Did that count? "I've never tried," she offered honestly.

"What? What kind of childhood did you have? That won't do, come on."

With that Bradley leapt off the prom onto the stones, holding out his hand. Declining his offer of help, Abby jumped down. The stones scrunched around her wedged heels; there was no way they were coming out of this unscathed.

"Pick your stone." With a grin Brad motioned at the array of stones before them.

Abby bent and picked a pebble she liked because it looked pretty. Brad studied the ground, sifting through stones and pebbles with a discerning eye. He looked up at Abby.

"That's it? That's your weapon of choice?"

Abby looked at the little round stone in her hand. "It's pretty."

"Abby, consider the physics of it."

Oh blimey, I hate physics! She gave him a quizzical look.

"Pick a stone that's flat."

As he spoke he opened Abby's hand, which had closed protectively around her pretty pebble, and brushed the stone away. He traced a circle round her palm with his index finger.

Abby drew in a breath and coughed to disguise it.

"About palm size." he added.

"OK." She snatched her hand away and looked down at the ground, scanning the stones. *Blimey, who knew stone-skimming was such a science?* "Smooth or rough?" Now she was putting her science head on; she didn't want Brad to think she was completely devoid of stone-skimming sense.

"Now there's a debate." Brad grinned. "Smooth for bounce or dimpled for less drag on the water, that's up to you."

Abby laughed. Was he actually taking it seriously, or was it a joke? She couldn't tell. She hoped he was joking. Looking down Abby spotted an almost palm-sized flat stone; it was slightly dimpled. She had a flashback to Simon holding a similar stone, chasing Jessica along the beach at Watergate Bay pretending it was a fossilised dragon scale – her squeals of laughter had ricocheted off the cliffs.

"Dimpled," she affirmed, picking up and tossing the stone in her hand, feeling smugly optimistic about its skimming qualities.

Brad picked his stone too. The challenge was on.

Reaching the froth of the shore, Abby swung her arm like a bowler with her eye on the wicket.

Brad looked at her, his head cocked to one side. "You really haven't done this before have you?"

"Umm, no."

Bradley moved in close to her, putting his arm along hers and taking her hand in his. *Oh!* She could smell him; clean, fresh and the distinct heady scent of Vera Wang aftershave. It was one Simon had worn a few years back. Brad's breath on her neck sent goosebumps tingling down her side.

"You need to crouch. Hit the water between ten and fifteen degrees, twenty tops."

As he bent her over, Abby could feel his weight pressed against her. She was sure he would be able to feel her pulse racing in her wrist; maybe even hear the thud of her heart it was pounding so hard. She didn't move. As if to demonstrate the throw he flung her arm in the direction of the water, his body pressing more firmly against her with the movement. Now she could feel all of him, oh so very close. *Oh!* She hurriedly freed herself from his proximity to retain her composure.

"Really? We're on maths now? You do know school's out for the day?" she mocked, hoping not to reveal how flustered she really felt. "I thought this was strictly adult time." *Oh God no, that sounds wrong!*

Brad laughed and stepped round in front of Abby. "Here, watch." Crouching, one leg outstretched, he held the stone between his thumb and forefinger, leaned and flung it, giving it a slight spin as it went. Abby couldn't help but notice how his stance pulled his trousers tighter, revealing flexing muscles as he moved.

"Five! Not bad – not great but not bad!"

"What?"

"Five skips, pretty impressive."

I forgot to look. "Well done! My turn."

Abby moved to the water, crouched in the style of Brad and emulated his grip on the stone; that much she had seen. Now the throw; *how did that go?* Unsure, Abby opted for what she thought was about a twenty-degree trajectory. *Two can take this seriously you know Mr Hunter!* Abby watched, mouth agape, as her stone bounced across the surface of the water. "Four, five, six, seven – SEVEN! Bloody hell Brad, SEVEN!"

Overjoyed at having made the stone skip she turned and flung her arms round him. "I am bloody excellent at ducks and drakes, I am! Did you see, Brad? I—" Abby abruptly halted her declaration when she realised she had moved from shaking his firm biceps to holding his face in her hands.

"It's great," he encouraged, his eyes sparkling in the last light of the sun. "Want to try again?"

It was too late. Abby was already clumsily ascending the stones on her way back to the prom. "No. No, no, I should quit while I'm ahead." She had made the stone skip, in fact she had made it skip quite far, but it was a complete fluke. She had no good reason to try again, no good reason to turn back. She waved as nonchalantly as her pounding heart would allow, adding an air of finality to her march away from the shore. "That must be a world record," she blustered.

Brad hurried after her. "I think that record belongs to a bloke I'm afraid. Russell Byars managed fifty-one."

"Fifty-one! F... blimey." Abby turned to meet his grinning expression.

"Yeah, he's American."

Of course he bloody is! Abby rolled her eyes and clambered back onto the prom, heading towards the café.

179

Chapter 27

Beautiful sky tonight. It made me think of you!

Abby smiled warmly and slid her phone away before Bradley saw Simon's name on the screen. She had no intention of inviting his opinion on her personal life again and she didn't want to find herself leaping to Simon's defence should he offer it.

As Brad returned to their table he gave Abby a wink. "A prize for the winner!"

"Brad, I've just been to the gym, I'm not sure cake will help my cause."

"Nonsense, you've earned it. Besides, teaming it with a Diet Coke must make it OK and... well... you're looking great." His cheeks flushed a little.

Unaccustomed to taking a compliment, Abby didn't respond. Instead she took the large wedge of coffee cake and a knife from the tray. She sliced it in half. "Perhaps it was all in the teaching. We'd better share." She couldn't really turn the kind gesture down but there was no way she was about to tackle sticky cake alone while Brad watched.

Having returned the empty tray and collected two forks from the counter Bradley hesitated, momentarily unsure whether to take the seat next to Abby or opposite her – both seemed quite intimate in the small booth the waitress had offered them. Abby slid his coffee to the place diagonal to hers. He took the hint and sat down.

A bit of an awkward silence fell across the table. Brad ate his cake while Abby picked at hers; the sponge was moist, while the cream was thick, sweet and topped with too many chopped walnuts. Abby watched as Brad devoured his half and wished she had sliced it more generously in his favour.

She broke the silence. "I wouldn't have picked you as a coffee cake man."

Brad laughed, looking at Abby's still almost whole piece of cake, realising he had attacked his a bit too keenly. "It was all they had left." Holding his fork poised in the air, he looked at her thoughtfully. "So what would you have picked me as?"

Abby pondered. "Fruit or carrot maybe – get one of your five a day in while indulging? No, I know gooey chocolate!" She motioned in his general direction. "You obviously only indulge occasionally, so do it in style?"

Brad smiled. Satisfied with her verdict, Abby sat back and took a long swig of Diet Coke.

"Actually it was chocolate I was after, you're right; it is what I would normally go for. But I think we have something in common. I have a thing for chocolate rolls, childish I know, and when I had one in my lunch the other day Melissa said I should offer some to you."

Abby choked and slapped her hand to her mouth to stop fizz spraying everywhere. *Oh, now she's for it!* "No. No, no not really," she spluttered.

Brad went to pat her back while Abby gestured him away, reprimanding herself for not making sure that Melissa deleted all evidence of her win at the lingerie party before anybody actually saw it. Wiping her mouth with a napkin and regaining her composure Abby decided to change the subject.

"Melissa was sorry she couldn't make it."

"Yeah, she text earlier. Is her ankle very bad?"

"I think she's scared it'll swell. You know, with the wedding only a couple of weeks away now." Abby didn't want to say more; she didn't want to imply that Melissa was being a bit neurotic.

"You're going to the wedding right?"

"Yeah, I'm pretty sure Si… I mean the girls should be all sorted so I'll be there." Abby still wasn't sure she would make a great wedding guest but she was excited to see Melissa on her big day and wouldn't let her down.

Brad smiled. "Good!" Realising his response sounded a little too keen (he really would have to try harder at this strictly friends thing), he added, "So how are Jessica and Grace?"

"All good thanks." Abby felt a bit weird discussing the girls with Bradley. *Did Simon discuss our babies with Helen Herne?* The thought slapped into her mind – why hadn't she asked that? How would she feel if he had? *Betrayed!*

"It can't have been easy for them, with everything."

Abby really didn't want to go further down this path; she could feel her mind beginning to spiral. She didn't want to discuss this – she was having a night off, and she could feel panic growing inside her. "Do you suppose the amusements are still open?"

"What? Why?"

"I want to go on the Twister." Abby had no idea where that came from but it seemed like an escape. She wanted to be flung round to loud music, like she used to at the fair. Her head couldn't go into meltdown if she couldn't think.

Bradley beamed. "Let's finish up here and go see."

Abby pushed her plate away, still with most of her cake on it. "I'm done."

"You didn't like it?"

"To be honest Brad, I don't like coffee." She laughed at her confession.

"Oh sorry… but you drink it all the time?"

"No, only recently, it was a phase. I'm over it."

Brad looked at Abby, bemused, as she stood decisively and headed for the door.

It was a Wednesday evening so the amusements were pretty empty but after a word with the tattooed man slouching round the rides Bradley returned, six tokens in hand. Abby giggled with excitement. It was mad but she was going on the Twister; she hadn't done that for years. As they took their seats Bradley insisted on going on the outside. Abby remembered that it was the worst seat to take, as once the ride got going all passengers would be flung in that direction. She winced and tried to insist that she should sit there. She really wasn't sure she was actually lighter than Bradley, whose physique was lean and muscular, and had a vision of herself flying across the seat and crushing him. But despite her protestations, he wouldn't budge.

As the ride got going Abby loved the feel of the breeze smashing into her cheeks. Her hair whipped at her face and she hoped it wasn't whipping Brad too. There was no music but the flashing lights above danced wildly in the darkening evening sky. It was a head-rush, a fabulous, distracting head-rush. As they moved ever faster, being thrust to the barriers and pulled back, she clung to the safety rail but it was no good; she had to let herself go. She bashed into Bradley who let out a roaring giggle and held her in place.

"Wait, I'll move back." She forced the words out against the buffeting wind.

"No way, you'll only slide back, I'll keep you here." Brad held onto her and she let him; their reddened cheeks close and their chests heaving in unison as they laughed together. She realised her hand had moved to his thigh and felt his muscles flex at the contact. Neither of them moved to prevent it.

The man controlling the ride seemed to be teaching them a lesson for disturbing his otherwise quiet evening and let the ride go on, faster and faster. It was so much more punishing than Abby remembered but she didn't care, she wasn't even sure she wanted it to stop. It was a moment; an exhilarating, mind-rushing moment. It felt wonderfully intimate, just the two of them; the darkening sky, the flashing lights, their bodies thrust together, Brad's deep laugh reverberating through her own chest. If she were a teenager it would have been enough to make her giddy for weeks. As an adult the charged air flashing around them made her want more – so much more – and for a moment her head was free of all other thoughts; it was as simple as the two of them and what could follow.

As the ride slowed their hair was ruffled and they both took heavy breaths. No longer having a reason to keep it there, Abby moved her hand. Missing the contact immediately Brad flicked his eyes at her. She inched back into her seat. It was over. The ride had ended. As she took Brad's hand and stepped down with wobbly legs, Abby felt slightly saddened to feel her feet land firmly back on the ground.

"Brad, this has been one of the most bizarrely enjoyable evenings of my life. Thank you."

Brad smiled, taking in her words. She looked so spirited and free. He held her gaze, enamoured by her sparkling eyes and flushed cheeks. He had to stay focused; he couldn't let his eyes drift to her lips – if he did he knew he'd be unable to resist them. He had promised their relationship would be strictly friends. He couldn't forget that; he didn't want to scare her away.

Reluctantly he broke eye contact and winked. "Happy to oblige, any time."

Chapter 28

No win, no point questions. It seems these are my new speciality:
Did you discuss our babies; did you show her pictures of them?
Yes? How dare you! You had no right to share them with her.
No? Oh, you really didn't give them a second thought did you?
Did you keep your wedding ring on?
Yes? Oh, I am so pleased my wedding ring has been all over
another woman's body!
No? How very premeditated; I really didn't matter to you at
all did I?

    I am good at these. Self-torturing questions with which to
entrap my husband – he can't win, but then again in playing
this game I'm not sure I can either.

Abby wondered what Mallory would make of that. She wasn't
proud of herself. It was all rather pointless. It wasn't moving
forward, it wasn't focusing on the future but sometimes she
just couldn't help it. Of course she wouldn't actually ask
Simon the questions; even she knew there was no point to
that. Her rehearsed answers ensured that he would give the
wrong response and would be maligned no matter what he
said. But she wasn't going to let the thoughts spiral out of
control either. She was putting them in her book to stop them
doing precisely that.

    Pausing, Abby flicked through her book. She could see
how far she'd come. From the person who couldn't bear
living in her own mind, who was obsessed, and at times she
feared possessed, to the person she was today; still sometimes
overwhelmed, still sometimes low or confused, but in so much

more control of it. She could use her book for the purpose for which it was intended. She could record her thoughts and feel the relief of them being out of her head. It had become her friend, her confidant. *How strange that a collection of pages and scribbles could become so very important.* She clung to her book; it was a part of her now. Her fear, anger, frustration, her struggle and her gradual rediscovering of herself all there, documented.

It was OK that she put her questions there. It was where they should be. She couldn't keep them in and it was pointless to batter Simon with them. She knew he was sorry. She knew he regretted what had happened, so what did she hope to gain by bringing it up over and over again? He had said he wanted to forget it all, he didn't want to remember *her* or the ugliness of himself, his selfish, uncaring behaviour – becoming a person he never wanted to be – and she believed him; after all his behaviour had been so unlike him.

It was funny; when she told Simon that part of her shock came from it being the last thing she expected – it being so very out of character for him – he had seemed relieved. He didn't want to be that person. He had watched how his dad had treated his mum; he didn't want to repeat that. The fact that Abby didn't see him in that way gave him hope that it wasn't who he really was.

Abby put her book away in her drawer. Next to it were the giraffe and elephant Simon had made for her; she stroked her hand over them and picked up her cyan gemstone. Sometimes, when she was feeling low, she carried it with her. She wondered when the lion would follow. Her original set had consisted of all three; if Simon were replicating them there would be a lion too. She felt the urge to Google its symbolic meaning, knowing that would give her a clue as to when she could expect it. She looked at her laptop sitting in its case across the room. She knew it was silly but having had the idea she suddenly felt an overwhelming need to know. Convincing herself that she would stick strictly to that search, therefore not breaking her promise to herself to stop wasting her life with needless nights of Googling, she reached for the bag.

Turning on her laptop, Abby waited and then clicked on Safari. Smirking at the irony she went straight to Google and typed in *lion imagery*. As hundreds of sites listing images of lions appeared before her she tutted. Trying again, she typed in *meaning of lions* and rolled her eyes as Google instantly offered a literal meaning of the word – *bugger!* But then, below the obvious *large, tawny-coloured cat that lives in prides* were the words *symbolism and the meaning of lions*. Her curiosity was piqued. She clicked the site open and read, her eyes flicking to pertinent parts of the text: *Renowned for their courage and faith… ultimate protectors of hearth and home.*

Reading it, Abby knew why Simon had left the lion until last. She lacked the courage to accept him back and wasn't yet ready to place her faith in him or their future together. With all that had happened she was protecting her hearth and home the only way she knew how. Not letting him back, guarding it, guarding herself. She stared at the screen. Is that what it was: self-preservation? Abby sighed. She wasn't sure she would be getting the lion any time soon.

Looking at the clock, Abby squealed. She had left the brunette-and-red-berry-burst hair dye on a little too long. With just over a week to go it was all part of her preparation for Melissa's wedding. Glancing in the mirror her eyes went wide; she looked pretty ridiculous and hoped the colour would be less vibrant once it was rinsed off. There was no way Melissa could complain this time. This was not a simple shade lighter; this was a colour change. With the dye, and a haircut she hoped to sneak in while Jessica had gym club and Grace was at nursery, she was aiming for a whole new look. Her fringe had grown, and with the addition of other layers she was excited to think that it might just start to blend in. While on a roll she had also made an appointment back at *Prrrr*imp Your Hide for the start of the summer holidays. Having tidy eyebrows (if she was brave enough on the day) and perfect nails felt fitting for Melissa's wedding and she couldn't deny she was more than a bit excited about being pampered too.

The shower looked like a massacre had occurred; Abby sincerely hoped her hair didn't look like that too. Giving it a rub she moved a bit of the slightly stained towel and peeked in the mirror. Relieved at what she saw, she shrugged the towel off. Initial impressions were good. The light gave it a warm red glow, and she hadn't gone ginger. That was a bonus. Deciding the ultimate test would be in the overall appearance once dry she headed for her bedroom.

Switching off the drier, Abby ran to get the door. She wasn't expecting anyone; if it weren't for Bramble's incessant barking, threatening to wake the girls, she would have been tempted to ignore it. As she swung the door open, with a big "Shhh" to Bramble, she was surprised to see Simon.

"I got my text."

Abby looked, not knowing what he was referring to.

"The text – when I didn't hear from you about yours I panicked. God Abby, what did yours say?"

"Simon, I haven't looked at my phone since lunch time, what are you on about?"

"Can I come in?"

Abby looked at his face; he was worried but she didn't know what about. She stood back, opening the door wider, letting Bramble excitedly rub himself all over Simon's legs as he stepped inside.

"Do you want a tea? Something stronger?" she revised, looking at his face.

"Abby, did you get a text from the clinic?"

Finally Abby realised what he was talking about. She had

tried to push it to the back of her mind as the two week results' deadline had come and gone, and now judging by the look on his face she shouldn't be expecting good news.

"Si, I... I haven't checked." She felt light-headed; what was it going to say? Abby went to the living room and scrambled in her bag for her phone.

Simon stared at her. She felt his eyes burning into her back. She saw the missed message highlighted on the screen and scrolled with fumbling fingers to see what it said. Relief flooded through her. Everything was fine. All her tests were clear. She didn't have anything. As she reread it and took a few breaths it suddenly occurred to her that Simon's news couldn't have been the same – he looked so scared.

"Simon, I'm all fine."

The relief on his face was clear.

"And you? What were your results?"

"Clear too," he announced.

"Christ, Simon, you scared me half to death! Why would you worry what mine said if yours were clear?"

"I was scared. Scared I might have passed something on to you. You know, like a carrier or something, and when I didn't hear from you I panicked. I knew I'd been careful but all I could think was what if I had given you something? It would be my fault entirely and I couldn't bear that. As dumb as it sounds, Abby, I never want to hurt you."

Abby made an exasperated noise; his logic was infuriating but she was very happy to be able to put the whole clinic experience behind her. She hadn't realised how much the late results had been weighing on her; she really felt quite giddy with relief. Moving forward, this was another step in the right direction.

She realised she could make more of it, make him suffer further, but he was clearly torturing himself with guilt. There wouldn't be a lot of point in making him feel worse – she wasn't sure she could. Also, she had been wondering if she had perhaps been a little over-the-top with the clinic visit. He had said they had been safe after all. It was a matter of trust. *Hmm, well maybe it was justified after all then!* She pushed the thought away.

"How about that drink then?"

Simon faltered, a little surprised. "What? I mean, what do you have?"

"Wine, martini, tea, Diet Coke, water?"

"Wine would be good, thanks." The colour was returning to his cheeks.

Abby went into the living room, carrying the glasses. The sight of Simon on the sofa reminded her not to drink too much, and to definitely remain in her own seat. Having seemingly regained his senses Simon looked at Abby.

"Your hair."

Abby touched her slightly damp hair. She had almost forgotten she had done it. *Oh no, does it look bad?*

"It really suits you."

Oh good. Abby smiled and shrugged. "It's a change."

"It looks great." He looked at her sincerely. "You look great."

Abby decided to change the subject. She would really have to learn to start taking a compliment. "Actually, I'm glad you're here."

Simon looked a little too pleased to hear that.

"I need to know that you're OK with the girls while I go to Melissa's wedding."

His smiling eyes grew jaded as he processed what she had said.

Abby was a little taken aback and sighed audibly; she thought he had moved on. "Si, I thought this was all OK with you now, that you enjoyed having them?"

"I did... I do."

"Well your reaction suggests otherwise. Honestly, don't worry; I'll sort it with Mum or Kennedy."

"No, I'll have them, of course I will."

"No, don't worry—"

"Abby, it's not them – of course I want the girls. I love having them. It's just… you… the wedding…"

"What?" It came out harsher than she intended.

"I just don't like the thought—"

"Don't worry Si, I'm not going to be an emotional wreck. I'm pretty sure I can go to a wedding without dumping all of our issues onto the situation." *Actually I'm not sure of that at all but maybe if I say it enough…*

"It's not that. I mean, of course I'm worried about you and I want you to be OK and enjoy it. But, well, who else is going?"

"Honestly, I'll be fine – about half the school are going. There'll be plenty of people I know."

Simon pushed his fingers through his hair, tension lifting his shoulders as he shifted in his seat. "What about him?"

"Who?"

"Him. Action Man."

Abby couldn't stifle her giggle. "Do you mean Brad?"

"Yes, I mean Brad." He drew out his name with a sarcastic tone. "Is he going?"

"I guess so, we were all invited, as were you before… well, before everything."

Simon let out a long breath. Abby watched the ticking muscle clenching at his jaw.

"I don't like him."

"I think you'll find that might be mutual. But what does it matter? He's not asking to be your friend and whether he is going or not should make no difference to you having the girls."

"Friend?" Simon spat the word. "Do you think he just wants to be your friend?"

"Yes, he wants to be my friend." *We've made ducks and drakes, been out for cake and on the Twister together.* Well, that sounded

191

ridiculous even in her own head; thank God she didn't say it out loud! *What the hell would you make of that?* "He's been supportive."

"Men like Brad don't do supportive Abby. He wants you." Anger flared in his eyes.

"You're being ridiculous; we've worked in the same school for years. He never bothered you before."

"He never wanted you before the way he does now... He knew you were mine."

"Simon," Abby looked at him, shocked, "it's not the bloody Dark Ages. I am not some piece of meat to be owned." She knew it was the right thing to say. But was it wrong that she slightly liked him going all caveman on her? It made her feel just a little bit tingly to see him all worked up and jealous. *He might just beat his chest in a minute.*

"Well I don't like him." He folded his arms decisively and raised an eyebrow.

"Well I didn't ask you to." *Damn, no chest-beating after all.*

Abby was aware she sounded like a petulant child and she did really want Simon to have the girls; organising her mum or Kennedy at this late stage would be difficult. She decided to tone the conversation down and to try a touch of honesty. "Simon, I am not going because Brad will be there, I am going to see my friend Melissa get married. She's been... she's been... well, a great friend to me over recent months and to be honest I don't know what I'd have done without her. I want to see her get married."

Simon couldn't really argue with that. He wasn't happy, but the tears that had welled in Abby's eyes as she spoke made his chest ache.

"Of course I'll have them." He reached across and stroked Abby's hand.

Abby smiled and moved to pick up her wine. She drank it in, swallowing past the lump in her throat. Grateful that he'd agreed to have the girls Abby added encouragingly, "Rachel said she'd stop by and help out."

Simon faltered. "Oh… did she?"

It wasn't quite the reaction she'd expected. He took a drink of his wine to release the tension building once more in his jaw.

"I thought you'd like her help. You can have some catch-up time before she's off again."

"Yeah, of course. That'll be great."

"Well don't sound too excited. What is it with you two? Normally I can't keep you apart."

Simon pushed his hand through his hair. "Yeah, I guess…"

"What is it?"

Simon hesitated. "Just the thought of sharing my time with the girls. I like having them."

"I can ask her not to come."

"No, honestly, it's OK. Everything's fine."

Not entirely convinced everything was OK, Abby smiled. Some time together might actually help Simon and Rachel sort out whatever their issue was. "Good, it's all sorted then."

Chapter 29

Abby felt good. She had emailed Mallory, asking if they could make their break a little longer. She felt she was holding herself together well, she was using her book and she was feeling optimistic about going to Melissa's wedding. If she needed Mallory afterwards she would be there and that alone gave Abby the reassurance she needed. She was actually proud of the way she had coped in Mallory's absence and she was beginning to believe that simply talking about her issues was never actually going to solve them: she wanted to be living, not procrastinating. She knew Mallory had pretty much told her that when they last met but she had to come to her own realisation in order to fully heed her good advice.

The summer holidays were underway. Abby loved that holiday feeling: no more working (at least not until she started her planning anyway), no more school runs to do, packed lunches to make, uniforms to iron or clubs to get to. The weeks stretched out before her, blissfully long and, with the exception of Melissa's wedding, blissfully empty. It was time to relax. She smiled to herself, thinking how nice it was to look forward to a lack of routine – a while ago that would have terrified her. Now it felt like an opportunity; for what, she didn't know but even that felt a bit exciting.

Abby looked at her open suitcase on the bed and back to the mirror. She mentally went through the list of things she had determined to achieve before Melissa's wedding: losing weight (Abby ran her hand around her waist: *check*), a new hairdo (she fluffed up her new layers: *check*), a whole new wardrobe (she glanced at her open wardrobe: *hmm, well some new clothes and a perfect outfit for the wedding, check),* saucy underwear (*oh yes, check!*). She smiled, *not bad!* And just to boost her self-esteem a little more she gave her expertly shaped eyebrows a run over with her perfectly painted fingernail. With Lucy brimming with excitement about her cousin's wedding she had insisted on giving Abby personal service so that she could talk at her about the coming celebrations. It didn't make for quite the relaxing trip to the salon Abby had hoped for; she was really trying not to overthink the wedding, but there was no denying that she was very happy with the results of the appointment.

Abby put on a t-shirt and the navy floral tube skirt she had bought with Melissa, smiling when she realised that it fitted her even better now she had lost a few more pounds. She knew she ought to donate some of her bigger clothes to charity but she didn't quite feel as if she owned her new size enough to let them go just yet. Perhaps she should get one of those plastic storage boxes and stash them under the bed, just in case they were ever needed again. Thinking how Melissa would scorn the idea, she dismissed the thought straight away; *they will most certainly not be needed again!*

"You look pretty Mummy." Jessica ran from the door and leapt onto Abby's bed, instantly fiddling with things in her suitcase.

"Thank you sweetie, so do you!" Abby beamed. A compliment from her gorgeous girly she could take.

"Can I paint my nails?"

"Not right now."

"Can I have red hair too… like Merida?"

Abby giggled. "Yikes, do I look like Merida?"

"No, your hair's too…" Jessica screwed up her nose, "flat."

Thank goodness for that.

"Can Daddy paint my hair red?"

"I don't think Daddy will be up for that this weekend but I'm sure you'll do lots of other nice things."

"Can we come to the wedding? I could wear these?" Jessica cheekily took Abby's pair of red glitter courts, with the slim three-inch heel, out of her case.

In a moment of madness Abby had bought them to surprise Melissa and had been attempting to get used to walking in them around the house ever since. She had backup wedges ready, as a precaution.

"How about I go to the wedding and wear these," Abby took the shoes from Jessica, "and when I come back we go and buy you some new sandals?"

Jessica grinned. "OK! And paint my hair?"

"Just sandals, and maybe we'll paint your nails... deal?"

Abby held her little finger out to Jessica, who linked hers around it, sealing the deal with a pinky promise. "Deal!"

"Me too, me too!" Grace bounced in from the door.

Jessica rolled her eyes.

"Yes sweetie, you too!" Abby scooped Grace up, giving Jessica a 'humour your sister' look.

Suddenly feeling a bit of pang in her chest at the thought of being totally alone at the wedding and how much she would miss the girls, she grabbed Jessica too and gave them an extra squeeze, causing them both to laugh. Obviously feeling thoroughly jealous, Bramble decided to get in on the action and rubbed himself in between and through their legs, dipping his head and barking in half-playful gestures, making them all laugh. *Silly old dog!*

By the time Abby was all packed, had said her goodbyes and managed to convince Simon to actually let her get out the door she felt a bit deflated at the thought of the journey ahead. She had declined a lift from Brad, feeling that it wouldn't have gone down terribly well. Now she was driving herself. It wasn't what she deemed a relaxing start to the weekend but she had decided to wait until seven pm to give the Friday night traffic time to ease and it was a nice clear evening; hopefully the M27 and A34 would be kind to her. She had a bottle of Diet Coke, some fruit pastilles, a few of her favourite CDs and her trusty satnav, nicknamed Sally by the girls, for company.

About to start the ignition she remembered to text her mum, fulfilling half of a promise to let her know when she was leaving and when she arrived safely. As she wouldn't be seeing her until the actual wedding ceremony she also decided to text Melissa to let her know she was thinking of her.

Hope you've had a really great time and you're feeling more relaxed now. Really looking forward to seeing you tomorrow. So excited... Dum-dum-de-dum... xxx

Excited was perhaps a bit of an overstatement. As optimistic as she was, in truth, Abby was still a little scared that watching the happy couple exchange vows might just tip her over the edge. Taking a deep breath she reminded herself yet again that she just had to get through the service and focus on enjoying the less formal parts of the day.

Before Abby reached the end of the road Melissa text back. Pulling in, Abby read: *Who, me? What makes you think I needed to relax? Haha, sorry I've been a bit of a Bridezilla lately. Thanks so much for the text. See you tomorrow. I'll be the one in white ;-) xxx*

Abby smiled. The pre-wedding spa organised by Melissa's bridesmaids as a hen do was clearly having the desired effect on the bride-to-be. She had been so tense with nerves over the recent weeks Abby thought she might actually explode before she reached the aisle. Whisking her away as school broke up was an inspired plan – clearly her friends from college knew her well! Abby was pleased that Melissa was at last sounding like she might relax and enjoy her day. Smiling, and with the sound of Take That in the background, she set off. *Only just over one hundred miles to go!*

After one hundred and sixteen miles, one toilet stop, half her bottle of Diet Coke, the entire packet of fruit pastilles, three CD changes and a slight delay at Newbury, Sally was announcing Abby's arrival at her destination on the left. All Abby could see was a long stone wall and dense trees beyond. *Typical*, she thought, wishing she had printed out the exact directions from Google Maps. Tapping her thumbs on the steering wheel she sat up taller in her seat as if that was going to make the place appear before her. She pondered pulling over and ringing somebody for help... *but who?* She couldn't trouble Melissa, Patty wasn't staying over until after the wedding and she didn't really want to confess to Brad that she was lost, having turned down his offer of a lift. She looked at her phone, deciding that there must be others from school that would help. *No signal, typical!* Attempting to remain calm she continued down the road; if need be she could ask for directions in the next village. The road seemed to go on for ages, testing Abby's patience and causing her jaw to ache as she realised she was clenching her teeth.

It wasn't until she turned the next bend that she breathed a sigh of relief and sat back in her seat at the sight of the large open gates of the Elysium Park Hotel. As she turned into the long, sweeping driveway her eyes goggled. *Bloody hell!* Melissa had said it was beautiful but this was quite breathtaking. The building, standing proud and elegantly lit in the evening light, looked like it belonged in a BBC Jane Austen adaptation; Abby was sure it must have once been a grand stately home. Winding her way along the gravel driveway she wished she had cleaned her car, or that she was driving a much posher car; or better still that she was riding a horse! That would have been oh so much more fitting to the stunning setting. Not that she could actually ride a horse (but that was an irrelevant detail in the scheme of Abby's fantasy). She couldn't see it all clearly in the evening light but the hotel seemed to be set in acres of idyllic countryside. It was quite perfect. The wall and dense trees she had followed along the road must have been hiding the grounds. *Sorry Sally, it seems you were right after all.*

As Abby got out of her car and stretched, she half-expected Mr Darcy to come striding through the undergrowth, wet from his cooling dip in water she couldn't actually see anywhere, white shirt clinging in all the right places. Oh yes, this was the type of place where such fantasies happened; Abby's imagination could go quite crazy in this stunning setting. She took a picture with her phone, which annoyingly didn't really do the place justice, and sent it to her mum and Kennedy with the message:

Arrived safely, just awaiting Mr Darcy and the weekend can begin! xx

Her hand hovered while she wondered if she should send it to Simon. But after his several 'don't forget I love you' statements as she attempted to leave, which she was pretty sure roughly translated as 'please don't get off with Bradley Hunter', she thought he wouldn't appreciate the humour. But she knew her mum and Kennedy would love it. Like her, they couldn't resist a costume drama. *Who can resist a bit of Mr Darcy from time to time?*

"You OK there?"

Abby swung round, taken aback by the deep voice from behind.

"Bloody hell Brad, you made me jump. I thought you were…" Abby bit her lip and thanked everything that was holy that she managed to keep the next stupid words from leaving her mouth.

Brad tilted his head quizzically and unleashed a very lovely grin.

As her heart pounded with what she thought must be the shock of being made jump Abby fought for something sensible to say. "Amazing isn't it… been here long?"

"Since six, it's a bit quiet." Brad did a frosty style shake.

Not that she would have believed it a few months back but peace and quiet and staying in that beautiful building sounded perfect to Abby. The weekend was looking better by the minute. She hoped she would have a room high enough for a good view.

"Dare I be a gentleman and offer to take your bag?" Brad motioned with a way-too-cheeky grin.

Abby blushed. "It's alright, honestly, it's not even heavy." *No stupid comments today, well done me!*

They walked towards the natural stone building, its grandeur and the heady scent of the roses around the door becoming more apparent with every step. As Abby needed to check-in they headed for the reception.

The receptionist on the phone motioned for another member of staff, who approached the large, swooping oak-topped desk with a broad, overly lipsticked smile. "Good evening."

Abby smiled. "Room for Turner, please?"

The young woman flicked her eyes down to the computer, clicking the mouse before lifting her head with a puzzled expression. "Are we expecting Mr and Mrs Turner?"

"No, no, no, just me…" Abby clarified, her cheeks glowing as she realised Brad had walked her all the way to the desk.

Brad coughed, a poor attempt at masking his giggle.

Chapter 30

Abby had slept really well; too well. Perhaps staying for one too many nightcaps as the school crowd had grown in the hotel bar hadn't been such a good idea. She had hoped to go down and sample the breakfast menu. Back when she and Simon stayed in hotels, when she used to wait for the weekend so she could join him at whatever conference or seminar he was attending, they always made it their mission to check out all the hotel facilities. It seemed rude not to when they were paying for it. Besides, it was all part of the fun, getting hot and steamy in the sauna, looking at each other longingly over breakfast, brushing up just a little too close in the pool. Abby lost count of the amount of times they had been almost caught in the lift, hands all over each other. Now the thought made her shudder. Those times had been theirs – now she couldn't think of Simon in a hotel without thinking of him with *her!* She groaned at the thought of perhaps never quite being able to enjoy her memories again without them being slightly tainted.

Looking at her watch Abby realised breakfast in the restaurant had almost finished. There wasn't really time to shower and make herself presentable enough to go down, not when almost all the hotel guests would be attending the wedding as well. She looked at the little kettle, bags of English breakfast tea, UHT milk and shortbread fingers on the dresser in the corner of her room. *That'll do*, she thought, feeling a little too excited at having an excuse to unwrap the shortbread.

After the thrill of the outside of the building Abby had been a little disappointed with her room. It was rather more Miss

Marple than Jane Austen in style. But at least it was clean and being located towards the back of the building, it was blissfully quiet. Yawning and stretching her way across the room, she opened the curtains; the evening light meant she had only got a glimpse of the view the night before. Abby smiled. It was beautiful; English countryside at its best. Despite the recent spell of hot weather the view was positively verdant. A velvet carpet of lush green grass rolled into the distance, merging effortlessly with a stretch of woodland where veteran sycamore and ash trees with their open headed canopies and irregular branches created an idyllic English skyline. Abby watched, amused, as a rabbit cheekily munched at the grass seemingly unaware of the peril of being out so boldly in broad daylight, and a male pheasant strutted out from the treeline. *Perfect!* It was only at that point that she noticed the golf buggy cutting across the green to the left. OK, so perhaps not quite perfect English countryside but she couldn't deny it was a very pretty golf course.

With the wedding only a few hours away Abby decided she ought to start getting ready. She didn't want to panic in the last hour and starting early meant she could have a soak in the lion-clawed bathtub before showering and straightening her hair. While the bath water was running she checked her phone: it was out of battery. Rummaging through her case Abby found her charger and plugged it in. As it slowly came to life, it buzzed repeatedly with several missed messages. Watching them all bounce up the screen she felt guilty for not having charged it before. She had meant to do it when she returned to her room. Unsure what had distracted her she reflected on her steamy shower and snuggling straight down between her Egyptian cotton sheets on her marshmallow bed. She hadn't slept quite so well for a long time. When the texts stopped coming in, she noticed missed calls from Simon and her mum. *Oh bugger!* Slightly panicked that something might have happened she listened to her voice messages.

"Abby, the girls said to say goodnight. Hope you got there safely, I've sent you a text. Maybe you have no signal. Anyway, let me know you're OK. We miss you."

Abby smiled; if she was honest, being away from home she missed them all too. She realised that after deciding not to send Simon the Mr Darcy text she had forgotten to let him know she'd arrived – with the weird mood he was in when she left she was surprised he hadn't sent out a search party. She decided she should text and apologise once she had dealt with her other messages.

"Abby, it's Mum. Everything's all fine but for goodness' sake turn your phone on."

Abby giggled; clearly her mum hadn't quite thought that through. Aware that she most definitely had fulfilled her promise to let her mum know she'd arrived safely she wasn't concerned; she would give her a call later when she could tell her all about the wedding.

Abby went to her text messages. Her interest was piqued when she saw that the most recent was from Melissa.

Missed you at breakfast, hope you're enjoying your room. Wish me luck! xx

Abby was a little disappointed; she hadn't realised Melissa would be at breakfast otherwise she would have made more of an effort to go down. She was also rather touched that she had taken the trouble to text her on her wedding morning. She text her good luck and sent her a hug.

The next in her long line of texts was from Brad: *Had truly hoped to share breakfast with you this morning. Ah well, there's always tomorrow xx*

Cheeky! Abby laughed. While she repeatedly reminded herself that she wanted their relationship to remain strictly friends she was more than a little flattered by his attention and she was beginning to quite like it when he occasionally blurred the lines. Abby grinned, reflecting on the previous evening when he had insisted on sitting with her in the bar, buying her drinks and walking her up to her room, giving her a friendly kiss on the cheek that lingered oh just a little too long. Remembering how that kiss had fuelled her dreams, she flushed and realised why she had slept so very well.

Simon had left several texts. Before starting on them she flicked to those left by her mum and Kennedy. Kennedy was answering her Mr Darcy text, weirdly telling her not to do anything she might regret – *what did that mean?* It wasn't the answer she was expecting. *It was a joke!* Abby rolled her eyes. Her mum had sent two texts, the first saying she was pleased she'd arrived safely, the next telling her off for not calling Simon. *What?* She flicked to Simon's texts. Feeling a pang of guilt creeping over her, she scrolled to the first left and read down the screen:

Hope the journey went well. You should be there by now. Let me know you're OK. Love you. xx

Abby? xx

Hope all is OK, text me. xx

Well your mum says you're there safely. Text me when you get a chance. Enjoy your weekend but not too much ;-) Love you. xx

Abby cringed; she hadn't wanted to worry him. The last text was sent at half ten – *Oh bugger, he must have woken Mum.* She read on:

Called your hotel. No answer from your room. Call me. xx

Oh no. She hadn't answered and she hadn't text or called either. She knew she didn't really owe Simon any explanations, it wasn't like she had to answer to him but really it all looked so bad. She searched for her bottle of water to refresh her dry mouth and slowly read the text again. *Does he think I…? That I actually would…?* Abby felt momentarily indignant before a picture of her with Brad, laughing, joking and drinking the night before, slipped into her mind. *Would I?* She shook her head and read on.

The girls slept well. Did you? They'd love to talk to you. xx

Saying the girls would love to talk to her was a way of getting her to call. She knew that, but now he'd said it she could hardly ignore it. She hesitated. Calling meant speaking to Simon and that would mean answering questions. The type of questions she wasn't sure she could face. Not that she had done anything to feel guilty about, apart from not letting him know she'd arrived safely, which was thoughtless. And perhaps spending an evening in the bar chatting to Brad when she had implied she would be doing no such thing. But that was all. Well, that and the slow walk up to her room, where their hands had brushed together a few too many times, and that kiss. *Hmm, that kiss!* Abby shook her head, forcing herself to stay focused. *It was just a kiss on the cheek*, she reminded herself, pushing away the memory of how it had sent quivers through her body. Abby chewed on her lip and turned off the bath taps. After thinking it over she decided to ring the home phone, that way one of the girls might answer. Simon picked up after the first ring.

"Hello." Abby's voice came out too high. All she had done was say hello and she already sounded like she had done something wrong. Her heart pounded a little too fast.

"Abby, I was worried."

Now she felt really guilty, he sounded genuinely concerned. It made her want to look him in the eyes; to reassure him the way she always did. "Si, my phone wasn't charged, I've only just got your messages. I overslept."

"Really? Why so tired?"

The tone of his voice made Abby defensive. "I don't know – the journey, it being the end of term at school, the fact I've been coping with quite a lot lately. What do you think?" Her voice was rich with sarcasm, her inkling to reassure him forgotten.

"Yeah, of course, sorry. It's just I rang you—"

205

"You don't need to check up on me Simon."

"I wasn't, I just wanted to know you were safe. I was worried."

"Worried about what? Did you call the hotel before or after you spoke to my mum, Simon? Before or after you knew I'd arrived safely?" She was aware she sounded like Columbo the way she was trying to catch him out. She knew the answer and deep down she knew she was reacting based on her own feelings of guilt.

"I wasn't checking up on you. I thought your phone must need charging, it's not like you not to answer. I was thinking of you in a hotel and it reminded me of when we used to have our weekends away, so I rang the hotel to surprise you."

"Oh…" Abby swallowed hard and tried to rub away the knot in her stomach. She was pretty sure that wasn't the only reason he'd called, but being jealous and reminding her of happier times they'd shared were hardly things she could be cross with him for. A part of her liked being able to stir those emotions in him, a part of her needed to know that he cared – enough.

"Did you like your flowers?"

"Flowers? What flowers?" Relieved to change the subject, she looked round the room but couldn't see any.

"I had them delivered this morning."

Ever since he had filled her lounge with freesias Simon had sent her a fresh bouquet every week. She had told him repeatedly he shouldn't but he insisted she should take them, saying that she deserved beautiful things. Secretly she had come to look forward to their arrival; they were always gorgeous and never failed to make her smile.

"Si, I can't see any flowers."

"Check outside your door."

Abby opened her door. Outside was a beautiful bouquet of hand-tied yellow roses with deep purple freesias. They were in a tall vase with a note: *Wish I was there with you, S xx*

She picked them up and inhaled their delicious scent. "They're lovely, thank you. You really shouldn't have." She bit her lip. *You really wouldn't have if you had seen me in the bar with Brad last night.*

"I like getting them for you."

She could hear the satisfied smile in his tone.

"Abby, when I rang, I just wanted to hear your voice. Honestly… and I know I have no right to question you—"

"No, you don't." *Except for the fact technically I am still your wife – I haven't cleared up the issue as to whether I do or do not want to be with you because what you have done to us is driving me nuts, and I told you I wasn't coming here to be with Brad and yet I spent the first available opportunity with him!* Abby rubbed her hand across the back of her neck in an attempt to ease the tension she could feel building there.

"But when you didn't answer—"

"I was just in the bar with friends from school." She meant it to appease him but as the words came out she realised what she had said; what she had implied.

"Friends from school?" It was a loaded question; she knew what he was asking.

"Yes, a whole crowd of us, we had drinks and we had a laugh." She didn't want to be drawn into this line of questioning. She knew she would end up sounding guilty over mostly nothing.

"So that was all? Just drinks?"

Now she was a muddle of emotions. Was it just drinks? Yes. Was that all she wanted it to be? She wasn't sure. Even through her guilt there was something about Simon reacting jealously that she liked. She hadn't set out to make him jealous. If she had she could have said oh so much more. But hearing him like that definitely did something to her. His protective tone called to something deep inside her, a primal reaction. A reaction her student feminism-studying self would have been ashamed of. "Yes, that was all."

He let out a long breath. She imagined him pushing his hand through his hair. "I'm sorry. I really am. Shakespeare was right: suspicion really does haunt the guilty mind. I know you, Abby. I don't know why I let my mind get carried away."

Abby swallowed, she needed to change the subject. "You said the girls wanted to talk to me. Can I say hello?"

After chatting with the girls, thanking Simon again for the flowers and remembering to point out that she wouldn't be taking her phone to the wedding she returned to getting ready. With only an hour and a half left before she had to get on one of the coaches that would be taking the wedding guests to the local church, she added more hot water to the bath and wished she'd got up earlier.

Chapter 31

The chill in the church made Abby's slightly damp skin feel cold. She fiddled with her order of service and looked repeatedly round as the throng of guests filled the pews all around her. She looked at the exit and wondered if she would be able to get out if she needed. Her pulse raced a little at the thought of not being able to escape without making a fuss. She wondered if she could move nearer the door. The ushers had been quite precise about where to sit, and she didn't want to upset things if Melissa had given them specific instructions as to where to seat people. She knew her friend was a stickler for detail. Only Melissa would have prepared a seating plan for the church as well as the reception.

Abby felt like the whitewashed medieval walls were closing in on her. She looked up to the high ceiling and attempted to steady her breathing. She was amongst friends – well, colleagues really. Having shared a section on one of the coaches the party from school were all now sitting together, with the addition of Patty and a few of the others who had made it to Oxfordshire that morning. She glanced round at the stained glass windows. Everybody depicted on them looked so frightfully sombre, so very foreboding as if they were waiting, goading the sadness inside her to join their sorrow. Abby knew she was starting to panic and needed to calm herself down. She tried to think what Melissa would say. She had rescued her when she'd been on the verge of losing it before and always seemed to know how to help. But Melissa was secreted away. This was her day. Abby knew she'd just have to cope without her.

A laugh from the right of the church broke her spiralling thoughts. It came from a pew of what looked like Adam's rugby mates. Their broad, suited shoulders and match-battered faces were a giveaway. *Either that or they must have had one hell of a stag do.* Abby glanced from them to the mostly diminutive sized young women, wearing brightly coloured short summer dresses, filling the adjacent pew on Melissa's side of the church. They had to be school or college friends. They all looked so fresh-faced and effortlessly glamorous as they waited excitedly for Melissa's arrival. Abby felt horrible for not feeling excited for her friend. She couldn't wait for this part to be over. In a fluster at how horrid she was being she dropped her order of service and watched helplessly as it slipped below the pew in front.

"Oh God, oh Christ, oh bugger – sorry!"

Guests from the pews directly in front of Abby turned, frowning, as she looked at the altar, convinced she was going to be struck down before the service even began. She pushed her foot under the offending pew in an attempt to drag the order of service back. As she did a sideways lean and crouch to see if she could see it she felt a tap on her arm from the pew behind.

"Here, share mine."

A friendly face, a distraction! "Thanks Brad."

Abby had been avoiding him. She wasn't entirely sure why but it seemed like a sensible thing to do. She sat away from him on the coach and had avoided searching for him in the throng as they entered the church and yet there he was, rescuing her again – albeit with a slightly amused grin on his face.

As the door to the side of the church closed Abby jumped. Now there really was no escape. Adam and his best man took their places at the front of the congregation. The vicar stood at the front of the church and grinned. Abby held her breath. But it was a false start. Instead of starting the service he stood and introduced himself, tested his microphone and requested that everybody turn their mobile phones off as even on silent they could interfere with the PA system. Abby mused at how long it had been since she had been in a church and how things had obviously changed. Once everybody had finished fussing around, checking phones in bags and pockets, the vicar adjusted his robes and finally seemed ready. With a nod to the organist he motioned for everybody to stand. As the organ surged into life with Pachelbel's *Canon in D* Abby's heart pounded against the silk of her fit-and-flare Audrey Hepburn-inspired dress. She could feel sweat pricking more readily at her skin and started to worry that it might show on the delicate fabric. She fanned herself a little with Brad's order of service and wished she had worn something more sensible, a jacket at least for hiding in as she melted into a sweaty pool of fractious nerves.

The doors at the back of the church opened and the congregation turned as one to see Melissa, arm linked with that of her glowingly proud dad, and looking stunning. Inhaling at the sight of her captivated audience she smiled demurely through her diamante embellished Italian tulle veil. She had an air of serenity about her. It was such a contrast to the crazed bride-to-be she had become as the wedding had drawn near. This was it. Her moment, and Abby was pleased at least to see that she was going to enjoy it. With a reassuring smile she didn't seem to need, Melissa's dad squeezed her arm – a silent gesture checking she was ready. As Melissa nodded her agreement Abby's first tear fell. She wiped at it with her hand and wished she had put more than three tissues in her bag. Taking a clutch bag had been a concession to achieving the perfect look for the day. Already she missed her usual rucksack – nothing sensible fitted easily into a clutch bag.

Melissa moved gracefully along the aisle to adoring looks and coos of appreciation at her exquisite dress. Her diamante encrusted sweetheart bodice enhanced her petite curves and merged seamlessly with the rich satin fabric that draped across her waist and fell elegantly to the floor. Beneath her veil her wavy auburn hair was styled in a natural-looking up-do. Abby had advised Melissa to avoid anything new that might look weird in favour of a slightly more glamorous version of herself. Pleased for once to be on the giving as opposed to the receiving end of good advice she had never revealed it was actually Kennedy's tip; seeing that Melissa had heeded the advice she felt a little guilty at having taken the credit. With soft tendrils framing her face and a faint braid going into a low, off-centre chignon Melissa had achieved a thoroughly romantic look that suited her more than any overly coiffed effort would have.

Abby wiped her eyes and formed a smile as Melissa neared her pew. Catching her eye Melissa smiled and gave her a little nod. That simple gesture of kindness was enough to make Abby pleased she hadn't yet fled the church. A lump formed in her throat as more tears threatened to fall. The bridesmaids went by in a blur as Abby wiped at her eyes with a shaky hand and attempted to hush her sniffles.

Adam beamed, enchanted by his bride-to-be, obviously besotted; his eyes didn't falter from her as she made her way towards him. His was a look of pure, untainted, untested love; full of desire, hope and promise. Abby remembered that moment well; how her breath had hitched when she saw Simon looking at her in that way. How nervous she had felt with all eyes on her, until she reached his side and held his hand. How right that had felt. When they had looked at each other and said their vows it had seemed like it was just the two of them standing there pledging their love for each other. It had all seemed so perfect. If only Disney had been right and happy-ever-after really did follow 'I do!' Now it all seemed so very long ago. So much had happened since. Not just the recent ugly things but also the happy things, the sad things, the wonderful things, the everyday things – life had marched on and now, before she had even realised, it might all be over. All that hope and promise lost. If only she could claw back that time.

Abby let out a sob as large, wet tears hit the skirt of her dress. She hadn't even noticed she had sat down – lost to her own thoughts she had followed the congregation. A woman in the pew in front turned to briefly stare. Abby was aware she looked a mess and as she wasn't wearing a sign that said 'this sadness is due to the mess of my own marriage' she had to look like the most emotional friend of the bride ever! She took a shuddery breath in and decided she had to get a grip. With her final tissue she wiped at the spreading wet blobs on her skirt. The silk crinkled at the moisture – *bastard fabric!* Abby couldn't believe it. She was a mess, she was trapped and all she could do was sit and try to contain herself while the vicar began the preface to the wedding. Wishing she really had been struck down she looked up at the miserable figure on the stained glass window. *There, happy you got your own way? The demons are itching to come out to play!*

Her thoughts were halted as she felt a warm hand take hold of hers. Bradley swept his thumb reassuringly across the back of her hand and leaned across to wipe her sodden cheek with a clean tissue. Realising that blubbering was the antithesis of the response expected to this kind gesture she braved a smile, mentally shooing away all thoughts of demons as she let herself take comfort in his kindness.

Abby tried hard to focus on the strokes of Brad's thumb across her hand rather than the words being spoken: "That as man and woman grow together in love and trust, they shall be united with one another in heart, body and mind..."

She had to focus on silencing the sarcastic voice in her head that wanted to mimic and mock the words.

"... The gift of marriage brings husband and wife together

in the delight and tenderness of sexual union and joyful commitment to the end of their lives. It is given as the foundation of family life in which children are born and nurtured, and in which each member of the family, in good times and in bad, may find strength, companionship and comfort."

Abby and Simon weren't married in a church. The words weren't the same but they had been similar; they had made lifelong commitments and promises to each other. She tried not to let the words sink in but the young vicar and his microphone were on a mission. Every word reverberated around her, bouncing off the ancient stone walls and ringing in her ears. She tried to quash her thoughts, pushing them away, feeling the rhythmic stroke of Bradley's thumb, staring at the array of hats in front of her, the organist, the light that kept hitting the sequins on Melissa's dress, fiddling with the Blissful Love buttonhole she hadn't put on for fear of spoiling her dress – anything for a distraction. But the more she tried to push the thoughts away the more they wanted to be heard: *Only if you don't give up on it, only if you work at it together.* Was it sarcasm about the past or a warning about the future? She didn't know. Her head hurt.

Chapter 32

Abby had never felt more relieved to hear Mendelssohn's *Wedding March*. At last the doors were thrust open and light flooded into the church. She welcomed the fresh air as it swept in. She felt like she could breathe again. She squeezed Bradley's hand and thanked him sincerely before letting it go. They were sitting amongst colleagues. If it wasn't too late after her performance, Abby hoped to keep gossip to a minimum. Brad had comforted her throughout the service, holding her hand, passing her tissues, glaring at anybody who stared whenever she couldn't control her tears and discreetly putting in silly words during the hymns in an attempt to make her smile. His kind intervention had quashed the voices in her head and stopped her spiralling into panic.

In readiness to leave the church, Abby opened her clutch bag and eased out her squished box of confetti. With that moved she could shove all her sodden tissues away. Despite her red eyes, blotchy face and tear-splattered dress she hoped to exit the church with some dignity still intact. As the bride and groom headed outside the bells rang out joyously. That was it: the service was officially over, it was almost time for a drink. *Thank God! Oh sorry!*

After waiting patiently as what felt like the entire congregation edged slowly out of the church Abby practically burst out the door, hurdling Melissa's wheelchair-bound auntie and forgetting to thank the vicar as she flew through the porch.

He called after her, "Confetti outside the lychgate!"

But she wasn't headed towards the happy couple; she needed a moment. Tucking herself round the corner, by the ancient graveyard, she leaned against the cold stone wall of the church and took long, deep breaths. It was refreshing after the confinement of the church.

Her dress was screwed up and still crinkled where her tears had hit. She decided that as much as she loved the shape and style of it, silk wasn't her friend.

"It's eBay for you when we get home!" she announced, swiping her hands over the offending material.

"That'd be a shame."

As Bradley sauntered round the corner Abby tried not to swoon at how very good he looked in his suit and tie. *Wow!* She wondered how she had missed that until now. It would have been a very welcome distraction. She attempted a sensible response.

"I don't know what I was thinking wearing silk."

"I think you look lovely in silk. I bet you feel good in it too."

Did he actually just say that? Abby's cheeks blazed.

Brad closed the gap between them. Abby held her breath.

"There you are. Ooh, hello! Who's this?"

Both Abby and Bradley turned sharply to see Mindy heading towards them, breasts first.

"Mindy. I didn't know you were coming." Abby felt her cheeks still blazing and stepped away from Brad as she flustered with introductions. "Mindy, Brad, Brad, Mindy." Abby watched as Mindy took Brad's hand, hoping she'd imagined her moving in closer so that her breasts were almost resting against his arm. Before she could stop herself Abby placed her hand on Brad's arm and pulled him closer to her. It was ridiculous. She looked like she was about to start a tug of war over this man who wasn't hers to claim.

"Brad works with Melissa and me. He's the PE co-ordinator." She said, attempting to cover her move by continuing the introductions. As nobody spoke, she went on. "Mindy works for Lucy, Melissa's cousin, at the *Prrrr*imp Your Hide salon. It's for humans. Not pets." Abby was aware she was rambling and over-introducing everybody. She forced herself to be quiet.

Mindy laughed, flashing her white teeth. Brad looked at Abby and slightly grimaced. Abby couldn't help but feel a little too pleased that he hadn't been distracted by the sight of Mindy's perfect teeth and cavernous cleavage.

"Hey you!" Lucy appeared around the corner.

Abby didn't want to seem rude but her little quiet spot was getting busier by the minute. She offered a tight smile. "And here's Lucy… the cousin." She cringed, feeling suitably embarrassed by her own tone.

"I waved at you inside, you were miles away."

Abby had been so preoccupied she hadn't even thought to look for Lucy in the church. "Sorry Lucy, I was distracted." She smiled at Brad, knowing he was aware of what a wreck she had been.

Both Mindy and Lucy misinterpreted the look and spoke in unison, laughing and winking at Brad. "Ah-ha!"

"It must be time for pictures," Abby interjected, deciding that trying to correct their erroneous interpretation would probably just make the situation worse. Smiling, she headed back towards the front of the church hoping they would all follow.

Abby watched as Melissa and Adam posed for rounds of photographs. She thought about her own wedding photograph in the drawer at home. She thought she might like to look at it again – maybe not put it up, but look at it. They had been babies when they married compared to the people they were now. She thought the girls might like to see it again; they always laughed at it, saying Mummy and Daddy looked funny.

When the photos were finally over and the confetti had been thrown – respectfully beyond the lychgate – it was time to head back to the hotel. The coaches pulled up. Abby looked at Brad; she didn't fancy getting on board with everybody else. She still needed a little space.

"How far do you suppose it is back to the hotel?"

"About three miles, I reckon. There's a footpath that runs along the fields."

Three miles – not too bad. Hmm, now which footpath is that? "OK, thanks." It was warm but Abby intended to change her dress when she got back anyway. If the walk made her too warm she could always grab a quick shower at the same time. She would only miss more drinks being served on the lawn while the happy couple were whisked off for private shots. She turned and started walking towards the road.

"Wait. Why are you asking?"

"I'm going to walk it. I need the space." Abby felt instantly annoyed with herself – she didn't need space away from him. She just couldn't face being confined again on the coach.

Brad looked a little deflated.

"Walk with me if you like." She surprised herself.

Brad didn't wait to be asked again and hurried after her.

Five minutes down the road and after watching the coach disappear into the distance Abby's feet were throbbing. She had worn her new shoes in on carpet; clomping them along a cobbled pavement felt quite different.

"It's no good, these have to come off!"

Brad laughed as she slipped her shoes off and wiggled her toes.

"It's been bloody ages since I've worn shoes like this out." Abby felt grit underfoot but her feet were more than happy to be free.

"The footpath is up here, it'll be grass then. Do you need me to carry you?"

"Pah!" Abby guffawed. "I'd break your back!"

"I could piggyback you."

Well that seemed like a ridiculous idea, what would they look like? Abby was pretty sure that would definitely break his back, plus she'd have to hitch her skirt up and wrap her legs around him while his hands were on her thighs... *hmmm!*

"No. No, no, I'll be fine honestly. It's refreshing walking barefoot." She almost convinced herself.

Once they were on the footpath, walking through a field, it really was refreshing. The grass was dry and tickly. It was peaceful, she felt relaxed and... happy. She reflected on how she had felt in the church: she had been on the verge of spiralling into panic and yet now she felt normal. It was such an improvement since the days spent engulfed by darkness, wallowing in her own sadness. The fact that it no longer consumed her in the same way made her feel more in control, like she was winning the battle.

"So Mr Hunter, where is your plus one? Why are you here alone?" The question came without preamble; it seemed feeling at peace made her relax a little too much. As Brad winced, she regretted her lack of filter.

"Honestly?"

Honestly? Yes, honestly – why don't men have honesty as their default setting? "Only if you want to tell me. Sorry... I wasn't trying to pry."

"It's OK. I'm surprised the gossip hasn't got round at work already."

Ooh, was there gossip? Perhaps she had been too wound up in her own problems to hear it. "I haven't heard anything."

"My plus one is in India."

The thought that there actually was a plus one hit Abby like a slap in the face. She tried not to look taken aback as she concentrated on keeping her feet moving forward. *But all the flirting...?*

"Though technically I don't think she can be called my plus one any more, since last I heard she had found a backpacker from Manchester to find herself with."

"Oh," was all Abby could manage.

"Autumn felt she was missing something. Apparently that something might be found in India."

Autumn? Did he actually say Autumn? Oh God, she's a hippy!

"I was getting ready to settle down, start a family and thought she was too. But when I was looking at engagement rings and honeymoon destinations, it turns out she was looking at backpacks and hostels." The hurt in his voice was clear.

Abby felt bad; all the time she'd been asking him to be her friend and yet she hadn't known this. She had never bothered to ask how he was, what was going on in his life.

"Simon was a dick for messing around on you. Honestly Abby, I'd love to have what he had."

Abby was shocked by the turn in conversation. Now it was Brad who had lost his filter.

"I want a wife who loves me and wants to be with me, I want children. I want a Sunday morning bringing my wife breakfast in bed, while our children play happily."

Abby thought about the reality of Sunday mornings in the past, of the girls waking her up too early while they squabbled over which toy to play with, and her succumbing to letting them watch *Milkshake* so she and Simon could sneak a cuddle that was generally interrupted by Bramble barking for his breakfast. It wasn't quite the picture Brad was painting but she got his point.

"I'm sorry I didn't know about... about... Autumn." She wanted to turn the conversation back round. Aware that Brad probably wasn't in the mood for it, she fought the urge to defend Simon and her marriage.

Brad sighed. "It's OK, there's nothing to know really. She's gone."

The final words carried weight, Abby could tell, but she wasn't sure Brad wanted to share. Perhaps it wasn't just her he was comforting at the wedding.

Following the edge of the woodland they could see the hotel in the distance and the guests gathered outside. Abby welcomed the distraction.

"Oh look, we're almost there."

"How about we arrive in style?"

Abby looked at Brad – he couldn't be serious. He was pointing at a golf buggy just a short distance from them.

"We can't just take a golf buggy!"

"It looks pretty abandoned to me."

"We both know that's not true, the owner has to be here somewhere."

"Um, well I don't see them." Brad shrugged assuredly as he jogged towards it and climbed in the driving seat.

"Brad, it's stealing."

"No, it's borrowing. Get in."

Abby knew it was a silly idea but her feet were aching and there was a drink calling to her in the distance. She could almost feel the bubbles tickling her nose.

"Oh bugger!" Abby leapt in, giggling wildly from nerves and excitement as Brad sped off. As they headed towards the hotel, Abby turned to see a disgruntled golfer emerging from the trees doing up his zip. *It's definitely stealing!* She turned, pretending not to notice. The golf buggy was at its limit around eighteen miles per hour but with the excitement of the moment and the hill leading to the hotel it felt faster.

"You do know how to stop this don't you?"

"Umm… yes."

With the hotel fast approaching Abby sincerely hoped he did. Arriving in style was one thing, crashing into drinks on the lawn was quite another. A few guests turned to see them hurtling towards them. Abby couldn't help but notice Patty's shocked face staring at them. *There goes keeping a lid on the gossip at school!* In true racer boy style Brad skidded to a halt, causing more guests to turn. Abby attempted a casual smile, aware that she was still holding her shoes, her hair was a mess from the ride and her dress was still screwed up. In fact she was looking thoroughly dishevelled. Brad offered his hand. Taking it and exiting the golf buggy with as much decorum as she could muster Abby stepped out and put her shoes on. As a waiter passed she took a flute of champagne and swigged it back. Oh, she needed that. Smiling at Brad and then turning to a wide-eyed Patty she excused herself and went to make herself look a little more appropriate for the occasion.

Chapter 33

Abby welcomed a quick shower. She looked in her wardrobe and pulled out what was to be her backup evening outfit; a tube skirt and sleeveless drape-necked top. It was slightly less formal than her dress and made her feel so much more comfortable. With no time to straighten her hair she scrunched it dry hanging upside down. While it wasn't as tidy as if she'd straightened it, she quite liked the slightly more ruffled look it gave her new layers. A quick check of her phone confirmed there were no missed messages – *good* – she slipped her shoes back on, emptied her clutch bag of soggy tissues and popped her phone inside. With a final check in the mirror she was ready to go.

As Abby arrived in the hotel lobby she slipped into the queue of guests waiting to formally congratulate the bride and groom before taking their seat for the wedding breakfast. Abby kissed Adam and hugged Melissa, who still looked amazing.

"Congratulations my lovely, I'm so happy for you." She meant it sincerely.

"Thank you, I'm so pleased you came." Melissa squeezed Abby, knowing how she would have struggled with the ceremony, before letting her go. As Abby moved on to the seating plan Melissa called after her, "Fab shoes by the way! Love them!"

Abby laughed: *mission accomplished.* Now all she had to do was find her seat and she could slip them off.

The tables were draped in white cloths while each chair was bedecked with an emerald green satin bow, matching the bridesmaids' dresses and the ribbons and foliage of the stunning floral displays distributed around the room. The large, round tables were all named after famous film quotes. Abby instantly spotted *LOVE MEANS NEVER HAVING TO SAY YOU'RE SORRY* and rolled her eyes cynically. Thankfully she wasn't on that table; it seemed the school crowd were sitting at *TO ME YOU ARE PERFECT* and *YOU COMPLETE ME.* Abby was pleased for Brad's sake that they weren't on *CHOOSE ME, MARRY ME, LET ME MAKE YOU HAPPY.* After some scurrying around the edge of the room she soon found her laminated place name and took her seat between Brad and Patty.

Brad stood and held out her chair. "I like this outfit too, but I miss the silk."

The slight drop in his voice made Abby shiver and laugh nervously. Patty's jaw fell south. Taking her seat, Abby decided not to attempt to explain.

Once seated and feeling generally more relaxed Abby looked around her. She spotted the cake, a sumptuous tower of Belgian chocolate sponge, coated in thick white chocolate and adorned with white chocolate cherubs. She recognised the *Choccywoccydoodah* style from her own wedding and her mouth watered a little.

Amongst the guests there was a multitude of outfits, in an array of colours, not all entirely appropriate to the occasion. Some looked stunning while others pulled at hems and fussed with collars uncomfortably. There was no doubting that everybody had made an effort and followed the universal rule of attempting to look posh for a wedding. Abby hadn't seen so many feather-and-bow mesh hats in one place since she and Kennedy used to try them on in Bentalls. She looked at the rather odd fascinator Adam's mum was wearing. She certainly wasn't a fan of them; Kennedy loved an excuse to wear one but to Abby they always seemed like some weird hat-hairpiece-hybrid. She couldn't imagine trying to keep one in place all day, and judging by the way Adam's mum was fussing with hers it wouldn't be staying put much longer either.

As the bride and groom – Mr and Mrs Wilson – were officially announced everybody stood, clapped and cheered. Holding hands they entered the room and made their way to *I PROMISE TO LOVE YOU EVERY MOMENT OF FOREVER*, aka the top table. In a break from tradition the bride and groom had decided to have the speeches before food. Melissa had explained to Abby it was because she wanted Adam's best man to do his speech before he got steaming drunk; however the official line was that it was so the men could enjoy their food without the fear of nerves playing havoc with their appetites. The young waiters and waitresses flew into action, swiftly placing open bottles of champagne on each table and filling champagne flutes. Clearly no expense was being spared.

Abby hoped for Melissa and Adam's sake they had a stonking savings account. Having been married a long time and having experienced the reality of starting a life together she couldn't help but feel a little cynical at spending so much on the big day. After all it was just that, a day. In keeping with the theme of the wedding she mentally compared it to blowing your budget on a stunning trailer while forgetting there was a whole movie still to make. As she glanced round at the grand setting she wished she had passed some of that wisdom on to Melissa along with her handy hair tip. Then again, Melissa had mentioned her dad was a very successful antiques dealer; perhaps he'd gone the traditional route and paid for it. *Does that still happen?* Abby pondered the question while sipping her champagne. The thought that it could be the product of benevolence on the part of the bride's wealthy parents and not Melissa and Adam's house deposit made it slip down oh so much more easily.

With a chink of a glass the father of the bride was announced and Melissa's dad stood, placing his hand on her shoulder. On behalf of himself and his wife, Judy, he thanked all the guests for attending, giving special mention to those who had travelled to be there. As he continued a lump grew in Abby's throat.

"Since she was a little girl it had been Melissa's dream to get married in the family church, and how lovely it has been to see her achieve that dream with Adam today. We remember her christening there as if it were yesterday, but now our little girl is all grown up and we couldn't be more proud of the beautiful young lady she has grown into…"

Abby's chest tightened. She missed her dad. She wished he were still alive. She missed his annoyingly sensible advice, his hugs, the too-strong tea he made at his allotment and his ability to always make her smile. She wished she could speak to him again, to tell him how much she loved him. She saw the tears that welled in Melissa's dad's eyes, the pride, the love and the way Melissa returned his smile. If only she could share a moment like that again with her dad.

Abby's mind slipped back to the conversation she'd had with Mallory about the loss of her dad. The thought that she had somehow coped with that loss better than her problems with Simon still sat uncomfortably with her. She remembered her dad's final days, when she had sat with her mum and Kennedy, watching helplessly as he slowly drifted further and further away from them. She recalled how Simon had held her up, hugged her, looked after her, been there for her and encouraged her to be brave. She thought about her dad's funeral, watching his coffin being lowered into the ground and struggling for breath as she sobbed mournfully in Simon's arms. He had guided her through it all, taken care of Eleanor and organised everything so she could have the wake she wanted for him, in the headquarters of his old cycling club.

In a moment of epiphany Abby knew she had only coped with it better because Simon had helped her. She had managed the grief because he had been there for her, holding her hand, helping her through, loving her, the way he always did. The way he had for almost half her life.

"Ladies and gentlemen, please join me in a toast to the bride and groom."

As everybody's glass was lifted in the air Abby was jolted from her own thoughts.

"The bride and groom," the guests echoed in unison and sipped their champagne.

Barely whispering, Patty nodded in the direction of Abby's glass. "You'll have none left for the other speeches at that rate."

Abby stopped drinking, realising she was positively swigging her champagne. She put her glass down and wiped her mouth, attempting to remind herself that getting drunk was not a good idea and that there were in fact two more speeches to come. Next to stand was Adam's best man. Within about sixty seconds of him speaking it was obvious why Melissa had wanted the speeches before the alcohol had too long to flow.

"As many of you know us both, you know I'm Tom and I *am* the best man." He paused for laughter while the room filled with groans. "Adam and I have played rugby together since we were at school. He is the best mate anybody could ask for and me and the team are all really happy to see him get hitched to Melissa – especially since by now, she must have discovered that in Adam's case, rugby really is a game played by men with odd-shaped balls."

The rugby crowd whooped. Abby's eyes went wide as she stared at Melissa. But Melissa's face was merely bemused. She obviously knew Adam's mates well and must have been expecting this style of cheeky speech. Adam's mum on the other hand looked a little horrified. If any more steam came out of her ears Abby feared her fascinator might actually wilt.

"Seriously though, when Adam asked me to be best man I was really honoured. I went home and I spent several hours searching the Internet. I found lots of really great stuff, but then I remembered I was going to be best man and thought I better get down to writing a speech…"

Brad laughed. Abby took a swig of her drink, wondering how much longer the speech could go on for while Patty listened intently, seemingly oblivious to the joke.

After finally delivering some rather sweet words about watching Adam fall in love with Melissa, acknowledging the maid of honour a little too lustfully with a wink, and thanking the other beautiful bridesmaids, Tom began his toast.

"So we all know Melissa's a stickler for detail and I got strict instructions about the film theme, so I had to do a little more research. But this time I had to go to my little black book – well, you know, the many ladies listed in my contacts anyway." He tapped his pocket, where his phone presumably sat. "And what they said was, all these films about love and stuff, when you watch enough of them you learn that the best relationships come down to a few simple things. And as I'm getting a bit Hugh Grant with this now, I'd like to apologise in advance for all the F words…"

Again the rugby crowd whooped, Melissa's parents tensed, the rest of the room stilled and Adam's poor mum looked in need of medical assistance.

"So here's to fate and finding the right one," Tom directed a smile towards the happy couple, "forging a friendship, falling in love, fostering forgiveness – everybody needs a little sometimes," he winked, "forming a family and making it last forever." Tom paused and pretended to shudder at his own words. "In short, because those ladies sure can talk and that's a bloody long mouthful, I'd like to propose a toast to all the F words, but especially 'forever'!"

The rather stunned audience echoed Tom's words in

unison. After drinking more champagne everybody clapped; Abby was sure it was as much out of relief as acknowledgment of the quite sweet toast.

With Adam's speech coming up next Abby decided to excuse herself. She knew he was besotted with Melissa and she really was happy for them, but she couldn't risk getting over-emotional again. Not only did she not want to make a scene, she was also on her last posh outfit; she couldn't risk another tear disaster. As she stood Brad caught her hand and asked if she was OK. Abby gave him a reassuring smile, nodded and slipped discreetly out of a side door. Moving away from the murmur of the main hall she found a set of sun-warmed stone steps and sat down. Bathed in warmth as she sat, momentarily enjoying the solitude, the words 'forgiveness' and 'forever' played in her mind.

Abby held up her hand and stared at her wedding and engagement rings. As the light caught them they sparkled. On the night she found out about Simon's affair, after she had told him to leave, she'd tried to take them off. She remembered sitting in her empty bedroom twisting and tugging at them, trying desperately to free herself of them, but with her having gained weight since they had married they wouldn't budge no matter how hard she tried. When she thought her finger might actually bleed from the frustratingly futile effort she stopped and cried pathetically instead. She knew it was different now. She had lost weight. She could take them off easily; she sometimes felt them slip round her finger. And yet no matter how many times she stared at them, no matter how many times she slipped them down her finger she never actually did it. She didn't want to. Something always stopped her. She had worn them for so many years, they had been a part of her for so long, she actually couldn't imagine herself without them. *Perhaps*, she thought, *some things are too much a part of you to simply let them go.*

Chapter 34

As the speeches and thank-yous overran, the wedding breakfast merged into the evening do. Dessert had barely been served to the back tables as more guests started to arrive and stand in open doorways around the edge of the room. It was the kind of thing that might have ordinarily tipped Melissa but she didn't seem to mind at all, in fact she was beckoning them in, much to the unease of the poor wedding co-ordinator who was trying to organise the waiters and waitresses as they attempted to ready the room for the evening around those still eating their orange crème brûlée with pine nut shortbread.

After a little flapping, and a good deal of ushering, the bulk of the guests were encouraged to go outside where it was decided that, as a cunning ploy to clear the room, the cake would be cut and served along with more drinks.

"Seen it on telly but never tried it," Patty announced as they all watched Adam and Melissa slice into the cake.

Abby looked at her, confused. "Did you not do cake at your wedding?"

"Of course we did, I've still got a tier in the freezer. It's lasted longer than the marriage."

"Oh… sorry…" Abby felt bad at having bought up Patty's failed marriage; she must have been dealing with her own issues at the wedding too. Chastising herself for not having thought of that earlier and checking Patty was OK, she smiled and ventured to change the subject. "Then what haven't you tried?"

"Anything from *Choccywoccywotsit*," Patty tutted, like it was obvious.

Abby laughed. "Oh, you'll love it! Our... my..."

Brad offered a small smile and headed off in the direction of the drinks table.

"I've had cake from there. It's delicious," Abby finished.

When Abby found Brad amongst the other guests he held out a napkin for her with something wrapped inside.

"Open it." He grinned.

Abby smiled at the sight of a white chocolate cherub. "I'm pretty sure you're supposed to take a piece of sponge from the plate, not a cherub off the side of the remaining cake!"

"It wasn't my fault, it kind of fell off as I passed." Moving closer he whispered, "Maybe it was destined to come this way."

Abby licked her lips – though she wasn't sure it was at the thought of the cake.

"That looks amaaaaazing!" Patty cooed, appearing at Abby's side. "How shall we divvy him up?"

Brad sighed. "I'll get more napkins."

When they returned inside there were fewer tables, a few more chairs, a dance floor, a disco and an open bar. It was well and truly party time. Having drifted back together the entire school crowd sat near the dance floor and the conversation turned to where the happy couple's secret honeymoon destination might be. It was the only thing Adam insisted Melissa should relinquish control of; he wanted to organise it as a present to his new bride.

"Well for his sake I hope it's bloody amazing!" Patty guffawed. "Ooh, Abby do you know if she got him anything? I mean, how do you top a honeymoon?"

All eyes turned to Abby as her cheeks turned a deeper shade of pink. "Not that I know of," she lied, remembering the gift Melissa had drunkenly ordered at Patty's lingerie party. She took a swig of her drink and added with an air of finality, "I'm sure they'll have a great time." *Thank goodness all orders were private!*

As the first dance was announced Melissa sashayed onto the dance floor looking relaxed and blissfully happy. She giggled wildly as Adam, on a post-nuptial alcohol-fuelled high, swept her into his arms a little too lustfully. Christina Perri's *A Thousand Years*, started to play and Jo Simms sighed.

"Seriously, do you think they'll go to the cinema less once they're married?"

Abby ignored her. Melissa loved a theme and besides, if Edward and Bella's music did it for her then so what? *Perhaps Mr Darcy is out and vampires are in!* They looked great dancing together, a little too great actually. Abby wondered if they had sneaked a few pre-wedding lessons. She and Simon tended to stick to the one-foot-to-the-other, slow-sway-and-spin version of slow dancing saved for such occasions as weddings and family parties. Melissa and Adam clearly had more flair to their moves than that. Abby wondered why Jo had come if all she wanted to do was be cynical, then she reprimanded herself for her own hypocrisy. If anybody had heard her inner monologue at the ceremony she might also stand guilty as charged.

As the happy couple's dance finished with a lingering kiss the party classics began and Melissa's friends rushed onto the dance floor, stealing her away from a begrudging Adam. They all looked stunning, a bit merry and certainly up for a party. Their colourful dresses contrasted with Melissa's and her bridesmaids' as they stood in a line ready to dance. Abby looked on with a tinge of envy as they all dipped and turned in time to the music. She could only imagine how many times they had all done it before, countless dances from sleepovers, birthday parties, school discos and clubbing, to being all grown up and dancing at each others' weddings; some of them had clearly shared at least a decade. They looked great and obviously knew the routine well. The *Macarena* had always remained an enigma to Abby, who had the general co-ordination of Bambi on ice.

The buffet table opened and was soon being obliterated by Adam and his rugby friends, their raucous laughter mixing with the loud music as they looked approvingly towards the dance floor. They were obviously a solid bunch of friends, proud of their mate on his big day and jibing him about being married at the same time. Not that Adam cared, the glint in his eye each time he glanced at his wife left everybody in no doubt that he was thoroughly smitten and couldn't wait to get her all to himself. With a dance-walk combo as he made his way across the dance floor, Melissa's dad joined them, putting his arm round Adam's shoulder and slipping easily into their alcohol-fuelled banter. Abby smiled.

Melissa's mum was obviously pleased the more formal part of the day was over too. Her hat had long since been forgotten and she sat with her legs a little too far apart, a glass of champagne, a cup of tea and a large slice of wedding cake set out in front of her as she entertained the two youngest bridesmaids. While Abby had barely noticed them in the church, she couldn't help but think how cute they looked now. The girls reminded her of Jessica and Grace: they had been so good all day, posing for pictures and sitting happily through the speeches and meal. Now their hair was looking a little ruffled and their sparkly silver shoes had been replaced with white Crocs. The glow of their cheeks reflected the dedication with which they had flung themselves around the dance floor in an effort to keep up with Melissa and her friends before commencing their mission to collect every piece of table confetti they could find.

Brad sat down next to Abby, his tie pulled loose and his top button open. His eyes sparkled, his pupils were dark and dilated; she wondered how many drinks he had polished off at the bar while getting the round in.

"Weddings are the best for people watching, don't you think?" Abby gestured across the room.

Not wanting to reveal that the only person he had been watching from the other side of the room was her, Brad placed Abby's drink on the table and looked across the dance floor. "I guess."

"Such a mismatch of people. Great isn't it? Honestly it's the only time you ever expect people from all areas of your life to come together. People you ordinarily wouldn't dream of putting in the same room all get invited to your... I mean, a wedding." *Shut up Abby!*

"Especially the evening do by the look of it." Brad grinned. "Who do you reckon was on the subs list?"

Relieved at the sight of his grin, and that she hadn't put her enormous foot in it yet again, Abby hit his arm. "Brad, that's bad!"

"OK, I'm missing the film theme now – do you think he might play something other than party songs if I remind the DJ of it?" Jo laughed with a roll of her eyes.

"Whigfield not for you Jo?" Brad asked cheekily.

Jo stuck her tongue out and headed for the buffet table. As she strutted across the dance floor the song changed; it seemed the film theme was back on and *The Time Of My Life* started. Brad, Patty and Abby watched in shocked amusement as one of Adam's mates threw himself on one knee in front of Jo and started miming the words in the style of Patrick Swayze.

"Oh no!" Abby blushed for her.

"This could be interesting." Brad laughed, expecting that the man might regret his move and be bent on one knee for a whole other reason any minute.

"Lucky cow!" Patty sighed; clearly her divorce wasn't playing on her mind in quite the way Abby thought it might be.

A stunned silence spread along their row as Jo, seemingly

unfazed, mouthed back the second line, put her hand out, pulled the man to his feet and started grinding towards him.

"What the… bet he didn't expect that!" Brad exclaimed.

"I certainly didn't," Patty laughed before booming, "GO JO!"

"She's actually dirty dancing! Jo Simms is dirty dancing!" Abby was gobsmacked.

Jo looked in her element and the man didn't seem to mind either.

"Who'd have thought?" Abby asked nobody in particular.

They all stared, eyes and mouths agape.

"Fancy giving them a run for their money?" Brad turned to Abby with a smile.

"Oh no! No, no, no. No way!" Abby shook her head, as if saying no five times hadn't quite been enough to make her point.

"But you can't just sit here all night," Brad protested.

"I will!" Patty leapt to her feet and tugged at Brad's hand before Abby could respond.

Brad looked at Abby and pulled a 'yikes' face that made her giggle.

"Go on Patty, have fun," Abby teasingly encouraged, but as she watched Patty press herself up to Brad and wiggle in ways she never saw in *Dirty Dancing*, Abby found it less funny. Jo was having a great time; who knew she had it in her? Patty had accosted Brad and Abby was left watching, and it was her own fault for not being brave enough. Now she was… well… *a bloody wallflower!*

Chapter 35

"Hey you, not dancing?"

"No… not yet anyway."

"Good, you can help me to the loo, my bridesmaids have gone AWOL and I've no idea how to go in this dress. I'm not sure how I've waited this long."

Abby laughed. A thoroughly sober Melissa would never have asked her to accompany her to the toilet, let alone stamp her feet and pull her to standing as a sign of her desperation; she was clearly enjoying the less formal part of the day and the free-flowing champagne too. Pleased to have a purpose to leave her post as wallflower Abby followed obediently. She remembered enlisting Rachel as her toilet buddy at her own wedding and tried to remember how they had co-ordinated the situation.

While Melissa's dress was far less meringue-like than Abby's it was still very much a two-woman task; it seemed all bridal attire from the full-length wedding dress to the complicated underwear conspired against dignity and practicality when it came to going to the loo. There was no way they could actually shut the door with Abby leaning in and holding up reams of satin round Melissa's ears. By the time Melissa was actually on the toilet they had said, "to you, to me," so many times Abby felt like she had auditioned to become the third member of the Chuckle Brothers.

"Oh no, I'm too bursting to go!" Melissa cursed before whistling.

Abby looked at her, perplexed. "Why are you whistling?"

"Apparently, it works for horses!"

With that they both roared with laughter just as Adam's mum entered the toilet, turned cerise at the surprise sight of her new daughter-in-law and hurriedly left. That was it; they both lost control, holding their stomachs and giggling like a pair of schoolgirls. At least the release of tension helped achieve the task in hand.

Attempting to regain their composure they fussed around readjusting Melissa's dress and straightening themselves out.

Abby paused and looked at Melissa. "I'm so happy for you. I really am. It's been a really lovely day. Thanks so much for inviting me and for... and, well... everything... you know."

Melissa pulled her into a hug. "Ahhh Abby, thank you too. I'm so glad you're here and you look bloody brilliant."

Melissa's enthusiasm was more than a little alcohol-fuelled but Abby welcomed the compliment – she had worked towards it over the preceding months; aiming to get in shape, both physically and mentally, for the wedding had kept her going at times.

"Savour every moment of today and every happy moment that follows Melissa, really hold on to what you have." Tears pricked at Abby's eyes, she wasn't meaning to get emotional and she was determined not to add *it could all be gone before you know it*, no matter how keenly she felt the sentiment.

"I will," Melissa promised, dabbing at her own eyes. "Now stop, or you'll have us both looking like pandas!"

Returning to the reception meant Melissa was in popular demand again and Abby had to let her go, but she was glad to have had the chance to say the things she wanted to say. A smile crept across her face as she saw Adam's mum, and faded abruptly when she met Brad's stern expression at the table.

"Where have you been?" he demanded, rolling his eyes in Patty's direction.

Oops. Clearly she was in trouble for deserting him. "I was on an important mission with the bride!" Abby insisted.

"Oh really?" Brad stood, removing himself from Patty's grasp. "Well now, Abigail Turner, you owe me this dance!"

Oh my, he's getting all masterful! Brad held out his hand. Abby took a moment to register what was playing. The dance tracks were back! DJ Casper's *Cha Cha Slide* had just started with the promise of getting funky. Abby felt fear, dread and anxiety building in her stomach – she hadn't been 'funky' for about a decade, if ever.

"Come on." Brad lowered his voice; it was slightly deeper from the alcohol anyway and the overall effect gave her tingles. Along with his dark brown, pleading eyes and the curve of his lovely mouth she found it all very persuasive. "It even tells you what moves to do, you can't go wrong."

Brad beckoned her as the song got going and everybody on the dance floor clapped as one. Abby looked across the sea of people and saw Jo, still dancing and very much entwined with her rugby man. *Sod it, if she can do it I'm sure I bloody well can!* Just as Patty was about to leap in, Abby stood and took Brad's warm hand in hers. About to head to the dance floor Abby turned and gulped down the remainder of her drink. As her knees slightly numbed she giggled – well, it wasn't like it was actually going to affect her dancing.

Feeling rather less ridiculous than she feared Abby joined in, following Brad's lead and giggling wildly as she got the moves wrong.

"Oh my God, it's like bloody Zumba," Abby laughed, remembering the DVD she had bought and promptly abandoned after tying herself in knots and falling over Bramble on her first attempt.

"You're doing great, besides, nobody cares."

Brad was right. Abby looked around the room; nobody was pointing or laughing at her, nobody cared if she made a tit of herself. Her own inhibitions were the only thing preventing her from really letting go. Feeling Brad move next to her, laughing with him and occasionally jostling into him – *oops* – increasingly freed Abby's mind. She decided to go with it; enjoy the moment. It was very liberating.

There was something about being with Brad that made her do things she wouldn't normally do. He brought something out in her, something that had been lost in the monotony of life. Perhaps it was her spirit for adventure, she didn't know. But whatever it was she could feel it awakening inside her. She was a little fascinated by it and at the same time a bit frightened about where it might lead. She didn't behave like herself when she was with Brad, or maybe she did and this was her new self, her post-Simon self. She dismissed the thought; she didn't want to think about that.

Even Abby felt that Steps' *Tragedy* seemed a little inappropriate for a wedding. Nevertheless it was a crowd-puller and Abby welcomed the fact that she knew some of the actions. *What girl doesn't?* Abby grinned, watching Patty and Jo throw themselves wholeheartedly into their moves. Even Melissa and her mostly loved-up friends were action-perfect, while Abby and Brad made up a few of their own – feigning tragedy and longing in equal measure as the song dictated, much to their own amusement.

Giggling and breathing heavily they stopped to have a drink. Though Brad offered to get her something from the bar Abby swigged down a glass of water. She wanted to keep a clear head. The water was cool and refreshing as it slipped down. Luckily the open doors around the room prevented it from becoming too hot, otherwise she would have combusted with the amount of dancing she was doing. Abby checked her shoes and bag were still where she had discarded them and momentarily considered checking her phone before being distracted by a familiar tune. Unable to resist *YMCA* she grabbed Brad's hand and led him onto the dance floor. As it was a school disco classic she knew she was on safe ground.

The children loved it when the teachers joined in and *YMCA*, along with Black Lace's *Superman* song, that she suspected wouldn't get played, were among the few songs that featured on her limited disco-dancing repertoire.

Once the song ended and the DJ announced a change of tempo with Take That Abby momentarily froze. She couldn't listen to *Patience*; it would call to the darkness she had shunned from the earlier part of the day. She didn't want to be pulled back down from the happy cloud she was occupying. As *Rule The World* began and Brad's arms slipped around her like a big, safe comfort blanket she relaxed too easily into them. If he had asked if she wanted to slow-dance she probably would have declined, but he hadn't and once she felt herself so close to him it was too late. She succumbed too easily to feeling herself entwined with him.

Oh God, it felt so good to be held in his arms. She knew she should set her hands somewhere appropriate and safe but she couldn't help herself. She slipped them inside his jacket and traced along the top of his belt line. She felt his taut muscles flex at her touch and inhaled when her fingertips came to rest on the dimples at the small of his back. Those dimples, the ones she had seen just above the line of his shorts, the ones she had imagined touching and trailing small kisses over just before she had dropped the hot chocolate. Blinking away how flustered she had been on that day, she allowed herself a moment to enjoy the feel of them. Beneath the thin cotton of his shirt she traced small circles around them with her manicured nails and heard his intake of breath.

She looked up; his eyes were dark and focused intently on her. She was affecting him. She could feel heat rising to his skin. She smiled a not-so-terribly-innocent smile and he bit his bottom lip. Heat rising to her cheeks, Abby wondered how it would feel to bite that lip. Unable to trust herself she looked away; focusing on his lips was not a good idea. Closing her eyes, she rested her head on his shoulder. She could feel the smooth, warm skin of his neck and the rhythmic hint of his pulse that had quickened there. He smelt delicious, of something familiar she had smelt before. She felt warmth spreading inside, awakening her nerves and causing her heart to beat faster. *What are you doing?* A small, sensible part of her mind was calling to her; attempting to get her to think this through. But she didn't want to. She needed this moment. She needed him.

With her eyes closed Abby's senses seemed to heighten. She felt Brad's hand touch her neck and trace slowly down her back. She swallowed as his fingers hitched over her bra strap before continuing to slide down her spine and coming to rest with his other hand at the small of her back. He sighed into her, a deep, soft groan that turned her insides to liquid. They were swaying together. Abby felt the need for him building inside her and she knew he felt the same. She could feel him warm and firm up against her. Everyone and everything else in the room melted away as all Abby could think about was how much she wanted Bradley Hunter.

As they danced she could feel his muscles rippling and couldn't help but imagine how they looked beneath his shirt. Without thinking she slowly traced her fingers along the top of his belt, allowing just her fingertips to slip slightly into the warmth at his waistband. He sucked in a deep breath and the air caught her neck as he exhaled slowly; goosebumps tingled down her side. She shuddered and moved closer into his warmth.

"Abby, you'll have to stop, or I won't be responsible," he whispered. She could hear the effect she was having on him in the quiver that rippled through his deep voice. It didn't make her want to stop. It made her want more.

Her conscience whispered *Simon* into her mind, while the word, "Brad" slipped breathlessly from her mouth. Hearing her speak his name in that tone was more than he could take. Abby felt his muscles ripple as she spoke and swallowed as she imagined what more she could do to him. Kissing her gently on the forehead, Brad stepped back. Abby looked at him, panic in her eyes, not wanting it to end. Needing to be close to him. Without speaking he took her hand and led her off the dance floor. Patty waved Abby's bag and shoes in the air and may have called something after them but Abby didn't stop to listen. She was lost to a world where only following Brad mattered and the draw of his hand taking her away from everybody and everything was all that she recognised.

Chapter 36

Passing through the foyer in a haze they slipped out the front door of the hotel into the cool evening air. Abby welcomed the sensation on her hot cheeks, and enjoyed the breeze against her enlivened nerves as goosebumps rose on her skin. She followed Brad silently as he led her away from the other guests, the light and the music, into the shadows. Part of her knew she should let go of Brad's hand, step away and break the spell, but she couldn't. The attraction flowing through their touch was too strong. As they reached the end of the building, Brad hesitated and turned to Abby. Still holding his hand she leaned back against the wall. The stone felt hard and cold against the heat of her back. She curled her toes into the grass and felt the damp earth below. Brad paused a pace away as they both stood, gazing at each other, catching their breath. The evening was calm and still. Abby could hear the thud of her own heart pounding over the distant sound of the disco music.

Don't do anything you'll regret. Kennedy's words slipped into her mind. Abby closed her eyes and pushed them away. Brad waited and Abby knew he was waiting for her, letting her make the next move. Her mind was scrambling and she couldn't (or didn't want to) draw any sense from it; instead she acted on impulse, drawing him in closer to her. She moved her fingers to the back of his neck, traced round his shoulders and down his firm biceps. She wondered if he could feel the heat from the lust-fuelled fire she felt spreading within, causing her skin to flush and her insides to quiver. Following her lead Brad traced gently along her shoulders and round her neck. His fingers tangled into her hair at her nape, causing her head to tilt towards his and her mouth to slightly open. Abby looked into his eyes; his pupils were swollen with desire and yet something about his gaze revealed a hint of vulnerability. His thumbs circled on her hot skin before he drew her closer and placed soft, gentle kisses on her full lips. She welcomed their touch and responded, kissing him back, feeling the effects throughout her body. She felt his tongue slip into her mouth and entwine with hers. He groaned, causing her legs to numb and her body to sag towards his. He leaned his weight against her, holding her to the wall. She could feel every inch of him pressed against her as their tongues tangled in their mind-rushing, desire-fuelled duel.

It was an amazing assault on Abby's senses. It was so strange and yet exciting being held and kissed by somebody new. She knew she was being driven by lust. It was so different to the intimacy she and Simon shared: they never made clumsy moves with their hands any more, they knew how to position themselves to kiss, how to elicit the most pleasure from one another. They were well-practised and more than good at it. But this, this was different and all new. It was an exploration – a much more impetuous form of arousal. Abby's mind couldn't keep up. She vaguely remembered wondering, some months back, if she could get the hurt and anxiety fucked out of her; was that what she was trying to do? Was that what she was about to do? She didn't know how far she wanted to go, but she couldn't stop her hands sliding over Brad's firm torso. She could feel his chest through his shirt and began to feel dizzy. *Oh God!*

In response Brad slid one hand down Abby's side, his thumb tracing the edge of her breast. Her cheeks burned at the involuntary moan that escaped her. Eagerly, Abby slid Brad's jacket off his shoulders. As it fell to the grass her hands slid down his back until she felt his firm glutes flex in her hands. *Oh fuck! You're going too far.* The movement sent him edging yet closer to her. She could feel herself drowning; drowning in her desire for him and the scent of his aftershave that she wanted to lose herself in – that smell, she loved that smell. His hands continued to trace up and down her sides; she gasped loudly as he slid one hand up inside her top and cupped her breast over the thin lace of her bra and traced his thumb over her tight nipple. She pushed herself unashamedly forwards into his hand, forcing him to grasp her more firmly. *Fuck!* Abby's world began to spin. Everything was happening so fast; part of her mind chanted *Simon* while her traitorous body succumbed to her need and Brad's touch. She clenched her hands, grinding him nearer to her, feeling the friction of his arousal so close to where she needed it. She heard her unrecognisable voice calling his name.

"Abby!" His voice was rough in response.

She knew he needed her too. Their clothes were all that were stopping them from going further, deeper into the abyss.

What was that? Abby thought she heard something, but with confusion still reigning in her mind and their audible panting she quickly dismissed it. She couldn't focus, not with Brad pressed so firmly against her; she dug her nails into his back and bit into his shoulder as he kissed her neck and across the top of her breasts. She wasn't sure how much longer she could continue. Brad began pulling at her skirt, tugging it upwards at her hips, *oh yes!* She needed to feel him closer still and began to part her legs as they were gradually freed from the constraints of her skirt. *Don't do anything you'll regret.* Kennedy's words slipped into her mind again. Abby growled into the air, fuelled by her building frustration and confusion.

"Is that you?"

Abby froze, sure she heard something this time.

"What is it? Abby, what's wrong?" Brad panted.

"Listen." Abby held her breath so she could hear over her own ragged breathing.

"It's nothing." Brad kissed her, but Abby didn't respond.

"Oooooh, Abby? Are you out here?" Patty's voice screeched through the evening air.

"Fuck!" Brad cursed and stepped back.

"Abby, Abby are you out here? Your phone was ringing."

Abby looked across at the light. Brad urged her to stay in the shadows, but she was flustered by Patty's presence and had started pulling down her skirt and straightening her top. Guilt flooded over her. *What was I thinking?* The lust that had fired warmth into her body and driven her desire drained away.

"Abby, don't. Let it be just us…" Brad pleaded, pulling her arm.

Abby paused; she could barely look into his eyes. The realisation of how far she almost went stung at her conscience.

She tried to pull her arm away. "Brad, I can't!"

"Abby please…"

The heat that had surrounded them faded and Abby felt the chill of the cold dark shadow they hid in. "But don't you see Brad? Don't you see… it isn't just us? It never has been."

Brad motioned to the light, his voice a harsh whisper. "She's gone now… listen."

Patty's voice had disappeared into the distance, but it didn't matter. She had broken the spell.

"I wasn't talking about Patty. You know that's not what I meant." Abby's voice came out harsher than she intended. She tried to move out of the darkness but Brad still held her arm.

"But you do want me. I know you do, God Abby, we almost… I know you want me, like I want you."

She looked into his eyes and stopped trying to pull away. "You're right, I do – I mean, I *did* want you. Part of me still does, believe me. But Brad, this is not who I am. Not really."

"But it could be, if you'd just give in to it." He sighed heavily.

Abby took a calming breath and swallowed. She wanted to run away but she owed Brad an explanation, probably more.

"Brad, you... you're great. You've been kind and lovely and you deserve someone who will truly want you back, you *deserve* that. What I was about to do with you, it came from a different need. And I shouldn't have let things get that far. I am so sorry Brad. You... you bring out the crazy in me."

Aware she was giving a parting speech but not wanting the moment to end Brad offered a smile. "I like you crazy."

"And I like this kind of crazy, believe me; it's a relief, but—"

Raising his eyebrows Brad interrupted, "I could make you feel more relieved."

Abby giggled. "Brad, you are so bad!"

Bantering felt more like their usual territory, like they were on safer ground. They both relaxed a little. Abby leaned her forehead against his lips as he planted a kiss there.

"If you let me I could show you how good I can be..." he pressed.

Abby recognised the bravado in Brad's voice, the self-preservation ringing through.

"Oh I know you could be good, I've thought about it a LOT."

"You have?" Brad brightened.

"Yes, but—"

"No, don't 'but'."

"But the truth is, I can't let Simon go." Abby surprised herself. Deep down she sort of knew it but that was the first time she had admitted it to anyone, even to herself.

The mood shifted again as Brad growled at Simon's name. "But you were about to... we almost..."

Abby continued to look at him sincerely. "I know and I'm sorry to have led you on, I really am." She pushed away an image of the two of them moments earlier. "But honestly Brad, I don't want what we've shared to be something I regret. I like you too much."

"If you like me then why not give this... this little bit of crazy we share, a go? He doesn't deserve to have you."

Abby sighed. "Oh Brad, it's just not that easy! Life, you know... it's complicated. We were so young when we first got together... we've shared so much. I can't just walk away from it all, he's a part of me, of who I am. The truth is... the truth is... I love him. Despite how hard I've found everything, I love him and I want to be with him." Abby hadn't expected the resolute tone in her voice, but suddenly she felt certain. She loved Simon.

Her words stung Brad. "A moment ago you wanted me, you can't deny it."

"Yes, my need for that moment with you was real but Brad, if we go too far, if I go too far, I might not ever be able to get back what I had. Simon and I will be too broken to fix and I don't want to be the one to do that to us. I want to... I have to be the one to let us try." Abby's words filled her with hope. She could see it all clearly for the first time. She wanted Simon and she was going to do all that she could to get her marriage back on track.

Brad had seen the look in her eyes as she spoke about Simon. He knew he had lost her, that he probably had never truly had her. "You know, this could be your chance."

Abby looked at him, confused.

"Your 'Get Out Of Jail Free' moment."

"What?"

"The only time you could get away with being with another man and your husband would have to accept it." It was a long shot, but he considered it worth a try. The cheeky grin, the self-preservation and the bravado were back.

Abby knew he was protecting himself and felt guilty that part of her had actually been ready to play that card. She sighed. "Ah well, it's a *Chance* I can't take... If you'll pardon the pun." She smiled and started to walk back towards the light and the music in search of Patty and her phone.

As she neared the corner of the building Brad called her name. She glanced back.

"If you change your mind, I'm happy to oblige… any time." He winked.

Abby took a long look at him looking slightly ruffled and still thoroughly gorgeous, smiled and said thank you. She knew he was making it easy for her; he was letting her go.

Chapter 37

I love Simon! I love my husband... We're going to be OK!

Abby loved having her notebook with her to confide in, she liked the new optimistic tone it was taking. She really had turned a corner, she was sure of it now.

She decided not to tell Simon how she felt on the phone. She spoke to him and they had a chat about the girls and Bramble and it was lovely. Since then she had called her mum to fill her in about the day, minus a few details, and lay awake most of the night, cursing the fact that she had drunk earlier in the day. As morning finally came she decided not to wait for breakfast, checked she had all her things, took the flowers Simon had sent from the sink, inhaled their lovely scent and left. She couldn't wait to wave Adam and Melissa off; instead she sent Melissa a text telling her to have a great time. She'd have to find out where they were honeymooning later.

Abby breathed in the crisp morning air. She was early enough for the dew still to be beaded on the cobwebs, like discarded jewels from the opulence of the day before. The sun was rising in the bright blue sky but didn't yet offer the full force of its warmth. It was that moment in the day where everything smells fresh, a new dawn, a new beginning full of hope and promise. Abby beamed; she genuinely beamed in a way she hadn't for too long. She thought about the unwritten future that stretched out in front of her and knew for the first time since everything had happened that she and Simon and the girls would be forging that future together. For a moment she almost felt whole again.

Throwing her case into the back seat of her car Abby noticed something attached to her windscreen. It was a bag containing wedding favours and a note. Taking it out, she read, *You didn't collect your favours, not that anybody actually likes sugared almonds (don't tell Melissa I said that). But I wasn't sure you would stop to say goodbye and I just wanted to say good luck Abby, and stay crazy (in a good way). Love Brad xxx*

Abby looked at the net of five coloured almonds. Attached to it was a label:

For life there are no retakes, no outtakes and no sequel; live each day as if it's your final take, make every minute count and be happy!

It was perfect and it was the kind of thoughtful gesture Simon would have made. It bought tears to Abby's eyes; she knew she was letting someone special go. But more than anything she knew that what she was doing was right. She wanted her life back, she wanted her family all under the same roof, she wanted her husband and she wanted it all now! Her mind was clear on that, blissfully, uncomplicatedly clear. She ripped the label off and tucked it inside her notebook.

Sitting outside the house, feeling a little sweaty now the sun was high in the sky and glaring through the windscreen, Abby wished she had spent at least part of the journey thinking how she should play it once she got home instead of driving like a lunatic, cursing at anybody who dared get in her way. Rachel was there, her car was outside, but that didn't matter. In fact knowing how excited Rachel would be to see them back together kind of built the moment even more in Abby's mind. She so wanted to get it right.

Trying to calm her nervous excitement she considered a few scenarios. Striding in and declaring her love seemed a bit over-the-top under the circumstances. Perhaps she should be more cautious; she didn't want to imply it was all going to be as simple as 'I love you and let's live happily ever after'. Besides, she didn't really trust her mind to allow things to happen quite that easily; she knew that even together, they'd still have to work at moving forward. *Perhaps couples' counselling?* She dismissed the thought almost as soon it popped into her head. Counselling felt like a step backwards. She'd had enough of procrastinating – for the first time in a long time she was ready to get on with living. She wondered momentarily if she should say what happened with Bradley. *No. No, no!* That wasn't quite the start she wanted for their new beginning. Though she realised, in the interest of honesty, she'd have to have that conversation at some point. Abby couldn't think any more. She needed some water. She needed to freshen up, to refresh her face and her dry mouth. Once she'd done that she was sure she'd be able to face Simon and then just go with whatever felt right – be spontaneous. *Arghh!*

Sneaking round the side of the house Abby decided to let herself in the kitchen. Bramble was in his bed but didn't bark when he saw her or actually even get up – *lazy boy!* Instead he banged his tail heavily against the floor. Abby crept over to him and gave him a stroke. Cheekily he rolled half onto his back and lifted his paw, insisting on a full-on chest rub.

"Good news, you funny boy, Daddy is going to come home," she whispered, unable to disguise the excitement in her voice.

Bramble rolled his eyes and snuffled back round to rest on his cushion.

On the kitchen side was a bottle of lime milkshake, Abby's favourite from her college days, and two packets of Love Heart sweets with a note saying **Welcome home my gorgeous wife! S xx** It was perfect; she imagined them sharing them later, the way they used to when they spent long hours talking or simply snuggling up on the sofa. Her chest ached and she realised that it was because she could *feel* she loved him again. It was a strange sensation. She had almost forgotten the feeling; she had shut it down for so long and yet there it was, not in its entirety, but nonetheless there. She welcomed it, like a little confirmation that this was right and it was all going to be OK. She loved Simon. Quietly Abby ran the tap a little and splashed water on her face. She looked at the cups but slurped some from her hands instead. It was messy, cool and refreshing. She still didn't know what she was going to say, but she knew she was ready to say it.

She wasn't due back until the evening but in her excitement she decided there was no need to announce herself; instead she would surprise them. They'd be shocked, she could reveal her feelings – however that came out – and they would all be so happy and hug each other like old times, *perfect!* Grinning to herself Abby snuck down the hallway. She could hear the girls playing upstairs and welcomed the sound of their happy voices. This was it. They were all going to be a family again. Everything was going to be OK.

Looking into the empty lounge she wondered where Simon and Rachel could be. She glanced round. The door to Simon's 'office' was slightly ajar. The room had been largely abandoned since he'd moved out. With the exception of the search Abby carried out for incriminating evidence after the fact (that yielded nothing but his flight itinerary showing details she already knew) she hadn't really felt the need to go in there. She tended to associate the place with stealing Simon's time when he should have been with her and the girls, the place that lent itself to working long hours while masquerading as being at home.

Ready to surprise him she crept towards the door, her excited steps making her look like a cartoon mouse sneaking past a snoozing cat. She had to stifle a giggle. As she lifted her hand to push the door open she paused. Something wasn't right. They were undoubtedly both in there, she could hear them, but why and what they were doing she didn't know. Something about the atmosphere and their agitated tones threw her from her stride. Lowering her hand she stilled to listen. She couldn't believe it; they were cross at each other *again*! She hadn't expected that; now she'd have to deal with that before she could share her happy news. The word 'What' forming at her lips, she stopped.

"Don't tell her Si, what if she can't forgive me?"

Abby held her breath. Realising she was trembling she steadied herself on the doorframe. She had to try and calm down. Panic rising in her chest made it hard to focus on listening.

"I can't keep it from her Rachel, she needs to know."

Abby bit her lip, her heart pounded against her chest. *Needs to know what?* What were they talking about? She wondered if she should just march in and demand an explanation or run before she heard any more. Her eyes flicked between the door and the hallway – her exit. Her feet felt heavy and uncooperative. She stayed still, holding her breath, desperately hoping not to be discovered.

"Don't Si, please, she's been through enough. Don't push her now, she's doing so well."

"That's why we should have told her in the first place!"

"Really? You told me what she was like Si, it would have finished her off."

"OK, but if there's a chance she'll come back to me she has to know everything. We can't keep lying to her. She has to know *everything*."

Lifting her heavy feet Abby took an exaggerated step backwards away from the door, moving as if in slow motion. The thought of more lies, heaped upon lies, and her two best friends in the world complicit in something – she didn't dare to think what. It was making her dizzy. She thought she might collapse. The air seemed to dissipate from her lungs. Gasping and walking as if in a daze she finally slipped back out of the kitchen door. The garden seemed to spin.

What could she do? A black hole was opening before her and she had to fight not to throw herself in and welcome the deep, dark oblivion. She flustered with her phone in her hand; she knew she needed help. Who could she call? She was sliding, slipping too fast towards the darkness. She couldn't call Melissa, she was surely on her way to some exotic paradise by now and Brad – *Oh God, Brad!* She couldn't turn to him. It wouldn't be fair. He couldn't be the one to rescue her this time.

"Daddy, Daddy!"

Hearing Jessica calling to Simon inside the house pulled Abby back from the brink. She threw her phone into her bag and ran to her car. She didn't want the girls to find her in a panic; she had to get away.

Chapter 38

"Good God Abby, speak! Whatever's the matter?" Eleanor pulled Abby through the door and shouted for Kennedy.

Abby felt barely conscious, she wasn't quite sure how she had driven there but she found herself at her mum's and wouldn't you know it, Kennedy was there too to witness her in her full, dark and spiralling-out-of-control glory. Abby didn't care any more. *That's right, this is me: out of control, lost, beyond help!* Her breathing was too quick and shallow. She couldn't fill her lungs with air; her chest was being crushed by the ton of misery that pressed upon it. Her head was light and dizzy. Kennedy put her arm round her. Abby didn't want sympathy, she wanted to wallow in a dark corner, but she didn't have the energy to shrug her off.

"Abby, speak! Tell us what's wrong."

"Mum, she can't – she's having a panic attack; leave her to me. Do you have a bag? A paper bag?"

Eleanor went to the kitchen and rummaged in the drawer searching for the paper bag she knew she had somewhere. Her fingers weren't as agile as they used to be and she was shaking at the sight of her little girl so stricken. Returning to Kennedy she passed it over. Kennedy cupped the bag and placed it over Abby's mouth and nose. Gently rubbing her back she told her to breathe slowly and deeply, her voice calm and reassuring.

"It's OK sweetie, we're here, breeeeeathe slowly," she said over and over again.

Abby wasn't sure how long they sat there but as she became more aware of her surroundings she welcomed Kennedy's soothing voice and the reassuring circling motion she made on her back. She became aware that Eleanor was holding her hand and hot tears spilt down her cheeks.

"I'm so sorry to come to you like this." Abby spoke groggily, feeling weirdly hung over. Her head ached.

"Nonsense, what are mums and sisters for if you can't go to them in times of trouble?"

"Abby, you know we're always here for you."

Kennedy's words bought fresh tears to Abby's eyes, though she wasn't sure either of them had actually been there for her over recent months.

Eleanor breathed a sigh of relief as Abby began to seem more like herself; at least the colour was returning to her cheeks. She patted her hand. "Now tell me my granddaughters are OK and we'll make a cup of tea and you can tell us what's got you in such a state."

Abby thought about Jessica and Grace back at home with Simon and Rachel and their dirty secret. She cursed herself for not bringing them away with her, but then she knew she had been in no fit state. She probably shouldn't have driven herself anywhere, let alone the girls. She stopped her whirring mind before it filled her head with images of herself and them in some hideous accident on the dual carriageway.

"So that's it, all you heard?" Kennedy stopped drinking her tea and looked at Abby, perplexed. "You didn't think to stop, go in, question them?"

"No, I couldn't breathe, I had to get out. It's obvious though isn't it?" The horrible realisation of what she'd heard weighed heavily on Abby.

"Is it? Because I'm lost." Eleanor screwed up her face and looked between her girls, a little baffled as to what conclusion she was supposed to have drawn from Abby's explanation.

"Yes Mum. It's obvious! It's Rachel. The other woman. All this time I thought it was some fictitious Helen Herne, from the name I saw on his phone, and yet it was Rachel. I've been so stupid. I never suspected... They must have been doing it right under my nose. Hell, I even arranged for her to go and keep him company at our house while I was away!"

"But you don't know that's what's been going on," Kennedy interrupted, "do you? Not really."

Abby thought for a moment. Kennedy was annoyingly like her dad with her 'stay calm and gather the facts' attitude, and in that moment when she just wanted someone to agree with her it made her seethe and desperate to prove she was right.

She folded her arms and wracked her aching mind. *Oh!* "OK, let's check Rebecca Giles' tour dates. If Rachel wasn't in Washington at the same time as Simon then I'm wrong, because I know for sure Simon was there and that's when it started because that's when he changed, when he went... weird. But if she was... well then... well then we'll know." Abby could feel her drive coming back, albeit spurred by hurt and anger. She felt back on familiar territory. Gathering the facts like a true Scott and Googling with intent, that was second nature to her now.

"We'll check the dates, but no matter what we find you need to speak to Simon. You can't just assume the worst," Kennedy reasoned.

"Assume?! You didn't hear them. They were talking about secrets and lies. Hiding things from me."

"From what you said it sounded like Simon wanted to tell you something, it hardly sounds like he intended to keep... whatever it is from you."

Eleanor sat like the umpire of a tennis match, her head swinging between the two, attempting to keep up with the conversation.

Firing up the dinosaur of a laptop Eleanor owned tested all their nerves. Everything seemed to take too long.

"Why have you still got this thing? Do you actually use it?"

Finally it surged into life and the home screen, a picture of Abby and Kennedy's dad sitting at the laptop, appeared. Abby no longer needed to ask why Eleanor kept it. She blew out a breath and reminded herself to speak more kindly to her mum.

"OK, let's do this."

Abby searched Rebecca Giles and her tour dates. Staring at the screen she saw a review of her *Uber-successful tour of Washington* appear along with the dates that were imprinted on her mind. *Fuck, it's real!* She started to shake. Without thinking she went into automatic pilot and clicked on the image results. She watched as the page filled with pictures of Rebecca Giles smiling, attending grand publicity events and book signings. Frequently next to her stood Rachel, her right-hand woman, always smiling, always looking stunning. Bile rose in Abby's throat as she scrolled down. And there, towards the bottom of the page she thought she saw… was it? *Is that? Simon!* The picture was a bit blurred but she was sure it was him – they were in the background, just visible over Rebecca Giles' shoulder, but it undoubtedly was Rachel and Simon. *Oh, Simon!* If she wasn't searching for him she might have missed it, but now, staring at the page, there was no mistaking him next to Rachel. They weren't touching or anything, but standing together. Not that them hugging would have been damning proof, they did it all the time. *Oh God!* Abby swallowed and pushed the laptop away. She had wanted evidence for so long, needed to see who it was Simon had betrayed her with and now she had it right there in front of her she wished she didn't. She couldn't look. She closed the laptop down.

"Abby, what are you doing?"

"I don't want to know. The girls and I, we were doing fine. We don't need *them*." She gestured at the laptop. "They can go to hell. I was wrong. Ignorance is bliss." Abby was rambling.

"Fuck that."

"KENNEDY!" Eleanor looked shocked.

"Sorry Mum, but she's got to wake up! It's true, ignorance is temporary bliss, but is that what you want, temporary bliss? Come on Abby, this doesn't mean a thing until you get all the facts, ignorance is shitty bliss but knowledge and truth is power!"

"KENNEDY, stop swearing!" Eleanor was stunned; she had never heard Kennedy swear and now it seemed there was no stopping her.

"Sorry Mum but she's wrong. You know Dad would agree!"

Hearing Kennedy play the Dad card made Abby instantly angry. As Kennedy was five years older Abby always felt like she never quite matched up to the achievements of her big sister in her parents' eyes. She was fed up with her always being the one in the right, who knew best. "Shut up Kennedy, you don't know anything. You just want to be right *again!* You don't care about me, not really. For months I've needed you. Where were you then? Did you care then?" Abby couldn't quite believe that came out of her mouth; she didn't even really mean it. Something about being in her childhood home and in the presence of her mum and Kennedy was making her behave like a stroppy teenager.

Eleanor stood up. "Is that what you think of your sister, and me… is that what you think of me too? Because believe you me, young lady…"

Oh no! The 'believe you me, young lady' was out; Abby knew she was in trouble. Eleanor rarely got angry but when she did she had a repertoire of sentences that let you know you were in trouble. Next she'd be calling her Abigail.

"You have no idea, Abigail."

Uh-oh!

"No bloody idea at all!"

Oh God, she said bloody! Bloody was the height of Eleanor's swear-o-meter; when she started saying that you knew she'd either hit the martini or was furious.

"You've no idea how much we've been worrying about you. Don't you think it's hurt us to see you so sad, so unreachable? Believe you me, we've tried to help you, spend time with you, be there for you and at every turn you've shut us out."

"We know you couldn't help it, I guess you've been… depressed." Kennedy was trying to calm the situation.

Abby went to protest but Eleanor jumped in again.

"How dare you put this on us now? How dare you think we didn't try to help you, when you kept shutting us out?"

Kennedy held her mum's arm and interjected, "But it's OK. Recently, you know… well… it didn't matter; we were just pleased to see you getting better."

Abby could see Kennedy was sticking up for her, it made her have a flashback of her doing the same in the past, defending her when they were little. "I was," Abby offered weakly. "I'm sorry, it's just I… I've never felt so low. I couldn't deal with myself, let alone others. Some days only the girls kept me wanting to breathe. I didn't want you all to see… To know I couldn't cope."

Eleanor swallowed past the lump in her throat. She hadn't meant to be so harsh but it came from months of frustration, watching her little girl seem so lost. Now Abby sat before her looking broken but finally talking about her feelings. Eleanor felt tears welling in her eyes, an ache in her heart and a strange sense of relief that Abby was finally letting her in. She held back a sob. She had spent long hours worrying about Abby, not sure how best to help her. But now she was sitting there confessing her feelings. It was a breakthrough – she knew it; that nice white-haired lady on *This Morning* had said so on the family therapy phone-in.

"Abby don't give up. Don't let everything go without knowing the facts." Kennedy's voice was softer, more encouraging.

Abby looked at her. "But you don't understand, everything's so perfect for you, with your doctor husband, no need for a job, perfect boys and big house. You've got it all."

Kennedy scoffed. "Is that what you think?" She shook her head and laughed. "Abby, I'm bored beyond belief. I gave up my dancing to have my boys and be the perfect wife and mother. Now the boys are teenagers and barely need me and Dave works such bloody long hours I hardly see him. That big house is not so lovely when you are rattling around in it alone!"

Abby was stunned. "But I don't understand... I never knew."

"You never asked."

Abby swallowed. "But why don't you do something, change it? Teach dancing again. You were so good at that."

"Because, Abby, I'm not as brave as you. I wish I was."

Abby was shocked.

"It's all a farce I've built for myself. With Nigella for company and all the committees I'm on I can pretend I'm somebody; that I'm living. When sometimes... well sometimes I just feel like I'm suffocating with the banality of it all."

"Bloody hell!" Eleanor and Abby said it in unison and looked at each other.

Kennedy started to giggle and the three of them laughed, a mixture of tears and giggles as they hugged.

"What a fine lot us Scott girls are turning out to be," Eleanor sighed. "You with your friend and husband doing goodness knows what, you so busy impressing others you forgot about yourself and me..." Abby and Kennedy were about to join forces in protestation at Eleanor's harsh summary of their lives when she continued, "well, I'm all alone now and who's to say I would have had any more fun if I'd married my Albert?"

"WHAT?" Abby and Kennedy stared at Eleanor.

"You know, the young detective with the sharp suit and the grin that melted my heart. I'm sure I must have mentioned him before."

"No Mum, you never did." Kennedy spoke for both of them.

"Ah well, that was before your father, well, before he proposed, well, before we actually got married anyway. I went with my head you see, married the man who was safe, not the one who lived on the edge – enjoying the danger, always up for an adventure. Funny that, isn't it – now I'm old I wouldn't mind a bit of an adventure."

The three of them sat momentarily in silence. Abby couldn't believe how strange the last twenty-four hours had been. Everything she thought she knew had been turned upside down. Nothing was quite what it seemed. Eleanor poured them all a glass of martini and they sat sipping it, along the sofa, taking in all the revelations.

Kennedy put her empty glass on the coffee table decisively. "Right, well the way I see it we – you – need to go and confront Simon."

"Hey, why start with me? Clearly it's not just my life that needs sorting, we're all as bad as each other."

"Because, sister dearest, you are the one who has most hanging in the balance right now."

"I think the scales are well and truly tipped."

Kennedy took Abby's glass. "Stop drinking – you need to have a clear head and you need to talk to your husband."

Abby picked up her glass again. "But really, I think it's too late. I was trying to sort it out. I was about to tell Simon I wanted him back when I heard… I heard what I heard."

"You heard part of a conversation. You don't know what they were saying."

"Honestly Kennedy, it doesn't matter. It's all too late now. I don't have the energy to work it all out again for nothing."

"Nothing? Abby, sometimes I wonder at you. You and Simon, you are special you know. You share something other couples could only hope to share. I don't think you've ever really known how much he loves you. He'd do anything for you. And the way he's reacted to this… he's a mess without you."

"But he had an affair!"

"He made a mistake. You don't really think he's the type…?"

Abby tried not to think how close she had come to making a mistake and pushed away an image of herself with Brad the night before. That was beside the point right now.

"Look Abby, I've spoken to Simon."

"You have?" The thought that Kennedy had spoken to him to check *he* was OK stung her a little, especially after what had happened with Kerry.

"I was cross that he'd hurt you, I was going to tell him what I thought. But I didn't need to. He was already beating himself up enough. He's barely coping with what he did—"

"What he did with my best friend."

"But you don't know it was with Rachel. Sure, she's always liked him, we all knew that—"

"You did?"

"Yes!" Kennedy and Eleanor chimed in unison.

Abby was taken aback.

"But he has never looked at her the way he looks at you. I can't imagine he cheated on you with her. He treats her like a sister and look how badly sisters get treated." Kennedy nudged Abby and offered a smile. "Abby please, don't let a mistake spoil what you have." Kennedy looked at her earnestly.

"But what if it *was* her? Or OK, what if it wasn't and it happens again? I'm not sure I'll recover after all this. I was wrong to think it would all be OK."

"It's been, as it seems Kennedy might say, a shitty couple of years!" Eleanor declared.

264

"MUM!" Abby and Kennedy could barely believe their ears.

"Well it has, with your dad's illness and then passing, your Simon's business almost going" – she mouthed the word "tits" with a nod of her head – "up. Things happen when life gets tough. Sometimes we all forget what's important and throw ourselves into other things when we should be looking out for each other."

"Did Denise Robertson say that Mum?" Kennedy teased.

"No, Mary down at the bingo, but it's true."

They all laughed.

"So girls, what's it to be – am I pouring us more martini to drown our sorrows and sit here and wallow or are we going to head to Abby's and get this business sorted out?"

"I'll have to drive, you two have drained your glasses. But it's OK; you don't need to come. I'll go and speak to him… to them." Abby stood, not quite feeling the conviction of her statement.

"Well you're not going alone, I'll come as backup." Kennedy leapt up from the sofa.

"Well I am not sitting here like a spare part. Somebody will need to entertain the girls while you do the talking." With that Eleanor grabbed her cardigan.

"Thank you." Abby hugged them. "I do love you both; you know that don't you?"

Chapter 39

Abby had never felt so nervous entering her own house. She felt sick. The memory of standing in the hall and hearing what she heard and the panic attack that ensued was too fresh in her mind.

"You can do this!" Kennedy urged.

As Eleanor held her arm reassuringly Abby climbed the steps and opened the front door. Bramble managed a wiggle and a token bark.

"Mummy, you're home! Auntie Kennedy! Nanny!" Grace was so excited to see them all she did a little happy dance in the hallway before running to Abby and giving her a hug. It was just what she needed and fortified her waning resolve.

"Oh, my gorgeous girly, I've missed you! Where's Jessica? Nanny's come to play."

"Yippee! Come on Nanny, Jess is glumpy in her room."

Wiggling from Abby's hold Grace took Eleanor's hand and started leading her upstairs.

"Grumpy, why?"

"I played mooval men with her dolls' house."

"Oh dear." Eleanor attempted not to show her grin. "And did you take everything out?"

Grace nodded and feigned a very wide-eyed sorry face.

"Come on then, let's go and sort it out shall we?"

As Eleanor and Grace disappeared upstairs Kennedy squeezed Abby's hand. Abby took a deep breath and headed to the kitchen where she could hear movement.

"You're back, I didn't expect you until later. I would have tidied more, packed up my stuff." Simon stopped fussing with the dinner things, smiled and kissed Abby on the cheek. He could feel it wasn't welcome. "Sorry."

Abby moved towards the table and Simon noticed Kennedy skulking in the doorway.

"Hey Kennedy, everything OK? What's going on? You two look… serious."

Abby spoke before Kennedy could answer. "Simon, is Rachel still here? I need to speak to both of you."

Simon's colour drained. "Yes, she's just taking the recycling out."

"Smoking more like," Abby sniped.

"Let's make some tea." Kennedy walked over, rubbed Abby's arm and went to the kettle. She needed to do something to break the building atmosphere otherwise she feared Abby wouldn't cope.

Simon looked at the gift he had got ready for Abby but thought it wasn't the time. When Rachel finally came in they were sitting at the table, sipping hot tea silently.

"Abby, you're back! Kennedy, it's been too long." She grinned before taking in their grave expressions. "Bloody hell, who died?"

Abby took a breath. "Sit down. I mean, please sit down, I need to talk to you and Simon."

Rachel faltered and then sat, but not before Abby noticed her hands were shaking. Seeing that Rachel felt nervous seemed to give Abby more strength, to drive her to say what she wanted to say. There was no point dressing it up so she got straight to the point.

"Are you two having an affair?"

"What? No!" Simon looked genuinely shocked.

Abby felt a little relieved at his reaction but then she remembered what she'd heard. She looked at Rachel, who had fallen silent. "Are you?" She pointed the question directly at her.

"Abby! Of course not! You know Si and I, we're close you know, but we're just friends."

"Friends who fuck behind my back?" Abby couldn't stop herself.

Rachel looked affronted and went to stand. "This is ridiculous!"

Kennedy stopped her. "No, you're not leaving just yet. I don't believe you two are having an affair but I do believe you owe my sister an explanation about something and that something is getting resolved now!"

Abby was beginning to remember why having a big sister had its advantages.

"But it's not true, there's nothing—"

"Don't, Rachel! She just needs to know, it was stupid not telling her straight away. I told you we should have just been honest when she found out about this whole fucking awful mess."

Abby sat trying to look calm, trying to look like she was ready to hear what they were about to reveal. Inside she wanted to run away. She couldn't handle it being Rachel, if it was her then that would make everything a lie; she wouldn't be able to trust anything from their past. Kennedy squeezed her hand under the table.

"There's nothing between Rachel and I. Abby, I'd never do that. She's just a mate. I love her, sure, but like a sister. What we share…" he motioned between himself and Rachel, "it's nothing compared to what you and I have."

Was it wrong that Abby enjoyed the slightly hurt look that flicked across Rachel's face?

Simon continued, "It's always been you Abby. I've loved you from the moment you raised your hand and waved at me with that nervous smile. Then when I bought you tea in the morning, do you remember? And toast—"

"Burnt toast."

They shared a brief smile.

"You had on that pink crop top, no makeup and your hair was all messy. You looked perfect."

Tears pooled in Abby's eyes.

"I wished desperately that I was in that bed with you, holding you. I knew then that I wanted to wake up next to you like that every morning of forever."

Abby didn't know what to say. He'd never said that to her before.

Kennedy coughed; she didn't want to interrupt the moment but she knew there were still questions to be answered. "So, what is it that Abby needs to know? What are you two keeping from her?"

Abby shook her head and wiped her eyes. "Yes, why were you two together in Washington?"

Both Simon and Rachel looked surprised. They hadn't expected that.

"You knew?" Simon stared, confused.

"No, not until I heard you both talking and then I saw Rebecca's tour dates… and the picture of you together, on the Internet."

"Abby I—" Simon went to speak but Rachel interrupted.

"It was a coincidence. Neither of us knew the other was there, until, well, until I saw him with that woman. Abby, I didn't know what to do." Rachel twisted her trembling hands on the table and shifted uncomfortably in her seat.

Abby looked at Simon, attempting to take everything in. "She saw you… She saw you there… with *her*?"

Simon nodded guiltily.

Eyes wide and heart pounding, Abby turned back to Rachel. "You saw them. You saw Simon with *her*!" She took a few deep breaths, attempting to control the hurt and anger she could feel building in her chest. "Rachel, you could have stopped them. You could have told me. You could have been a bloody friend!" She fought back tears.

269

"Abby I know, I know all of that but I was shocked. I'm sorry. I'm so very sorry." Rachel went to hold Abby's hand but she snatched it away. Swallowing hard, she continued. "At first I didn't know what to do, then eventually I called Simon and got him to meet me at one of Rebecca's signings. I was working; it was the first opportunity I had."

"Is all this the truth?" Abby glared at Simon.

"Yes."

"And what did the two of you decide the best course of action was? Because you obviously decided not to bloody well tell me!"

"I told her I'd made a huge mistake, that I was scared of losing you. That I didn't know what I'd do if I lost you."

"I told him not to tell you. Abby, I'm sorry. I know that was stupid but I didn't want you to get hurt."

"Really? And the two of you keeping secrets from me – that wasn't going to hurt?"

"Well, no not until you found out," Rachel new it sounded pathetic when she said it.

"It's not her fault."

Abby rolled her eyes. She couldn't believe Simon was about to defend Rachel. "No?"

"No, it's mine, I should have told you. Well, I... I mean it shouldn't have happened in the first place but after I behaved like... after *it* happened, I should have been honest. It didn't matter what Rachel said, I should have been honest."

OK, so that's a good point. "Yes you should have, you *both* should have."

Abby felt a weird whirr of emotions. She was relieved it wasn't Rachel. She had been wrong. Her husband and her best friend weren't having an affair. There really was a Helen Herne; it was a strange thing to feel grateful for. But then they had both lied to her and kept secrets. *Bloody secrets!*

"You've both hurt me! Rachel, you could have told me."

"Abby, I couldn't be the one to tell you, I'd have betrayed Simon and hurt you. I loved that we were – that we *are* – all friends together. I felt pulled in the middle. I couldn't break my best friends up and when Simon looked so crushed at what he'd done I gave him what I thought was the best advice."

"To lie!"

"Well it seemed like the right thing at the time but what the hell do I know about relationships? Look at the fuck-up of my love life!"

It was true. Rachel had never managed to sustain a long-term relationship.

"So why didn't you say anything once I did know? You didn't check I was OK or anything."

"Simon said how hard you'd taken it, and I didn't want to be the one who'd betrayed you too. I thought it might send you over the edge."

That was scarily close to home. If Abby had known it really just might have tipped her; it might have been more than she could take.

Rachel continued. "I wasn't comfortable with lying to you. So I said nothing. I hid. I stayed away and acted like I was too busy to notice. It was stupid because I knew you needed a friend, but I convinced myself you'd be OK, that you had Simon and your mum and Kennedy."

Abby looked at Kennedy and smiled weakly, as Rachel continued.

"When Rebecca's tour ended I came here to tell you that I knew, but I got scared. You were getting better and you were making... new friends. I was scared I'd lose you. Abby, I'm so, so sorry. I've been such a bad friend. If I could change the fact that I've lied to you and my bloody awful advice I would."

"You need to watch *This Morning*." Eleanor spoke from the door, relieving the tension.

Abby looked at Simon, groaned and thrust her head onto the table. "Oh, what a bloody mess, and just when I knew I loved you and wanted you back!"

Simon stilled. "What?"

Abby looked up, realising what she'd said. "But that was before…"

Everybody was staring at her.

"Say it, don't let this stop you. Please Abby, say it."

"Well I… I…" She looked at him. She loved that face, she loved the fact that he had one or two wrinkles around his eyes now and the odd grey fleck in his hair, she loved that they'd spent almost half a lifetime together, been there for each other for so long and she loved knowing that she loved him. She could still feel that little feeling inside; it was real. "I love you!"

With that they hugged and kissed and it felt warm and familiar and like coming home. Bramble got out of his bed and weaved himself around them, wagging his tail excitedly. It wasn't at all how she intended to say it, it wasn't time for happy ever after, it wasn't all sorted but they were together again. It was a start.

Chapter 40

Six Months Later

Picking up her bag, Abby gave the girls a cuddle and bent to give Simon a kiss. As she went to walk away he pulled her into his lap and kissed her again.

"Oh, you're going to make me later than I already am," she giggled.

"OK!" Simon pressed another kiss to her lips, pushed her to her feet and cheekily smacked her bottom. "Enjoy... I'll look forward to seeing what you've learnt later."

Abby laughed and teasingly swiped her hand at him. "Behave!"

As she reached the door Simon called after her, "You'll be back about eight, right?"

"Yeah, sure, if I survive this."

Jumping into her car, Abby checked the clock. *Bugger!* Adhering to the safety-in-numbers rule of starting any new exercise class she was collecting Melissa and her mum en route. She fired them off a text to let them know she was finally on her way. Running late was a side effect of being able to read again. She loved the fact that she could pick up a book and read it without her mind interjecting. Her head finally felt free to enjoy it. She'd missed owning her own thoughts. Even just being able to read made her feel more alive. Though being a bit too engrossed in Rebecca Giles' book was making her late for almost everything.

Abby hadn't become a great fan of exercise but she liked the way it kept the pounds at bay and helped keep her head clear. The gym remained part of her weekly routine and she'd discovered some long-forgotten stomach muscles as a result; muscles she hoped might help her out in the class she was about to attend. *At least it's not pole fit!*

Melissa waved and tapped her watch in mock scorn as Abby pulled up outside her house. Her high ponytail bobbed as she sprung down the driveway, still looking thoroughly bronzed from the tan she'd been secretly topping up with lotion since her month-long honeymoon in the Cook Islands. Her Lycra exercise tights, Bébé et Moi fitted t-shirt and pink tasselled hip scarf accentuated her slight bump perfectly.

"You did get permission from the midwife to do this didn't you?"

"Yes Mum!" Melissa laughed as she got into Abby's car.

"You're not funny! I promised Adam I'd keep an eye on you."

"What's he like? I promise to be good and take it easy, OK?" Melissa tugged at her seatbelt. "Besides, Adam won't mind; the midwife said it's actually good for keeping your back supple and your pelvic floor muscles—"

"La, la, la – too much information!" Abby laughed.

"Anyway, I could hardly miss Kennedy's debut could I? We promised her a full class and a full class she shall have. How's she doing? Did you speak to her today?"

"Of course. She's nervous, but she's been training hard and actually sounded really excited."

"She'll be great! I can't wait. Lucy's coming and bringing Mindy too… there won't be a lot of jumping will there?" She shook her head and whistled. "Imagine the black eyes!"

Abby giggled. "Melissa, that's so bad! Honestly, it's the kind of thing I'd say."

"I know… you're such a bad influence on me."

They both laughed, until Abby remembered she had to be on her best behaviour where Lucy and Mindy were concerned.

"No, stop – we have to be nice. I think they've only just forgiven me for being so blunt with them at your wedding. I swear Mindy's been pulling the bloody wax strips from my eyebrows much slower than necessary."

"Ouch!" Melissa chuckled.

"It's not funny, if you'd told me they were a couple before I would've behaved less like a nutter when she rested her boobs on Brad... not that I was jealous or anything."

"Of course not." Melissa over-emphasised the words and shook her head slowly.

Abby glanced at Melissa, and as they caught each other's eye they burst into laughter.

Abby's *thing* with Brad seemed strange to her now. She was pleased they had managed to stay on good terms and would always remain grateful to him for being there when she needed someone. Under the circumstances Simon had been fairly understanding about the whole thing too, much more so than Abby had expected. She told him she and Brad had 'shared a moment' and that she'd been tempted to go further but didn't. She'd started with a basic outline and decided to elaborate when he asked; she wasn't going to lie but she wasn't going to embellish unnecessarily. It turned out Simon didn't want details. *Men – such different creatures to women!* He was happy she hadn't slept with him and in the scheme of things having her and the girls back with him eclipsed everything else. It was a very lovely thing to say, though Abby was pretty sure the situation was also eased by the fact Autumn had returned from her travels and was very much on a mission to sort things out with her man. Who knew life with the lovely Bradley Hunter would turn out to be more appealing than trekking around India with a backpacker from Manchester? *Derrrr!*

Eleanor was waiting on her front porch. Her exceptionally white trainers and Angela Lansbury inspired salmon tracksuit came into view before she did. Abby smiled. Melissa jumped out of the car and stood holding the door in the style of a chauffeur.

"Hello Mrs S, all set for a bit of a jiggle then?"

"I am indeed, Mary's meeting us there and I told her to bring along anyone else she could muster."

"It's great you girls are getting in shape." Melissa shifted Jessica's car seat and sat in the back of the car.

"It'll be worth it you know, when we jet off on our travels! Did Abby tell you we're off to Jersey?"

"Of course I did!" Abby laughed.

Eleanor was enjoying telling everyone that she and Mary were soon to be 'jetting off' on their travels. She was so excited about her trip. Abby and Kennedy were both surprised and hugely proud of her for booking it. Eleanor and Mary had gone and done it on a whim after a win at bingo – *just like that!* For as long as she could remember Abby had watched her mum visiting the places her dad had wanted to visit and doing the things he had wanted to do. This was something purely for her, a holiday of indulgence. It was what she deserved. Just thinking about it made Abby beam, especially when she imagined the look on her mum's face when she saw the red Triumph Roadster 2000, aka 'Bergerac's car', which Simon had secretly arranged to take her out for a spin during her stay.

Practically running along the corridor of the leisure centre and bursting in just after the initial introductions Abby blushed, Melissa grimaced and Eleanor apologised to the group before proudly introducing herself as Kennedy's mum. Kennedy's cheeks reddened and she gestured for them all to take their places.

"You're just in time, we were about to warm up."

Abby glanced round. It was quite an eclectic group of people. There were a few she didn't recognise and while their barefoot-and-all-the-gear appearance made them a little intimidating

Abby was pleased to see Kennedy's belly dancing class had attracted more than just friends and family. Eleanor joined the bingo crowd at the back who looked a little surprised at what they'd let themselves in for, while Melissa and Abby stood in a line that contained Lucy and Mindy in pink leggings and *Prrrrimp* Your Hide vest tops. Patty waved from the front and Abby wondered how she had missed her in her leopard print catsuit. Abby waved back and her heart swelled a little; *bless her for coming; bless them all for coming!* She knew Rachel would have been there too if she hadn't been called away to work as preparations for the next leg of Rebecca's tour got underway.

While Abby was hurt by Rachel not telling her about Simon, she realised she couldn't stay angry with her for long, it was tiring and undermined her mission to move on. Besides, Rachel had seen Helen Herne; getting her drunk meant she could fill in all the missing details Abby wanted to know. She could even identify her on Facebook, as Simon could have if Abby had been brave enough to ask him. It had been a bizarre and intriguing night. All those things that had eaten away at Abby and seemed so important culminated in one night of discovery. And the most important thing Abby discovered was that it didn't particularly matter who Helen was or what she looked like; Abby had sat there and looked at Helen's face, even had it within her grasp to contact her and for what? There was nothing to gain from doing it. It wouldn't change what had happened. Nothing could change it. Though accepting that knowledge was – *don't tell Kennedy* – empowering.

At the front of the class, Kennedy looked lovely, just as Abby remembered her from her earning-cash-to-get-through-college bellygram days; like a blonde Princess Jasmine in her crop top and chiffon harem pants. Abby stared a little enviously at her fabulously lean stomach; *after three babies as well, grrrr!* Kennedy handed out scarves for those who didn't have them to wrap around their hips or wrists. It gave everybody something to focus on and relieved the tension. Abby wasn't sure she needed anything to accentuate her hips but chose a sparkly purple one, popped it on and wiggled to test out the jangling noise of the shiny penny tassels. She was never going to be a great dancer but she was learning that not caring what others think and throwing yourself into it could get you quite far. The hypnotic rhythm and beat of the Middle Eastern music started and the slow, sultry warm-up began.

It wasn't long before they realised Patty was quite the star of the class: her hip circles were smooth, her arm movements fluid. In contrast Abby felt that her hand movements looked as out-of-control as her *Incy Wincy Spider* hands that had always got a laugh at Grace's baby boogie class. In fact Patty's hip thrusts, clearly punctuated at the four points on her imaginary hula hoop, were carried out with a conviction the rest of the class couldn't help but admire. When it came to hip shimmies, a little fun towards the end of the class, everybody threw themselves into it with gusto, though Abby had to admit hers were more what you might call all-over-body shimmies. She knew she was supposed to keep her upper body still; her mind was saying it but the thought got lost somewhere in translation to her chest. She made a mental note to sneak a bit of extra tuition with Kennedy before the next lesson.

Chapter 41

Feeling refreshed from her shower, positively invigorated and more than a little sexy from the exercise (*it's all in the hip rolls you know*), Abby sat outside the house and smiled at the thought of Simon waiting inside for her. Things were going well between them. They were having fun again – adjusting their work-life balance together to suit their needs. And it seemed their need for each other had grown in all kinds of exciting ways since being apart!

Of course it wasn't all easy. In fact she still had the occasional dark day – moments that overwhelmed her triggered by memories, films, somebody saying the wrong thing. But they were becoming fewer and no longer haunted her. She found it strange that the whole experience had affected her like that; it was as if it had opened something inside her, a darkness she never knew was there before. She didn't know if it would ever go completely but she did know it no longer scared her in the same way. She didn't let it define her. She was learning to control it – her relationship with Simon was more than that moment in time and ultimately she knew that.

In fact she knew it in more ways than one – *his week, which technically thanks to Rachel's intervention was less than a week, was one out of the at least seven hundred and eighty we'd spent together, less than seven days out of the over five thousand four hundred and sixty we'd shared.* As much as Abby wasn't about to admit it these facts, provided by Kennedy, were reassuring!

Bramble greeted her warmly as she walked into the house. The smell of her Simon-safe M&S dinner cooking tantalised her taste buds and caused her mouth to water. She heard music coming from the lounge, it was familiar; it was their song. Abby grinned, slipped her shoes off and went to find Simon. As she entered the room he smiled and stood up. Abby swallowed. He looked lovely, all fresh from the shower and dressed to impress. *Oh!*

"Should I change?"

"No need, you look beautiful."

Abby looked down at her clothes, momentarily questioning his judgement, but as Simon moved towards her all thoughts of going to change were forgotten. Unable to hide her smile she took his hand and allowed herself to be pulled into a hug. They fitted perfectly in each other's arms.

As their bodies met and the music continued to play they began to dance in their own familiar rhythm. Abby welcomed his fresh, clean smell and rubbed herself into his neck. The dance was slow, sensuous and perfect. Abby was pleased she could listen to *their* song again. It had taken a while but gradually she was accepting the fact that what Simon had done didn't make everything that had come before meaningless. Their song would always be their song and nobody could undo the things they'd shared; the moments and things that were theirs would always be theirs.

As the song ended another of Abby's favourites began. She looked at the stereo. "Did you make me a mix-CD?"

"Maybe," he teased. It had been years since they'd made each other mix-tapes; it was a very sweet gesture.

"Thank you."

Simon kissed Abby's nose and took her hand as he led her into the kitchen. He'd laid the table complete with candles and fresh white freesias. Her pulse raced a little and she wondered, as she watched him pour two large glasses of wine, if she'd forgotten something. She knew it wasn't their anniversary.

"Simon it's lovely, but… why?"

He motioned for her to sit down. It was only then that she

noticed the origami lion on her plate, sitting on a ring box. It was her lion, to go with her elephant and giraffe, the complete set, together again only this time made better by years of practice! Tears welled in her eyes.

"You know how you said you wouldn't marry me again…?"

Abby sniffed back her tears and laughed. "That's not what I said; I said I didn't want to renew our vows. We don't need to start again, we have a whole life together – our life. What's been is a part of us now."

Simon looked at her, knowing how hard that actually was for her to accept, and smiled. "I didn't think it was possible but I just might love you even more for that, you know." Kneeling before her he took the ring box from her plate. "OK, so you don't want to renew our vows, but Abby… will you accept this?"

As he opened the box she saw the most beautiful gold, diamond-studded, understated and thoroughly gorgeous eternity ring glistening in the candlelight.

"I used to say to achieve and truly appreciate what you want you should deserve what you get. I don't deserve this chance you've given me, I know how much I stuffed up, Abby. But I want you to know I do really appreciate you, I appreciate us, our beautiful family and how lucky I am." He slipped the ring on her finger. "The thing is, Mrs Turner, I love you and I know it may take forever to prove it to you but I am never going to risk losing you again."

Abby fought back her tears and looked at the ring sitting on top of her engagement and wedding rings, each with their own little bit of history. "The thing is, Simon Turner, you'd better bloody mean that because I love you and I don't ever want a reason to let you go."

Abby's Notebook:

I once told Mallory I was scared something might come along to put Simon's affair into perspective. It turned out life put it into perspective!

It wasn't the worst thing in the world to happen, I always knew that, but at the time it felt like more than I could cope with. When I think about the dark depths I plummeted to I am grateful to my beautiful children who gave me a reason to keep going, and my friends and family who helped me through.

In the darkness that still sometimes touches me I have found new weaknesses I never knew I had, but through my journey I've also found new strengths.

I've found me again and I am happy.

Acknowledgements:

I am very fortunate to have lots of lovely people in my life who have helped me along the way, but special thanks must go to my wonderfully supportive husband Mason, whose encouragement in helping me see this whole project through has been amazing. It wouldn't have been possible without you. I really appreciate all you have done. Thank you so much!

Kirsti, despite being one of the busiest people I know, you always make time to listen to my ideas and to read first drafts and rewrites for me. I really appreciate your honest opinion, and continued support. Thank you! Amelia, Madison and Edward, thank you for your love, hugs and encouragement. I am very lucky to have four such wonderful and supportive children.

Angela, thank you for reading drafts and for letting me text and call you at all hours to discuss various aspects of my book. Big sisters really are invaluable!

Mum, I had never seen you read a novel until you picked up my manuscript, thank you. That meant a lot. Also I'd like to take this opportunity to thank you and Dad for all the love and support you have given me through all the twists and turns of life. I hope you know how much I love and appreciate you both.

Thank you also to Rebecca, Max and Julie, for reading *Crazy Over You* at various stages of development and for helping me to make tweaks along the way.

On the technical front, I must thank my very talented nephew Drew Bristow (www.twitter.com/Drewvis_UK), who had more emails from me about book covers than I'm sure he ever imagined possible when he agreed to help me. I love the cover image you created for me, thank you so much! And to all the people at Troubador Publishing Ltd, thank you for answering my many questions so promptly and for helping me publish a book I am proud of.

And finally I'd like to thank **you** for reading my book! Your support is truly appreciated ☺

If you enjoyed reading

Crazy Over You

you can find out more about books by Carol Thomas here:

www.carol-thomas.co.uk
www.facebook.com/carolthomasauthor
www.twitter.com/carol_thomas2